MURDER OF AN IRISH SONG

MURDER OF AN IRISH SONG

❖

Bill Dougherty (signature)

William A. Dougherty

Copyright © 2007 by William A. Dougherty.

Library of Congress Control Number: 2007903078
ISBN: Hardcover   978-1-4257-6781-5
                Softcover   978-1-4257-6767-9

All rights reserved. No part of this book may be reproduced or transmitted in any form or by any means, electronic or mechanical, including photocopying, recording, or by any information storage and retrieval system, without permission in writing from the copyright owner.

This is a work of fiction. Names, characters, places and incidents either are the product of the author's imagination or are used fictitiously, and any resemblance to any actual persons, living or dead, events, or locales is entirely coincidental.

This book was printed in the United States of America.

To order additional copies of this book, contact:
Xlibris Corporation
1-888-795-4274
www.Xlibris.com
Orders@Xlibris.com
35657

Acknowledgements

The late Dr. Robert Smith and William G. Wilson, two native Vermonters, born a few miles apart—whose crossed paths have made my journey possible.

Tireless readers and editors: Tamara Joyce, Ellen Johnson, Kathy Kent, Ron Smith, Carl and Lynn Hoar, and Tim Griffin.

Many readers from Gosnold TSS to whom I owe a great deal of thanks and a prayer for their recovery.

Author and teacher James Murphy, Falmouth and Newton friend, who offered early encouragement and direction.

Authors Michael Palmer, MD and Archer Mayer who gave me a framework to begin writing.

Technical advice from Lt. Conrad Prosniewski, Salem Police Department who took the time to give me the basics. Also, Falmouth, Massachusetts Police officers Mark Deutschmann, Paul Driscoll, and retired Captain Don Price, who each added a new perspective.

Medical and forensic details from Herb Gray, MD, Falmouth Hospital and Arthur Bickford, MD, Cape Cod Hospital

In Vermont, former Vermont State Trooper Peter Barton, Lynsey Buzz Cole, the late Dr. George H. Humphreys, former Dover police officer Keith Clark, and my dear friend Eric Swanson who has always managed to laugh at my madness.

My parents, Mildred and Frank, who gave me my love of Vermont, and my late brother Franny who would relish this story. My sister Mary who remembers it all.

My daughters, Brady and Libby, who patiently guided me on my early adventures on the computer, and our wonderful friend Jenny, whose presence, constant encouragement and humor supported my family and me. And finally my wife Debbie, who has gently guided my writing and editing every step of the way, and who has loved me through it all.

INTRODUCTION

ONCE UPON A time, there was a fifth season in Vermont. It was the period between the end of foliage and the arrival of the first skiers. It was a season of anticipation prior to the advent of artificial snowmakers—a frustrating yet exciting time of the year. In the valleys of Vermont, those who lived and died by the ski trade would watch the late fall skies and breathe deeply as they went about their November chores. It was the period of last-minute fix-ups—time to complete long-overdue tasks, a time of laying in provisions for lodge owners and getting equipment ready for those who manned the mountain. The days grew shorter; wood fires burned brighter. It was a time of final inspection by the liquor board or the health department. This season held the greatest promise and the greatest anxiety.

This season would end when the magic day would come, and the sky would gently loose its first flakes of soft white powder. The cold would turn from brisk to bitter, and the village barber in the town of Warrens Mills would turn to his wife and exclaim, "Skiers, Thelma!"

Prologue

December 27, 1963
Warrens Mills, Vermont, 6:00 AM

THE SKIER STOOD in inches of soft, new powder and looked delightfully perplexed. Morning sun cast a warm shadow over the four empty lifts that beckoned him to begin his Vermont ski holiday. His boots seemed comfortable, his skis tuned and ready. His goggles were perched atop his woolen hat. His smile was infectious, and his teeth were gleaming white. He was a perfect person in a perfect winter world until a dart penetrated his skull and a voice rang out:

"Bingo!"

The muffled thud caused Bob Matthew to awake with a smile, smiling because an up-to-date mortgage payment was headed for the bank. Outside, the snow continued to fall as it had since three days before Christmas, bringing a full house to his family-farm-turned-ski lodge. Matthews gambled in 1961 that the ski business was here to stay, and he busted his ass and borrowed heavily to make the conversion from rough to rustic. The constant white powder barrage and the green cash receipts told him that he had made the right decision.

"Morning, Ruth," he said as he entered the immaculate kitchen ruled over by Ruth Parsons, a Warrens Mills native like himself. Ruth had come to work for him at High Meadow Farm when her husband of only three years had been crushed to death in a logging accident. Like many of the locals, she tolerated—but did not particularly care for—the skiers who jammed the roads and markets of this tiny village.

Parsons was busy throwing darts into a poster that the state Department of Tourism had sent to over four thousand potential clients in an attempt to capture the elusive weekday skier. The tagline on the poster read, "The best skiing in Vermont is Monday morning at nine o'clock."

"I'll have the linen order ready when you get back from the bank," she said as she turned to him and handed him a plate of blueberry pancakes. He carried the plate to the woodstove, where a cast-iron pot simmered with the farm's own dark maple syrup mixing together with butter.

"By the way, the guy who checked into room 3 couldn't be a bigger asshole if his life depended on it."

She laughed and threw another dart toward the wall where she had hung the tourism poster, this time skillfully placing the dart in the skier's stomach.

Each week, they chose a candidate for their "Skier of the Season." In the spring, when mud season slowed their pace, they gathered with the other lodge and business owners at a valley tavern to award the dubious prize for grandiose or obnoxious behavior. This activity was aimed more at their own entertainment than at condemning skiers. It was replete with costumes, live music and generally a way to reward them for putting up with city people for three months.

At this point, their leading candidate was brushing his teeth, unaware that his name was being added to the kitchen wall of infamy. Marty Leonard checked his smile in the mirror, unscrewed the cap of his diet pills, swallowed a black capsule, and knew today would be another great day on the slopes. His shiny Chevrolet Corvette with the New York orange and black vanity plate MART MAN was stuck in a snow bank just a hundred yards from the house and would probably need a tow.

Bob started his truck and let it idle against the cold mountain air. He looked at the Corvette stuck near the house and shook his head. He walked back in the main house to his small office just off the mudroom. He unlocked the small metal chest, which held his and Uncle Sam's share of the long weekend's receipts. He counted the cash and checks, made out a deposit slip for the lodge account and his personal account, and then zippered shut the leather and canvas lock bag.

As he backed out onto Townhill Road, he noticed his neighbor and best friend Clyde Turner heading into town. Bob hit the horn and gave his friend the finger as he deliberately tailgated Turner's truck to the bottom of the hill.

At 7:00 AM, the bank was already half filled with Warrens Mills business owners or their employees. The sign on the door read, "We have instituted a policy of opening at 6:00 AM on Monday morning in order to process the increasing amount of cash and checks that have expanded our business volume from December through March. Thank You. Green Mountain Trust."

"Need a deposit slip, Bob?" the teller asked.

"Shit, Amanda, he ain't got enough to deposit to need a whole slip."

Turner had quietly walked up behind and goosed Bob so hard that he almost banged his head as he lurched forward toward the brass bars that separated the teller from the public. They had been playing the grab-ass game with each other since they had met years before at Warrens Mills Regional School.

"Move along, jerk offs."

An irritated voice broke through their continuing banter as they stood before the teller's window, blocking the flow of traffic. It was the voice of backhoe operator and part-time town constable Porky Atkins. Porky was assigned to the bank on Mondays in order to have an armed presence when the heaviest deposits were made.

"Up your ass," they said in unison as they walked out together. Bob turned his head and looked back at the bank.

"You know, Clyde, I hope someday that somebody shoots that fat prick."

At ten forty-five that morning, 243 depositors had taken advantage of the bank's early opening policy. The largest depositor was Snow Valley Resort with combined holiday weekend revenues totaling over $1.2 million. The bank then closed its doors to the public, packed the cash and checks in three canvas bags, and awaited the bonded carrier who would transfer the deposit to the main branch in Brattleboro, some twenty miles east.

* * *

Searsburg, Vermont, 10:50 AM

"The snow should accumulate no more than six to eight inches today and will end tonight. The temperature dropping into the midteens. Looks like tomorrow will be a dream for you skiers out there in mountain radio land."

Part-time bus driver and former collegiate skiing all-American Billy Latimer turned the radio off. He adjusted his windshield wiper speed to high, in order to see through the whiteout effect that the snow had created on the highway leading from Bennington to Brattleboro. This stretch coming off the backside of Searsburg Mountain had long been a death trap for truckers. Billy pulled between two truck drivers ferrying their precariously balanced load to the sawmill.

The object was to "get there safely" and to "keep his passengers happy," he reminded himself. Today was a straight commercial run and involved no passengers on the final leg to Brattleboro. The sun burst through as he rounded the last double hairpin turn leading to Warrens Mills. He let out a sigh of relief and consciously relaxed his shoulder muscles. He slowed as he approached the shops and restaurants that lined the postcardlike Main Street of the town. The streets, he noticed, were already plowed and sanded.

He smiled mischievously as he pulled over directly in front of the Green Mountain Trust Building that dominated the intersection of this one-stop-light town.

* * *

Snow Valley, Vermont, 11:00 AM

Meanwhile at Snow Valley, Marty Leonard was cruising blissfully behind the ten milligrams of amphetamine he had taken before breakfast. He cut parallel turns on Snow Valley's wide Sundown slope that led to the enclosed bubble lift at the base of the hill.

"Track," he shouted as he sped by slower skiers on his week-old Head 220s. Marty felt elated. Filled with the promise of a sparkling Vermont day, he dug his poles in as he headed up the slight incline toward the last drop to the bottom. As he reached the crest of the tree line, he couldn't believe his eyes.

Nothing was moving. The lifts had stopped—every lift in sight. There were skiers queued up as far as he could see. A skier's nightmare coming true in the middle of Marty's chemically enhanced *winter wonderland*.

Snow Valley, Vermont, 11:10 AM

For ex-logger turned ski lift attendant Dave Jackson, the amphetamines he had stolen from the owner of the Cave Nightclub were having a decidedly different effect than the euphoria felt by skier Marty Leonard. The drug made him agitated and caused him to chew at his lip. Adding to his foul mood was the fact that his wife had left him and moved to Rutland a week ago with a minister from some church he'd never heard of. Now Joe Phelps, the lift engineer, was looking at him as though he had caused the power outage.

"Fuck Phelps," he muttered and walked inside the warming hut. He pulled a half pint of coffee brandy from his parka, unscrewed the cap, and swallowed, feeling the warmth immediately in his stomach. He pulled one more swallow from the bottle, capped it, and returned to his immobile chairlift; and the crowd of brightly attired, Ban de Soleiled and very annoyed vacationers who had chosen this day to complicate Dave's life even further.

Snow Valley, Vermont, Manager's Office, 11:13 AM

The third floor of Snow Valley's base lodge was lined with large glass sliders that opened to a wraparound red cedar deck that overlooked the main chairlift area and the ski school. General manager Tim Kane loved this view. He had spent recent mornings enjoying the silent flow of skiers that colorfully dotted the meticulously groomed expanse of south-facing slope, but not today. The mountain was his baby, and at this moment, his baby had stopped breathing. He felt helpless.

"What do you mean?" he screamed at the receiver in his hand.

"How can we lose our power? And then you tell me you don't know when it's coming back on line! Where the hell is Harry?"

He continued to scream at the secretary, who had tried to remain professional as Green Mountain Power Company's largest customer turned apoplectic on the other end of the line.

Meanwhile, office manager for Green Mountain Power Harry Martin was enjoying his second cup of coffee at Dot's Deli. He was reading the *Brattleboro Reformer* sports page when Dot leaned out of the kitchen door and yelled, "Harry, the whole goddamn upper valley has lost power!"

Snow Valley, Vermont, 11:30 AM

It had been thirty minutes since the chairlifts had gone down. The assembled crowd grew larger as the skiers began to finish their runs. Those in the overhead chairs and enclosed gondola cars became increasingly apprehensive as Red Cross-emblazoned ski patrolmen reassured them that they would all be taken down safely, should this emergency continue.

For ten-year-old Kit Miller, this day couldn't have been more fun. He loved to climb, and the thought of lowering himself by rope to the snow below was the icing on the cake of his Christmas vacation. He only had one greater passion, wrestling.

"Mom, this is great," he yelled with glee. "They're wrestling under the lift."

With an audience of three thousand surrounding them and hundreds more looking down from their Plexiglas-enclosed box seats, the first ever Vermont ski riot was well underway. Skiers and employees were rolling over each other in an attempt to gain leverage on the slippery surface beside the main gondola.

What had started out as some disgruntled words between Marty Leonard and Dave Jackson had escalated to fistfight status when Dave bellowed, "New York cocksucker," and threw a roundhouse right hand that toppled Leonard into ski school director Franz Vogel. Vogel was trying desperately to stop the pugnacious Jackson from causing any more turmoil.

Marlboro, Vermont, 11:30 AM

"Wilson to dispatch." Pete waited and a tired voice came back.

"Dispatch."

"The accident below Hogback has been cleared, and I'll follow the wrecker into Warrens Mills."

"OK, Pete."

The dispatcher signed off, and Patrolman Peter Wilson got out of his state police cruiser and inspected the sight one last time, then retrieved his flare kit from the roadside. The driver had been lucky. The car obviously skidded out of control in the icy conditions on the Marlboro side of Hogback Mountain. This stretch was flat, and the driver managed not to panic as most city dwellers did when they drove out of their element. He took off his heavy parka and lit a cigarette as he, again, started out on patrol.

His patrol area covered sixty square miles and incorporated twelve towns stretching from the Massachusetts border at Searsburg to its northern limit at Stratton

Township, Vermont. Wilson was working on very little sleep, which was par for the course for Vermont troopers on long holiday weekends.

"Dispatch to Wilson."

"Pete. Get up to Snow Valley immediately. They're reporting a power outage and a riot."

"Say again," Pete replied in disbelief.

"The security guard says there is a brawl going on and they ain't got a bit of power. He can't do nothin' about the power and he surer than shit ain't going to do nothin' about the brawl."

Wilson flipped his cigarette out the window, hit his overhead light, and with siren screaming, he accelerated toward the Auger Hole Road that would take him the back way to Warrens Mills and Snow Valley Resort.

Snow Valley, Vermont, 11:45 AM

"Stop rocking the chair, Kit," Valerie Miller yelled at her son.

She spoke loudly, but her voice landed on deaf ears. Kit Miller was in prepubescent heaven as he and the spectators below cheered each new player who entered the fray.

Against the background of sunlit snow, the ski patrolmen tried to maintain order as lumber-shirted lift attendants came to the aid of their buddy. Dave, by now, had moved to take on the ski school instructors, most of whom spoke no English. Tyrolean curses echoed as ski poles and yellow-lensed goggles were strewn across the now-bloodied lift entrance.

As one pocket of stretched-pant warriors were calmed by the levelheaded patrolmen, another exploded in a flurry of quick verbal taunts followed by gloved hands reaching out and yanking monogrammed turtlenecks over their opponents' heads. This chaos probably would have spread like a dry prairie fire, except for the intervention of two booming shotgun blasts that reverberated across the slopes like thunder.

"The next person who throws a punch gets this shotgun up his ass." Six-foot-three-inch-tall state trooper Pete Wilson introduced himself to the assembled mob, entered the fray, and in less than ten minutes restored a reasonable truce, while the ski patrol began the arduous task of safely removing those trapped in the still-silenced lifts.

December 28, 1963

On any other day of the year, the story of the Snow Valley riot would have headlined the papers from Brattleboro, Vermont, to Boston, but not this day, or many in the days that followed. Instead, the headline of the *Brattleboro Reformer* read "Driver and $1.1 Million Missing in Marlboro." The story went on to say that William Latimer, twenty-two, a part-time driver for People's Bus Line, disappeared at approximately 11:45 AM, Monday, December 27, 1963. The bus was found abandoned, and approximately $1.1 million in cash and checks were missing.

CHAPTER 1

July 5 1997
Salem, Massachusetts, 6:30 AM

THE WHINING HOUR was beginning—anxious minutes between waking and physicians' rounds—ushered in by sounds of shift nurses changing; rubber-soled shoes squeaking, as the night shift hurry to exit; coffee and bacon smells wafting from breakfast carts coasting over freshly waxed floors, between the aging, creaking elevators and the detox unit. For the chronic alcoholics, lulled to sleep by the Librium sandman, it was the hour of shaking, cold sweats, nausea, another day in paradise.

Hangover horrors subsiding, Johnny Dwyer walked out of the Salem Hospital detox at the end of the July 4 long weekend. He read and then discarded aftercare instructions handed him by a tired charge nurse when he exited the unit against medical advice. He mentally counted each floor as he descended on the snail like elevator to the hospital entrance. Humming a song that had been his trademark for more than twenty-five years, he let the words play out gently in his mind.

Tempted to sing one last time "So be gentle and free when you're drinking with me . . . ," he managed to laugh to himself instead.

He was dressed in weathered jeans, a collarless navy T-shirt, and worn but comfortable deck shoes without socks. His wallet contained $816. Plastic inserts held pictures of his long-dead parents plus a color photo of a raven-haired smiling runner in a singlet and tight shorts being crowned the winner of Boston's prestigious marathon by the diminutive swarthy Greek governor of Massachusetts. He would miss Megan, he thought.

Now, his entire being was screaming for a Bushmills, but Dwyer knew he had finally lifted his last jar of the creature. He studied his reflection in the small glass safety box that hung above the floor buttons and smiled. Dwyer was graced with a sailor's deep tan, long curly grayish-brown hair, trimmed beard, and piercing sky blue eyes. A tiny gold ring hung from his left earlobe. His ruggedly handsome face had graced the covers of twelve well-known CDs.

His presence in traditional music circles was minor legend. A penetrating tenor voice, the quality of his songwriting and his total inability to put down the sauce were all a part of the Johnny Dwyer myth.

Approaching the exit, he was still feeling the lingering neutrality of Librium that had been used to calm his body and lower his blood pressure during his twenty-third medical detoxification from alcohol. Except for the clothes on his back, he had no baggage to speak of, but under his arm, he cradled a Martin and Company D28 acoustic guitar in a lined black leather case. He waved cautiously to the familiar driver parked in the hospital's No Parking zone and started toward the vehicle.

After taking a few steps, he stopped, put down the case, and said without hesitation, "It's all over, you can't stop me."

With gloved hands, the driver raised a worn-looking shotgun from the seat, fired, then pumped, ejecting a shell, and fired again, pumped rapidly while watching Dwyer fall, and fired again.

With each pulse of the shotgun Johnny Dwyer's face, neck, and chest exploded. His head, a bloody piñata opened by more lead than usually expended in a midsized Mexican revolution.

Four of the eleven slugs fired from a pump shotgun caught him directly in the front of his face and neck, clipping the left carotid artery and causing a still pumping heart to push his blood out like a crimson fountain, while it tried to compensate for the trauma registering ever so quickly in his brain. The socket that held its once twinkling blue eye was ripped apart, leaving a dangling eyeball suspended from his facial hair. Whisky-laced blood splattered across the brick wall of the hospital and hung like a spider's web. The shooter paused, looked around the empty parking lot for witnesses; seeing none, he waved, as if to say farewell, and drove off across the parking lot and out the barely deserted main road and thought, *I can and I did, Johnny, and for you it is finally over.*

Chapter 2

July 5, 1997
Salem, Massachusetts

THE LAST THING Detective Brian Rooney wanted to hear on that hot July morning was the dispatcher's voice reporting a shooting at the Salem Hospital. He was tired. He had returned late the night before from a job interview and vacation on Nantucket Island, his boyhood home, taking a late ferry to cover the twenty-six miles from the island to the Massachusetts coast. He was busy trying to find a letter that he hoped would be stacked with his mail, and he finally found the letter from the Nantucket Review Committee buried under a pile on his desk.

He opened it slowly as if it was a bomb, which it very well could be, a career bomb if nothing else. Laying the envelope aside, he cautiously read that he was one of four candidates still being considered for the job of police chief.

"I'm still alive; I'm still alive, Kate Rooney. I will be there to watch you grow."

He read it twice and sipped his coffee, savoring the congratulatory tone and looking at the picture of his four-year-old daughter that sat prominently on his desk.

The letter went on to ask if he would give them dates that he could return to the Island for further review of his application. Rooney put the letter aside, and put away the idea of catching up with two weeks of accumulated paperwork. He grabbed his radio and car keys from his desktop, retrieved his nine-millimeter Chief's Special from his top drawer, inserted a clip, and headed for the municipal lot next to police headquarters.

"I'm sick to death of goddamn drug deals," Rooney muttered to himself as he drove out of the station parking lot and flipped on the flashing lights that adorned his unmarked Crown Victoria. The Salem cops were acutely aware of the amount of high quality heroin and a new version of ecstasy that had begun to infiltrate the streets of this North Shore Massachusetts community, known more for its infamous witch trials than its role in opening trade routes to the Far East.

As he cut behind the three-tiered, fortresslike police station and proceeded to travel the four minutes to the hospital, he was sure he would find some gang activity from the neighboring town of Lynn was to blame for the interruption in his paperwork.

"There are some still here that will hold your temper against you Brian."

"I can live with that, Dad."

"Some don't forget the beating you gave the Folger boy."

"I don't forget the beating he and his asshole friends gave Timmy."

He remembered the conversation that he had with his widowed father just three weeks ago when the Nantucket chief's job had been posted on the bulletin board at Salem Police Headquarters.

Rooney's family had been on the Island since 1851, his great grandfather Thomas, having been rescued by Nantucket mariners after surviving the wreck of the ship *British Queen* that had gone down off her coast.

Rooney's father, Michael, had built a mini-island dynasty, serving fresh donuts and pancakes at his downtown breakfast shop, capturing the appetites of the new wave of ACKholes as Rooney jokingly referred to the wealthy off-islanders who had discovered the island in the seventies and had quickly taken the airport designation of ACK as a status symbol, adorning casual clothing and Range Rovers. By the nineties, their wealthy presence had driven real estate prices to the point of absurdity, destroying the middle class dreams of home ownership for the dwindling working class population of the Island.

Now Brian Rooney wanted to be the police chief on an island he had long ago deserted. He would be coming back to Nantucket to watch his father age, a daughter grow, and prove his own maturity with his brother and others on the Island that had written him off as an angry kid with quick hands. His mind drifted to his last conversation with his father as he drove to the crime scene.

"Your brother can help in the politics, Brian. He's done good in spite of your misgivings."

"I can do this on my own, Dad. I don't need Timmy's help."

"What about Janet's new husband. How's he gonna feel if you're back on the Island?"

"She left me, Dad, and I really don't give a shit what he thinks. He's an ACKhole. I just want to be there, see my daughter grow up and spend time with her."

"I'm on your side, Brian, just watch out for your temper, and remember, there's a little bit of ACKhole in all of us."

Orange, broomstick-mounted witches appeared to leap from the door of the blue and gray police cruiser—still flashing lights—while parked in front of the four-story hospital building. Officer Thomas "Red" Nolan and a rookie patrolman that Rooney didn't know were busy stringing yellow crime scene tape. Nolan was a long time beat cop who had recently been transferred to patrol in order to better use his people skills learned over twenty-two years as a liaison between Salem's citizenry and its police force.

"What's gone down, Red?" Rooney asked as he walked past and nodded at the attending paramedics.

"It looks like a drug hit, Brian, but I can't get a lot done. Martin hasn't stopped throwing up since we got here."

Nolan pointed to the uniformed officer who was gagging and trying to remain inconspicuous behind a nearby dumpster.

"I haven't been able to do much except get the medics in and keep the crowd of hospital employees out. I called the Southern Mortuary office and the State Police Crime Scene Unit once the doc from detox confirmed he was dead."

Rooney kneeled and looked quickly at the bloody corpse, observing first a drying, detached eye staring at him. He felt his stomach turn queasy. Not wanting to join the distressed and ghostly-white rookie, he quickly turned his head back to Nolan, who read from a small spiral notebook.

"Shotgun from about eight feet, multiple wounds, mostly face and neck. He probably bled out quick. I found four shell casings in the street, which are in the cruiser in an evidence bag. So far no witnesses, but as soon as the Sergeant gets here, we will start a canvas of those apartments across the street and get the statements from the employees who were coming on this shift."

"Thanks, Red." Rooney walked toward the entrance.

"Hey, slugger." Rooney turned from the front doorway and looked back at a smiling Nolan.

"Can we call you Chief yet?"

Rooney laughed and flipped him the finger.

"Not yet, and stop calling me slugger"

The entrance to the Salem Substance Abuse Unit was crowded with frantic staff and patients trying to find out what happened in the street beyond their view. Brian produced his wallet and flashed his detective shield to a balding, middle-aged man with a large, spider-veined nose, who appeared to be restoring order.

He was greeted by a "thank God you're here" look. Rooney assumed him to be the man in charge of this odd-looking crowd of unshaven, pajama-clad men and women with matted hair and sickly pallor, all trying to get a look at the body being loaded into the Salem emergency vehicle.

"I'm Paul Taglia," he said. "I'm the nursing supervisor on the detox unit. What the hell happened out there? It sounded like a fucking war zone. Someone started screaming like hell and then nothing. It was weird. Our medical director went out and hasn't returned. Is he OK?"

Rooney nodded affirmatively and assured Taglia, that the doctor was assisting the police and would return as soon as the medical examiner arrived.

"I'm going to need some information on your policies if it turns out the victim was one of your patients. No one is to be let out of here without seeing me or one of the other detectives when they get here."

Rooney pulled his cell phone out and dialed the station requesting detective backup.

"OK," said Taglia. "No discharges and I'll hold anybody trying to leave against medical advice. In the meantime, I need to get the boss down here and find out why we did a discharge this early in the day."

The street door opened, and a tall white-jacketed doctor Brian had seen attending the victim entered the area where they were standing. He leaned over to Taglia and said, "Jesus, Paul, it was Dwyer; somebody shot the hell out of Nelson's Vermont buddy."

Taglia looked ashen as he turned to the doctor and blurted out, "I gotta tell Karen."

At that moment, Karen Nelson, clinical director of the Salem Substance Abuse Unit, was sitting through the third meeting in as many days, discussing the changing role of the treatment team. The forty-four-year-old blond nurse practitioner, whose specialty was behavioral medicine, sat rubbing her allergy-ridden blue eyes, wondering why housekeeping hadn't sent the coffee cart she had requested.

Her staff was frustrated and rebellious as they increasingly saw their unit composition changing from an alcohol and cocaine based population to one comprised of what she referred to as the second generation of junkies.

She reviewed what she had written on the blackboard for them as if it might help them to understand the changes in street drug use that occur every two or three years. Most staff members had little experience with treating high numbers of heroin-addicted patients, and most, couldn't handle the constant whining that the increasingly middle-class opiate addicts brought to the detox milieu.

"Paging Karen Nelson."

The voice seemed to blast over the administration building's speaker system.

"Karen Nelson, call extension 221."

"Oh shit," she said aloud. "I knew this day was going too smoothly."

As soon as she dialed the detox extension, Paul Taglia answered nervously.

"Karen, get back here quick. Somebody shot and killed a patient outside the unit." He spoke hesitantly, almost in a whisper. "It was that buddy of yours from Vermont."

Her stomach knotted as she looked around the room at the other staff members. In one phone call, she had lost an ex-lover, an old friend, and her best friend's only brother. Somehow, this thing with Johnny was her fault. She knew something was different when he checked himself into the hospital.

She sat back and could feel the tears starting to creep from that sad place she had learned to live with forever. *Oh God, Meggy, Meggy, Meggy. Not again.*

Chapter 3

July 5, 1997
Boston, Massachusetts

MEGAN DWYER ANSWERED the door of her Beacon Hill apartment shakily, her thoughts locked in the screaming silence of her brother's death. She hugged Karen Nelson and sobbed painfully, her face contorted in memory. She stood, clinging, as if begging like a child, not to be hurt. Repeatedly, she flashed back to that horrible day ten years ago when the priest from Sacred Heart and her cousin Billy Regan held her and tried to comfort her as they told her of the accident that had claimed her parents' lives. And now, she stood powerless again. Bleak, disordered images of death battered her consciousness as she tried to make some sense of what the red-haired detective was saying, as he explained the brutal circumstance surrounding the murder of her brother. She dizzily sat down in a wing chair that had been her parents', gripping the arms, and trying to slow her breathing. She motioned Rooney to sit on a large couch near a window that overlooked the bustling pedestrian traffic on the street below. "This is not happening to me again."

"Do you want us to call someone, Meggy? What about Cooper?" Karen asked, referring to Megan's longtime coach and on-again-off-again lover. Megan shook her head.

"No. I don't want to see anyone right now. I'm just having a hard time believing this could happen to Johnny. Not this way, the booze maybe, an accident maybe, but not murdered. I just don't believe it."

"Can you think of any reason that anyone would want to kill your brother?" Rooney asked. Megan Dwyer smiled faintly and looked at Karen. Brian looked at both women trying to understand the shared secret that would bring a smile in the middle of this tragedy.

"Let me tell you a little about Johnny," said Megan. As she spoke, she reached behind her chair, and picked up a compact disk and handed it to Brian.

"This was Johnny's last CD, a collection of traditional maritime music he called *Remember the Fishing.*"

On the front cover was a picture of a bearded Johnny Dwyer dressed in a heavy wool sweater and jeans, set in what looked like a New England or Canadian fishing village. He was playing a penny whistle and smiling as he looked out on the harbor. Behind him sat a handsome-looking man in his forties holding a five-string banjo.

"Johnny and Ben Latimer spent eight months researching and writing for this album; when they finished it, and went on tour, Johnny proceeded to get drunk for every performance from Salem to New Brunswick, until Ben quit in disgust, and John finally ended up in detox at his home away from home in New Hampshire."

Brian looked puzzled at the New Hampshire reference.

"Oak Hill. He dried out there so much he should have had stock in the place."

She stopped and caught her breath. Her face drained of color.

"I can tell you that every pub owner in the northeast has wished my brother dead at one time or another. He pissed off just about everybody in the business when he would show up drunk for a performance, or worse than that, not show up at all."

She spoke softly picturing Johnny's smile and pointed around the room to concert posters and pictures of her brother with various politicians and celebrities. There were framed letters prominently hung on the living room wall. Rooney could make out some signatures that he knew including one from the family of a past president of the United States who had lost his life in the same senseless manner as had Johnny Dwyer.

"I can guarantee you these same people would walk on fire for the privilege of bearing his casket. My brother was a good man," Megan wept and rubbed at her eyes with the back of her hand to clear the tears.

"Ms. Dwyer," Brian interrupted, "I hate to ask this right now, but could Johnny have been involved in any drug activity, or owed any money to someone who would seek this kind of revenge? What about any relationships, an ex-wife, perhaps?" He paused and said, "Could he have been a batterer?"

"Detective," Karen Nelson interrupted, "let me answer that. I'm as close as any ex-wife could have been. I spent a lot of years with Johnny. He never married, but definitely had quite a few relationships. He was smooth as silk and could be a heart breaker, but he wasn't vicious. In twenty-five years, I never saw him really angry; in fact, like most drunks, he usually ended up hurting himself, one way or the other," Nelson continued while holding back tears.

"I met him in on a ski trip to Snow Valley in Southern Vermont. At the time he was singing in a small after-hours coffeehouse and bottle club where we went when the bars closed." She looked over at Megan and they both smiled.

"That's the same night I met Megan as well. We were both underage, but Johnny got us in." Nelson leaned over and held Megan's hand, gripping hard while she continued fighting tears as she spoke.

"The place was candlelit with maybe thirty tables and a huge fireplace. Johnny walked on stage that night and opened with his "anthem" as we called it. For twenty-five years, he always opened his show with the same song, which all the locals seemed to know. "So be gentle and free," she sang in a strained, but lyrical voice. "When you're drinking with me, I'm a man you won't meet every day."

She looked over at Megan and both sang together, as if on cue, of a man you won't meet every day, and never again after this bloody July morning.

"Sorry, Detective," Megan said. "It seems that maybe this grieving has been planned for a long time. The doctor who runs Oak Hill warned us that we would lose my brother at an early age unless he stopped drinking. Her eyes were puffy red now, and when she spoke, it was to no one in particular.

"My grandmother used to tell us there are only a few things that can mask the pain of death—Whiskey, the church, or a song. For me, the whiskey and the church went long ago. We have been left with some very good music." She continued to hold the CD, turning it repeatedly, as if a talisman that could stop the reality of the moment.

Brian was uncomfortable with this woman's feelings and wanted to move on.

"What about money? Could his drinking have gotten him in hock to anyone, any mob connections, any loan sharks?"

"No," Megan shook her head and said, "Unlike most people in his lifestyle, Johnny seemed to have an uncanny ability to make money. He gave away a lot to charities and drank away more than most."

"His singing earned him that much?" Rooney asked skeptically.

"Yes, but more than that. He was a partner in the recording studio where these tapes and CDs were made. It started in the early sixties when he was still shipping out in the merchant marine, playing the bars on Cape Cod in the summer and the ski areas in the winter. He got to know a lot of the happy hour singers who were developing the same following of people who liked their music and wanted to buy records and tapes, which most of these groups couldn't afford to make."

She paused for a moment to catch her breath. "He thought up the idea for a niche recording studio. He catered to the pub performers then, but now the studio crosses a whole range of music. It's located it in Southern Vermont, on the grounds of Frost College, which was about six or seven miles from where he lived in Vermont."

Rooney wrote down the address on the back of the CD cover.

Megan seemed more composed as she spoke, obviously taking pride in her brother's accomplishment, and using the story to let this policeman know that her brother was just not some stumblebum. Rooney had seen this so many times in his career when the relative of a criminal or a victim would go out of their way to extol their good points. He let her speak and took more notes as she went on.

"He allowed his performers to come in their free time and record the stuff their audiences liked, plus whatever new songs that were flooding the folk music scene at the time. He also provided studio musicians. It was a good cheap deal for everyone concerned. As music became more electric, the Frost Studio became a haven for the small band of folk purists who wanted to retain an acoustic sound. Frost provided records and tapes to sell in the small number of coffeehouses that remained loyal to traditional music. He also attracted Gaelic performers whose circuit was beginning to flourish when Irish pubs started to spring up from coast-to-coast. At one point, he even began a charity with some of the Irish singers. He's done hundreds of concerts to support kids from the North and South of Ireland to come here and live with American families."

"What is the name of the group?" Rooney turned a page in his notebook.

"It's called the Holy Ground Society. They're located here in Boston and New York. My brother was on their board, and even though he hated formality, he always made a point to come into town for their quarterly meetings."

When she finished speaking, she began again to weep, and then sob. Karen got up from her chair and hugged her, rocking her gently, like an infant, and placing a shawl over her as the sobbing turned to a wail. The primordial cry told Brian that there would be nothing gained by continued questioning. He felt awkward and uncomfortable as he always did when facing another person's grieving.

"Ms. Dwyer, just one more question. Can you think of anyone who could benefit from this?" She looked like a gaunt scarecrow as she spoke. Shaking, she pulled the quilt around her like a giant multicolored cocoon.

"If you mean financially, it's just me, and I'm sure he left some money to the Holy Ground Society, but you probably should talk to his lawyer in Vermont. His name is Ed Romano. His office is in Warrens Mills. He handled everything for my brother."

Rooney jotted down the lawyer's name. As Megan reached over to hand him her phone directory, the phone on the writing desk began to ring. She looked at it as though it was a foreign object. She tentatively answered it.

"Hello. No he's not. I'm sorry. Who's calling?" She looked overwhelmed and handed the phone to the detective.

"I can't handle this today, please."

Brian identified himself to the caller and heard, "This is Peter Wilson in Warrens Mills, Vermont. I'm trying to locate Johnny Dwyer. I run a home security firm here, and in the last couple of days, his house on Valley Road was broken into. It looks like whoever did the break was looking for something specific, but I can't tell whether there is anything missing or not. I'm going to need some help on this from Johnny or a family member or friend who has been in the house lately."

"Can you do me a favor? Please alert the locals and the Vermont State Police that this could be connected to a homicide investigation that is ongoing in Massachusetts, and we would appreciate it if the scene could be sealed. Mr. Dwyer was shot to death at six thirty this morning."

Wilson paused as if to digest what he had just been told. He then spoke assuring Rooney that he could call in the Vermont State Police "They have to come out of Waterbury from the State crime lab," he explained. "I'll alert the locals to seal the house and place somebody here till we get a handle on this thing."

"Thanks, Wilson. By the way, are you ex-law enforcement?"

"Twenty-eight years, seven months, six days, Vermont State Police. "But who's counting?"

CHAPTER 4

July 8, 1997
Salem, Massachusetts

CHIEF OF DETECTIVES Angus Martin had the confident look of a man who had never been bullied, and had never bullied. At six feet four inches, set on a solid Nova Scotia fisherman's frame, he had the cut of a man, whose presence always seemed to lend comfort to his surroundings, no matter how hostile. He was as comfortable with politicians as he was with street thugs, and had developed a reputation for never taking bullshit from either. He was Brian Rooney's boss, friend, and longtime mentor in the Salem Police Department. Martin's speech still had the remnants of his childhood on Cape Sable, even though he had been a U.S. citizen for thirty-five years.

"Were they tough on your childhood fisticuffs, Bry?"

"Considering the fact that I beat the shit out of one of the selectmen when I was in high school, and the fact that I'm known to visit the Island's most notorious criminal while he's doing a stretch in Walpole Prison raises some eyebrows. But having a gay brother with more money and real estate than brains seems to scare them more than I do."

"How you and brother Timmy doing?"

"Don't ask, I still think he's got something to do with some of the so-called medical marijuana coming onto the Island"

"I won't ask, but how about the boxing, you know the home town hero stuff?"

"That went OK; my old coach from the Boys Club showed at the hearing, but he wasn't allowed to say anything. It's funny, I never really knew how he felt when I walked away from Munich. I was his pride and joy, but I never felt that anybody would be hurt because of my decision, but he must have felt something. He's never said a word."

"Do you want the job, Brian?"

"I want to be back on the Island as my father gets older and watch my daughter grow up. I realize how much this divorce is kicking the shit out of me when I see that Kate's living with a new man in her life. Christ, Cap, I don't want that idiot raising my kid."

"Don't blame you, I'd do the same. Did you spend much time with her this trip?

"Every minute I could, but her asshole stepfather's not making things easy."

Rooney sipped at his coffee and then asked, "What do you think my chances are Angus?"

"A lot depends on the other candidates. If there were thirty, and it's down to four, that's a damn good sign. You've got the time, and the administrative experience, and I told you that master's you earned at Northeastern would come in handy. Now you've got a major case to figure out."

"You want me to finish up the Dwyer murder?"

"All the way. Hand off what you've got pending to other guys in the squad and get extensions on anything else you've got in court. I want the mayor and the city council off my ass on this thing, so I'm assigning you full time to it. Keep in touch with the DA's office and the state police, but this is yours. Work with Sheila and Red. Keep them in the loop. Let her do the local interviews while you're in Vermont."

Ten minutes later other members of the ten men, one woman Salem detective squad plus Patrolman Red Nolan sat down to their weekly meeting. Rooney led off reading from his well-worn notebook.

"I've got a fifty-eight-year-old deceased white male shot within twenty feet of a hospital at 6:30 AM with no witnesses. There is no apparent suspect and his wallet and belongings were untouched. I've got four expended 12-gauge casings found at the scene by Patrolman Nolan. Our canvas of the area around the hospital has turned up nothing so far and the other patients we spoke to were either too "mocus" or too medicated to make any sense. We are interviewing the morning shift employees, but so far, that's turned up nothing to speak of. Beyond that, I've got absolute horseshit. It seems he was a loner, and only connected to one quasi-political charity, some Irish fund raising group located in South Boston. We're checking on them as we speak."

"Sheila, what are you coming up with on the streets?"

Martin turned to his one female detective who spent most of her time on gang activity and narcotics. Sheila Merino was a former gang kid who found her way out of the streets through martial arts, and now after six years of paying dues in uniform, had become a highly respected member of Martin's detective force. Her discipline and sense of integrity culled in a New York dojo were subtly hidden beneath dark eyes, flawless olive skin, as well as small but perfectly formed breasts and sculptured butt.

"It's quiet, boss. This guy seems to have no connection with any drug activity in the Latino community, and my snitches haven't got a clue. The weapon doesn't fit the street profile; the gangs don't use twelve gauges. Whoever this guy pissed off was more than likely Anglo, and from somewhere in Boston, probably Southie or Charlestown." She looked at Rooney as she spoke, "Maybe there's something in this charity we ought to know about Brian?"

Rooney nodded in agreement with her. "I think you're right, Sheila. Check out any possible links between this Holy Ground Society and anything that smells dirty, especially weapons or money laundering."

"Where are you going next with the investigation?" Martin asked while sipping at his brewed tea and taking notes.

"I'm checking the gang activity with the Lynn PD. Who knows, maybe this guy was involved in some shit he just plain didn't belong in. But I doubt if we tie this guy to anything going on in town. If you want, I'll continue to handle the media, but they've already made their minds up that it's drug related."

Sheila held up the *Salem News* story that suggested the murder was related to the heroin traffic on the North Shore, and had the usual "sources close to the investigation said today . . ."

"Where did that shit come from?"

"The reporter talked to a guy who was in the unit with Dwyer and he thinks he got the story from the horse's mouth."

"Anything to it?"

"Nope, turns out the guy was in full-blown withdrawal when Dwyer got hit. He was in a separate unit and never even saw him, let alone speak to him. The reporter stumbled across the guy when he was leaving and assumed he was straight, so he bought the whole package. The reporter got scammed, and the patient mysteriously ended up with enough cash to score another bundle. The guy's back in detox today, laughing his ass off at the news."

"Keep up the no comment, Sheila. I do not, I repeat, do not want this to turn into a feeding frenzy for the papers."

He paused, turned to Rooney. "Brian, do you want to handle the press conference?"

"Why not let Sheila handle it all, boss. I'll be in Vermont for the next three days and it will be a hell of a lot easier to coordinate from here than long distance."

"OK, Sheila, it's yours. Set it up for the front steps. Keep it short and focus on our ongoing efforts and appeal to anyone who might have knowledge to come forward."

"Red, have we got the autopsy back yet?"

"The MEs office gave me a prelim this morning over the phone. He took eleven direct slugs to the face and neck severing the carotid, causing him to bleed out rapidly. He was probably dead in less than eight minutes. They're faxing over the total report this afternoon."

"Any forearm hits, Red?" asked Rooney.

"None, Brian. He never tried to cover up."

Martin looked around the table. "Whoever shot Dwyer could have been someone he knew, and maybe trusted, since the natural reflex is to raise your arms and hands defensively when accosted by an assailant or suspected assailant."

"Brian, before you march off to Vermont with the sister, you better know goddam well where she was when he was popped."

"I hear ya, boss, but I'm not liking the sister for this."

"Ya, but you're obviously liking the sister for something."

Desk Officer Barbara Poole interrupted the meeting.

"Cap, you aren't gonna believe what just came in." She came around the conference table and inserted a tape in the VCR at the end of room. As she rolled the combination unit forward and adjusted the sound, there appeared on screen the apparent ghost of Johnny Dwyer.

"Woody wrote his best music while wandering the Pacific Northwest talking and singing with the Okies who were eking out a living as scrub farmers and living in government camps."

Dwyer was speaking to a small audience in an auditorium. As he spoke, he began to tune his guitar. The camera focused on the Martin Company trademark on the guitar head, then slowly panned to Johnny's face as he continued rambling and continued tuning.

Johnny began to trace the migrant experience in a song American songwriter and dust bowl balladeer Woody Guthrie called "Pastures of Plenty." His voice growing stronger as he walked his listeners through "California and Arizona I've worked on your crops," he smiled as those who knew the song began to sing. "Then Northward up to Oregon to gather your hops / dig the beets from your ground, take the grapes from your vine / to set on your table that light sparkling wine . . ."

They followed him like schoolchildren as he closed with Guthrie's wonderful line that summarized so well America's conflicted depression paradox. "My land I'll defend with my life if need be, my pastures of plenty must always be free."

"What the hell is this and where did it come from?" Rooney looked puzzled while turning to face Officer Poole.

"The date on this tape is the third. If he needed to detox, his blood alcohol should have been off the charts."

Rooney looked at the tape closely watching Dwyer.

"Christ, he looks like some professor giving a lecture and not some stew bum headed for the Salem detox."

"The Peabody Essex Museum curator dropped it off and took off like a bat out a hell. Turns out Dwyer had been booked into their folk performers series for a couple of months," Poole answered.

"No shit," said Rooney. "We'll call him and tell him he's got twenty minutes to get his ass over here and talk to us about our dead minstrel boy."

Poole headed for the Plexiglas enclosed station front while the others compared notes on other criminal activity in Salem. They broke twenty minutes later, and as Rooney prepared to leave, Martin pulled him aside, and for the second time that day reminded him that the sister was still a suspect and to watch his ass until they knew more.

Brian agreed, yet still felt in his gut that this murder had to do with something far different from family arguments or insurance policies.

"Brian, you got a call from a Chief Atkins, in Warrens Mills, Vermont."

Rooney picked up his messages as she spoke.

"He said to tell you to try and get an elimination print from Dwyer's sister. And also ask her if she can think of anybody else who stayed at the house on a regular basis, or worked for her brother whose prints they might need."

"Thanks, Barb, and do me a favor will ya."

"Sure, Bry. Waddya need?"

"When the sister comes this afternoon, would you do the print?"

"No problem, I'll handle her with kid gloves," Poole assured him.

Rooney had two hours to kill before meeting with the sister. He went to the locker room and changed into a T-shirt, shorts, and high-topped boxing shoes. He taped his hands and spent a half hour on the heavy bag that the chief installed in order for Rooney to help win back his Massachusetts police boxing title.

Slugger signs sprouted up around the station after his last fight and he was living with the nickname somewhat unhappily. As he pounded at the Everlast symbol printed on the bag, he thought of the Boys Club where he had learned to box and the place that probably saved his ass. Sweat poured out as he worked the lower part of the bag, crouching lower, feeling the pain spreading across his forty five year old back.

He thought of his Boys Club coach Sandy Renucci—pot bellied, bald, and always admonishing to stay inside and hammer the body. Rooney pictured the twenty-eight-year-old state police corporal who had taken his title with a head butt the year before. "Not this year, asshole."

Chapter 5

July 8, 1997
Boston, Massachusetts

"THANK YOU, SEAMUS. That's a beautiful way of describing Johnny's life. I know how much you loved my brother, and I promise to call you when we find out about a service." A weeping Megan Dwyer hung up the phone and leafed through pictures and wandered in memories as she sat with her cousin Bill Regan.

Regan was now her last male relative and had always been there for her. After the death of her parents, when Johnny decided to drink his way through the funeral and the burial, it was Regan that had finally been able to reach through and pull Johnny back from the pit of depression long enough to honor his parent's death.

Bill had spent the night at her apartment rather than return home to his wife and four girls in nearby Watertown. They drank Megan's specially brewed dark roast coffee and ate bagels from the shop next to the Sevens. The Sevens was their old drinking and lusting hangout on Charles Street, near the base of Boston's Beacon Hill, a short distance from the golden-domed State House and the Massachusetts seat of government.

"Look at this, Meggy."

Bill handed her a black-and-white photo of all the cousins draped together in better times, smashing into the surf at Silver Beach on Cape Cod.

"Look at Barbara and your brother. They were thick as thieves."

Barbara was Bill's older sister, who had married early and wealthy, then found cocktails and diet pills. Barbara at the age of forty-four, succumbed to the ravages of liver cancer, while her husband and two daughters looked on helplessly.

The black-and-white photos chronicled the history of this second-generation Irish family that prospered in a postwar economy.

"God, we were lucky kids," Meggy said aloud. She wiped her eyes as she looked at the photo of her parents who had saved for years to vacation in the old country and ended up dying together, as their overloaded plane could not hold the runway at Boston's Logan Airport. The yearlong investigation had hinted at pilot error and icy conditions, but was never fully resolved to Megan's satisfaction.

Their insurance provided her and her brother with economic freedom, not that either needed the money since Johnny's studio was doing well in spite of his drinking. Megan had won enough prize money on the road race circuit and through her sponsorship deal with New Balance shoes and Perrier, to live comfortably in her condo, and travel to other races throughout the world. Now she felt alone and beaten. She knew it was time to run again, as she always had, but this time to Vermont. When she found some answers there, maybe she could stop running. *Maybe stop running for good,* she thought to herself.

She stacked the pictures neatly and gave them a soft kiss as she put them in the chest that had come from County Cork so many years and too many tears ago. Seamus Flynn had said so well, "Johnny's life had been an Irish song, full of hope one morning and sorrow the next, but never defeated. Johnny was a man you won't meet every day."

Chapter 6

July 8, 1997
Salem, Massachusetts

"DETECTIVE, BEFORE WE start any investigative process, or take any fingerprints, why don't we agree on some ground rules for this afternoon."

Bill Regan spoke with the authority of fifteen years as a defense attorney. Rooney wasn't used to confrontation in dealing with family members this early in the process. Controlling the interview was his goal from the outset, and he really didn't feel like sparring with some Boston College double eagle. Megan sat in the second-floor conference room of the Salem Police Station with her cousin Bill and drank coffee.

"Do you have a problem, Mr. Regan?"

"I have a problem with Megan giving a print until we know if she's a suspect in her brother's murder."

Brian backed off slightly from the table and raised his hands as if to signal a truce in the discussion.

"Sorry Megan, maybe I should just ask where you were at the time of your brother's death."

"That's easy enough," she replied. "I run every morning at six, and usually wind up at the Bagel Bonanza by seven thirty."

"Do you run the same route every day?"

"Usually, unless I'm training for a marathon. Then I throw in extra miles or add more of the steep hills across from Mass General."

"Did anybody see you running on Monday?"

"Probably ten or fifteen people," she said without hesitating.

"How can you be so sure?"

"Because I always run with the same group. The Greater Boston Track Club." She sat back and gave him a slight grin.

The conversation became less confrontational as the interview progressed. Rooney began to trust his first instinct that this woman had nothing to do with her brother's death. Bill Regan also became friendlier as he saw the detective as a willing ally in the capture of the person who shot his cousin. They talked somewhat painfully about Johnny's alcoholism.

Rooney asked if they could explain the tape that he had viewed earlier. "He appeared sober, but—"

"He was in a blackout," Megan interjected. "I've seen him do it a hundred times and never could I tell until the next day or even two, when he would crash." She told a story of her brother reciting "A Child's Christmas in Wales" to a college audience.

"He was a master at creating the right mood for the season. It was at a homecoming weekend at Middlebury College and Christmas was a few weeks away. I swear that if you closed your eyes and listened, you would think you were ten years old and experiencing the holiday in the British Isles." She was drawing a picture with her hands as she spoke.

"The audience hung on his every word then waited as he appeared to be resting on his stool. Just when they thought he was about to deliver the ending, he fell face first to ground and never woke up until the next morning, remembering nothing of the event or the poem. He spent the morning drinking vodka, and then just as suddenly as he stopped the night before, he began again to recite right where he left off. Karen Nelson and I were treated to a one-man show."

Rooney spent a good part of the afternoon listening attentively to Megan and Bill as they outlined Johnny's history of blackout drinking. He made note to check with Karen Nelson for her opinion on whether a crime of a serious nature could be committed while in this phase of intoxication. Perhaps there was a key somewhere in the booze that would unlock the puzzle of the gentleman from Warrens Mills, Vermont, but for now he had very little to go on and even less with which to comfort the family.

"I am planning to meet with the chief in Warrens Mills on Tuesday. If you are comfortable going through Johnny's house, I would appreciate your input as to what might be missing."

Megan looked first at Regan then to Rooney and answered.

"Detective, I believe his whole nightmare has something to do with Vermont. The last ten years it seems that something or somebody that was destroying him haunted my brother. He wouldn't talk about it or even let me try to help him. When it got too bad, he ran like a child to Oak Hill.

She paused and brushed back a tear. "As of next Tuesday, I'm not leaving Vermont until I find who killed my brother. If I have to spend every cent I've got, I'll see that person rot in hell," she added bitterly.

As she spoke, Rooney began to see another side of Megan Dwyer and hoped it would not be a problem. This woman was strong and angry. She was no longer a victim to be comforted, but was acting more like an avenging angel who no longer spoke softly, but with conviction and venom.

When they finished making arrangements to meet on the following Tuesday to travel to Vermont, Megan and Regan left to meet with officials at the State Police Crime Lab and find out when they could retrieve Johnny's body for burial.

Rooney went to the computer room and pulled up the archives from the *Boston Globe* looking for information on Dwyer. There were a series of concert reviews as well as gossip column material attesting to his larger-than-life status as a performer, songwriter, and drunk. It was at the end of a gossip piece that reference was made to his sister.

Rooney entered Megan's name and found to his surprise that there was much more written about Meagan Dwyer than on her late brother. Her ability to make the transition from college amateur to professional athlete was covered thoroughly by both male and female Globe staff. Her prize winnings from major marathons and 10K races were estimated at over a half million dollars, and the reporter was convinced that she had received under-the-table appearance money as well. What caught his eye was a piece speculating that her relationship with her coach may not be the healthiest, and in fact the writer, a female sports columnist named Pam Swift, speculated that in the long run, this Svengali, Cooper Adson might hinder her career rather than help it. Rooney printed three of the articles and placed them in his briefcase.

Chapter 7

July 13, 1997
Salem, Massachusetts

THE VOICES OF doubt wandered into Brian Rooney's waking moments.

"Whose battles are you fighting, Brian?"

"I don't get you."

"You told me you've been fighting since you were a kid. Why? What were you fighting about?"

"Some were about my brother. I couldn't stand to see him get picked on."

"Who picked on him?"

"Kids are cruel as shit to other kids who are different."

"How was he different?"

"He was always considered a sissy, you know what I mean."

"Your brother is gay?"

"That's what they call it now, but not when we were kids."

The therapist had been mandated after a possible suspension faced by Rooney for punching a fellow officer. Officer Edward Wells had clearly violated the civil rights of a gay man. The man, a Methodist minister from Beverly, brought to custody for a violation of a public morality charge, soliciting at a rest stop, was being housed overnight in the holding cell. Rooney found the man beaten, silent, and shame-filled a few hours after his confinement. Rooney had taken the patrolman into the male officers' locker room and asked him what happened. The answer "he's just a faggot, he'll keep his mouth shut" was the wrong answer for Rooney. He proceeded to stomach punch the officer, leaving no marks on his face, but leaving him gasping for breath with a broken rib behind the last row of lockers. The chief tabled the incident on the condition that Rooney get counseling for anger.

"Do you and your brother get along now?"

"All right I guess, I don't see him that much. He's my brother, you know how that goes."

"I'm afraid I don't know Brian."

"I mean I love him, but I always had a hard time, as we got older, with his lifestyle."

"You mean his homosexuality?"

"Yes, and some of the risks he takes."

"What is it about his lifestyle that bothers you the most?"

Rooney made coffee and buttered a bagel as he tried to push the memory of the therapist from his mind, but knew he couldn't run from the session that played like film in his head. He remembered being uncomfortable sitting in an armchair and looking straight at the therapist.

"At Christmastime, the year my mother died, we had a family party at the White Elephant. My brother brought his lover who appeared to be very sick. I didn't know the man very well; he was from off-island. His name was Barry Ahearn. He was almost blind and couldn't have weighed more than a hundred pounds."

The words choked in his throat.

"Before dinner, we had drinks, and my brother played Christmas carols on the piano. It was snowing and the fire in the fireplace was blistering hot. I could almost feel my mother's presence in the room. Maybe it was the wine or the snowstorm, but it all felt wonderful."

"It sounds like a perfect New England Christmas, Brian, I'm envious."

"After caroling for a while, my brother dedicated a song and sang it to this man. Jesus, Doc, he sang like we weren't even there."

"And that bothered you, being left out of your brother's affection, or was it just watching him caring about another man?"

The therapist paused and watched Rooney's reaction.

"What did you do?"

"I left."

"How did your brother react to you leaving?"

"I haven't spoken to him since the incident, so I really don't know."

"Have you tried to talk it out with him?"

"He's called me and written me, but I'm just not ready to talk about it."

"How are things with your ex-wife and your little girl?"

"My ex and I speak occasionally, but she's happily remarried. I see her when I pick up my daughter and we talk when we need to."

"Are you angry at her for getting remarried?"

"Not really. I was never around when she needed me. Three miscarriages and I managed somehow be unable to comfort her. Thank God for Katie. She was a miracle kid."

Rooney felt himself choking up when he thought of his only child.

"Do you think you're going to lose her too, Brian?"

Rooney put the thought away and began to pack for his upcoming trip to Vermont.

Chapter 8

July 13, 1997
Boston, Massachusetts

AS MEGAN DWYER FINISHED packing to go to Vermont, she stopped and looked over her condo. Her trophies took up an entire bookcase that had once belonged to her parents. There was a picture of her winning the National women's cross-country that had been taken at Franklin Park by a *Boston Globe* photographer. Another showed her third-place finish in the first ever Women's Olympic Marathon Trials.

The same picture used to hang on the wall of the now defunct Eliot Lounge, along with those of Frank Shorter, Bill Rogers and Joan Benoit. The Eliot, as it was known in the Boston running community, had become Mecca for the thousands who came each year to run the twenty-six miles from the village of Hopkinton, Massachusetts, to downtown Boston. Boston Marathon guru and full-time bartender

Tommy Leonard, who had befriended Meggy's entire team from the time they were college juniors, assembled the gallery of pictures there.

Distance running had given Megan fame in Boston, as well as in national athletic circles. She had parlayed that fame, as well as a marketing degree from the University of Vermont, into the creation of the Beantown Belle Road Race. The race was a world-class 10K that wound through the streets and neighborhoods of Boston with sometimes as many as ten thousand women sharing pride in this annual event. *Runner's World* called it "A sponsor's dream that reaches across a full spectrum of female runners."

The event also propelled Megan into Boston's social and political circles as well. It forced a shy, quiet, and extremely attractive woman into public speaking and charitable work that sat well with potential sponsors and kept her name in the forefront of Boston's female athletic contingent.

Her resignation as director did not surprise the press in light of her brother's death. But very few people knew the real reason for her move to Vermont and she hoped to keep it that way. She looked at her old cross-country trophies and remembered the thrill of competing in all sorts of foul weather. She smiled as she reflected on her ability to kick near the end of races when her competition had stopped looking over their shoulders. Meggy Dwyer was a strong closer, and that she owed to Cooper Adson.

His picture graced more than half the wall space that she had devoted to her running accomplishments, for in great part she was a testament to his coaching. They met in her senior year at UVM, as the University of Vermont is called. He was a former distance runner who had landed a job working to build a team for the

New Balance shoe company. She was one of the first women recruited and he not only became her coach, but her first bed partner as well.

He had called twice in the past couple of hours, but she knew there was nothing he could say now to make up for his open disdain for her brother's lifestyle. After twenty years of dependency, she had finally gathered the courage to tell him to "fuck off." Their parting was made easier by the fact the her lover was supposedly sleeping with a Boston College running "phenom" who was half his age.

The doorbell rang, jarring her back to the present.

"Are you all set?" Rooney asked entering her sunlit living room. He sat on her brother's favorite couch, where Johnny had slept-off many a hangover.

"Give me a few minutes to finish this note for the real estate company."

Rooney looked around the room, focusing on the trophies.

"Are these all yours?" he asked, feeling inadequate for having not observed them on his first visit.

Another life, another time," she smiled a bit and felt embarrassed as she continued to write.

"Are you seriously thinking of staying in Vermont?"

"Absolutely."

"And you have actually spoken to someone about finding your brother's killer?"

"Yes, I spoke to Wilson, the ex-state cop who called about the break-in at the house."

"Did he recommend someone?"

"I told him that you and I would discuss it when we got up there."

"Hold on Megan. I can't speak to him about helping out, this is a police matter."

"No, Detective, it's my matter. And as much as I hope that you guys find the murderer, I'm not hedging any bets. When my parents were killed, we were told we would have an answer to the reason for the crash within a year. It's been ten years Brian and I still don't know, so pardon my cynicism."

"These things can cost a lot of money to investigate," Rooney reminded her.

"Brian, let's cut out all the crap. Do me a favor and look around this room. Do I look poor to you?"

Rooney wasn't sure how to answer, so she answered for him.

"I'm worth a little over a million dollars just from the airline settlement, and I've inherited another four hundred thousand from Johnny's insurance. Now I own two homes outright and the major interest in a profitable recording company. I have no husband and no children. All I want to do is grieve for a brother I loved and find out who could have done this to him and to me."

"I'm sorry, I don't doubt your ability to pull this off, but there may be more at stake here than just finding your brother's murderer, like your personal safety." Rooney could feel himself walking a line between anger at her naiveté and wanting to protect her from herself.

"Your million dollars won't protect you from your brother's killer if there is another motive that we don't understand. The person who killed your brother was a vicious and a cold-blooded son of a bitch, either that or a professional killer. The same person would have absolutely no qualms about killing you if you interfere."

She was at first taken aback by his apparent anger, then quietly said, "Pardon me, Detective, there is someone I need to call before we go, so could I have a little privacy?"

Nice going, Rooney, he thought to himself. *This is going to be a long trip to Vermont.*

CHAPTER 9

July 13 1997
Marlboro, Vermont

BEN REMEMBERED THAT the ride from their home was eight hours of boredom, bathrooms and carsickness, until the pavement ended and their Vermont odyssey began. He and his brother Billy had been coming to Lake Bomoseen since infancy. Their suburban world of brick schools and supermarkets was transformed into a world of sweet-smelling hayfields and crisp mornings that came alive with the first crackle of kindling. The brothers' Latimer hid their heads under their blankets until the warmth of the wood stove permeated the thin walls of their lakeside cottage. They arose to the smell of bacon cooking in a large black skillet and the sound of eggs being dropped into hot grease. Fresh eggs the boys had selected the day before as they did chores on the nearby farm of a fourth-generation Vermonter and his two sons.

In the early morning, they rode in the back of a rusted, prewar pickup, cottage to cottage, collecting trash and garbage. They then dumped it in large metal containers and hauled it away to the landfill near the main house on the property. They were careful to keep separate the edible waste to feed the pigs that were penned up at the rear of the barn. Later, they sat on three-legged milk stools and learned the art of milking from the Barton boys who were more than willing to pass on the work to the city kids.

After milking, when the truck was emptied and hosed down to the satisfaction of Delbert Barton, the owner's eldest son, they began their favorite chore of delivering ice to the cottages. By now, their white T-shirts had begun to show the badge of sweat they wore so proudly as the July morning turned hot. They made a point never to ride in the cab; instead they stood in the flat bed holding on for dear life as Delbert caromed down the birch and maple-trimmed dirt road. Finally, he turned into his grandmother's driveway headed for the icehouse attached to the long yellow house.

Sawdust was everywhere they walked as they began to separate out the twenty-pound blocks that would be halved and cleaned with a hose to remove the dark moist coating. The sawdust had insulated the ice since February, when it was placed in the barn after having been cut from the lake. The sleighs used to carry the ice effortlessly along snow-packed roads now rested in this cavernous, frigid barn until the winter.

The boys lugged the blocks with heavy metal tongs that bit and held their frozen cargo until they deposited them on to the bed of the truck. Delbert would then bring the scale and they would be off to peddle their melting wares and flex their freckled biceps as they made their way from cottage to cottage. There they would carefully chop with wood-handled picks and weigh out the right measure to keep cool the provisions tucked inside the wooden iceboxes with gleaming brass handles.

When they finished for the morning, they would usually stop at the wood shop overlooking the seven-mile long lake. It was here that Harry Barton spent his summer days working to repair and paint the many screens, doors, and miscellaneous furniture damaged over the long harsh New England winter.

Harry would reward them for their labors with coins or maple sugar candies from his pocket. If he had time, he would fashion them wooden tomahawks. Some days he would fuel their imaginations with stories of the Abenaki people who roamed the King's Grant woodlands long before the farmers tried to cultivate the rocky and unyielding soil.

Just as their curiosity began to fuel their energy level, he would send them to lunch across the open meadow, with the white metal swing set that always invited them to stop and climb aboard. Filled with the unbounded gift of joy they thought they would swing forever or at least until lunch.

After a lunch of egg salad or peanut butter sandwiches, they would usually go with their father to buy night crawlers to be used for bait for the afternoon's fishing. Then armed with poles, leader and bobber, they would sit quietly beside the man who gave them the gift of this wondrous place, and wait for the first strike of the hook that sometimes came, but most times did not.

Ben Latimer slowly opened his eyes and focused on his breathing. He could feel the sense of well-being, which usually followed this period of focused meditation. He had learned the technique almost twenty years ago as a way to cope with the absence of his brother. At the time, he still struggled constantly with the "black hole" in his heart created by Billy's disappearance.

When the phone began ringing, Ben was barely conscious enough to recognize Meggy's voice. She sobbed as she told him of her brother's murder. He remembered the last time he had seen Johnny. They had gone from dinner at the tavern to Dwyer's house to rehearse for an upcoming album.

Johnny got drunk. Ben got angry and said he would see him later. Now he was dead.

"I will be coming up with a Detective Rooney from the Salem Police Department to meet with the Warrens Mills' police and an ex-state trooper named Wilson who handled security when Johnny was gone. Rooney wants me to walk through Johnny's house and try to gather any possible evidence that may help the investigation of his murder."

She had asked if Ben would help plan the service and arrange for some musicians to play as well. The arrangements were still up in the air pending the autopsy required in all homicides in Massachusetts. This delay gave them time to call those old friends who may not have heard through the grapevine about Johnny's death.

When Megan hung up, Ben could feel himself starting to dredge up the old feelings associated with the former state trooper, Wilson, who Meggy said was somehow involved with all of this. He could feel the bitterness that came back whenever he thought of the day thirty years ago when the tall uniformed trooper walked into his American literature symposium on the Frost College campus and demanded to talk.

"Can I ask what is so important that you would interrupt me in the middle of a class?"

"Sorry, Professor, but I'm afraid there is something more important than school to talk about. You have a brother who drives a bus for the People's Bus Line?"

"Oh God, is Billy OK? What happened to him?"

"I thought maybe you could tell me. Have you heard from him today?"

"No, I thought he was working until three today. What the hell is this all about, Trooper?"

Wilson went on to explain what he knew about the disappearance of the bus and spent two hours getting the names of Billy's family members and close friends. The trooper was relentless in his questioning, wanting to know every detail of his brother's life. He left, letting Ben know that detectives from the Vermont Bureau of Criminal Investigation as well as the FBI would interview his family. He warned Ben not to leave the area, and to call if he heard anything from his brother.

As Ben thought back to that winter, he felt as if he were trapped in a Kafkaesque nightmare that took such an emotional toll on his mother that she never recovered. It was bad enough to have a child disappear, but the constant pressure from the FBI and the questioning of relatives and neighbors, many of whom his parents had known for years, finally caused her emotional collapse four months after Billy's disappearance. He knew that with his father's death three years before and no close relatives to lean on for support, she would not survive in their large Newton home.

He soon placed her in a nursing home less than three miles from her home. Although she seemed to gain some physical strength, there was a quiet desperation about her that finally drove her to silence within a year.

Strangely enough, the entire process of investigation ended for Ben when he and Wilson drove to Montpelier to the Redstone building that housed the Vermont State Police Polygraph Unit. Ben sat through a polygraph investigation, and when it ended, Wilson drove him back to the college and made it clear that he would no longer be investigating him. No apology, just some mumbling about pursuing other leads.

Ben rose from the couch where he had been talking on the phone to Meggy and walked to the refrigerator. He opened a cold bottle of beer and thought about a reunion with the cop who had altered his life.

"You son of a bitch, Wilson. All you bring into my life is death."

He put the beer down, walked out of his house to the front porch, and screamed silently, "Dwyer, what the fuck have you done now!"

Chapter 10

July 13, 1997
Warrens Mills, Vermont

PETE WILSON APPROACHED the house on Townhill Road with a vague feeling of anxiety and a mile-long hangover. He gulped down two of the green and black capsules that helped ease the anxiety and thought about the upcoming day. The meeting with Megan Dwyer was set for eleven o'clock at her brother's house and he couldn't help feeling that her insistence on meeting with him had more expectations on her part than anything he wished to be involved in.

He had been retired for four years and found that the home security business was just right after twenty-eight years as a member of the Vermont State Police. Putting away the late nights and barroom brawls that had taken their toll over the years, he was finally beginning to sleep with just a few drinks, and an occasional pill. Many nights he got by without the nightmares coming back to haunt his bed. Lately, he caught himself dwelling on the early years of the job when half the roads in his district were still dirt and the hardest drug he dealt with was homegrown pot and Donny McArdle's distilled apple white lightning.

Out-of-towners came mostly in the month of June. They spread out over the Handle Road in their big summer cottages, keeping mostly to themselves and the relatives and friends who would came to buy up the cheap property that was so abundant in the Valley.

Many of their children had stayed and became part of the community. They were mostly good people and they made the Deerfield Valley a better place. The problems began to arise when the State finished the roads, and the skiers started to flow into the Valley. It seemed to him that police work changed and probably a piece of him as well. No longer a few beers after work, but time and time again, the whisky-induced vagueness carried with him as he patrolled his twisting mountainous territory.

Fear came then, sometimes like a jolt, and left him shaking with shallow breathing. He had learned to mask his dread behind his large frame and gruff manner.

His time as an investigator made it easier to hide. He was alone more and not bound to a barracks. He knew the town's people and was trusted as any cop could be by Vermonters who made a point of social anarchy as far as lawmen were concerned.

Then the day came, a peaceful fall day, when at the end of a dirt road, surrounded by the sounds of chickens squawking and pigs snuffling, all the masks fell off in the face of a violent assault. From that day on, he knew that he had changed and it was time to get out.

Chapter 11

"Take a right at the lights, then go up Townhill Road on the right." Megan Dwyer had just awakened as she and Brian Rooney pulled up to the stoplight in Warrens Mills Center. "Jesus, where did I fall asleep?" she half-muttered while stretching out and yawning.

"Somewhere around Athol," he replied as he made the turn.

"Sorry to leave the conversation like that." She was surprised that she was comfortable around this man whom she'd known only a short time and under such painful circumstances.

"What did the state trooper want; is he a friend of yours?"

They had stopped for coffee at a rest area on Route 2, and as they came out, a Massachusetts state police cruiser was parked, blocking their exit. A young black trooper was behind the wheel.

Rooney tried to remain cool as the trooper looked him over without speaking and without giving way for him to exit.

"I'm on duty trooper and I'm with a homicide victim's sister, so fuck off or we'll settle it right here."

"Rumor has it your gunning for my ass in October, peckerhead."

Rooney stepped back and tried to calm himself, while Megan sat staring straight ahead oblivious to the tension between the two former boxing opponents. He knew she couldn't hear.

Rooney smiled and walked closer to the cruiser, shifting his Chief's Special, and watched as the trooper realized his joke was over the edge. He leaned in the open window as the trooper looked startled. Without hesitating, he slammed his head into the man's forehead, quickly and viciously, and then withdrew while the confused trooper sat and grabbed his forehead and swelling nose.

Megan still wasn't paying attention, so Rooney kept his smile as he walked away and waved. Occupants of four other cars curiously looked over at the blue and gray cruiser as it raced out of the parking lot.

"Ya, the trooper and I haven't seen each other in a while, but I'll guarantee I'll hear from him again."

"About two hundred more yards," she spoke quickly, and then pointed to a long circular dirt driveway that hid the converted barn and thirty-five acres. For the last sixteen years, this place had been her retreat, now it was her home, as she somehow always knew it would be. That recognition made her feel an even deeper sense of loss.

There were two vehicles blocking the circle, so Rooney pulled to the right allowing them to exit if needed. The yellow tape sealed all but the entrance, which was cleverly concealed behind sliding barn doors that had been allowed to weather and discolor. A tall, tanned, fiftyish looking man dressed in faded denims and an aging Lacoste shirt greeted them.

At first glance, he had the look of a man content with his place in life. His handshake was firm and Brian could see how they both began to size the other up, as cops do when confronting new situations.

"I'm Wilson." He addressed Megan directly and said, "I'm sorry for the phone call the other day, but it was the only number listed in my emergency directory. And I had no idea of your loss at the time."

Brian then introduced himself and showed his wallet badge as a courtesy. He could smell yesterday's liquor on the man's breath, but thought to himself, *This guy could have been an old friend of her brother's and probably threw a few down at the shock of hearing he was dead.*

"The crime techs said it would be about an hour before they would be finished," Wilson informed them. "Why don't we go into Warrens Mills, pay a courtesy call on the local chief, and grab some lunch at the Mill Tavern."

Warrens Mills' police chief, Porky Atkins, saw Peter Wilson's jeep from his office window on the second floor of the municipal building—spotting Megan and Rooney heading up the stairs toward his office. He shoved the brownie he was eating into his desk for safekeeping until they left, which as far as he was concerned could not be fast enough. He knew the sooner he sent the city cop back to Massachusetts, the easier his life would be. Porky liked life easy.

"Good morning, Chief Atkins, and thanks for your cooperation."

Brian spoke first and again displayed his badge while handing Porky a business card. Porky Atkins looked directly at Megan as if she were an old friend.

"Sorry for your trouble, miss," he said. "I heard your brother sing and play that guitar many nights when I was workin' constable over to the Cave."

Megan now recognized the chief and almost started to laugh as she remembered Johnny's stories about Porky's eating habits. The chief was a former town constable, who was forced on her brother's nightclub payroll to keep the peace politically. After hours, when they were closing the Cave down for the night, Johnny would mimic Porky going from table to table, finishing uneaten sandwiches and pouring half-empty beers into large plastic containers. When he finished collecting his goodies, he would then sit in front of a roaring fire, unbuckle his belt and consume his hoarded loot, then belch and fart till he fell asleep.

"Thank you Chief. Johnny used to mention you a lot," Megan replied, smiling internally at the still-graphic picture painted by her brother.

"Are you going to have a service here in town? Or is there anything else we can help with before you go back to Boston?"

"Right now we are planning to have a memorial service here sometime in the fall. I will be meeting with the funeral director today to find out the details of interring my brother's ashes. As soon as you clear it, I will be moving into my brother's house and meeting with his attorney to try and settle some insurance matters and look further into finalizing his estate issues."

"You should be able to move into his house by tomorrow at the latest. The state boys will be out by then."

"Thanks Chief; until then I'll be staying over at the college with a friend of Johnny's, Ben Latimer."

Porky wondered if that little college prick was getting it on with the sister, but he just smiled and said, "OK. I have his number and I'll call you if there's any problem with the house."

Megan started to walk away then turned back and said, "Pardon me, Sheriff, but how do you happen to have Ben's number. Is he a friend?"

Porky spoke with some sarcasm as he answered, "Me and the professor go back a long way miss, a long, long way."

Chapter 12

THE MILL TAVERN looked and smelled like Vermont. It sat overlooking the Deerfield Branch River, from which the converted sawmill drew its power when it processed the logs that were abundant in years past.

Today, the former sawmill, with its original blades suspended from the ceiling, produced seasonal hospitality and ample New England food. It was an example of what Peter Wilson called "good progress." It was well managed and there was always a sense of comfort no matter how overrun with tourists it became. In the summer, they served food barbecue style on a deck overlooking the river. It was there that Megan and Rooney found Wilson. He was leaning over, bantering with a fisherman in waders who was casting flies into a pool of water created by the rock foundation at the base of the old mill.

When he saw them, he ushered them to a long bench and table and settled back.

"What's the story with Chief Atkins and Latimer? My instincts tell me there is some bad blood," asked Rooney.

"You could say that," Wilson laughed. "Porky has had a problem with Ben Latimer ever since the day Ben's brother Billy disappeared in 1963, and I guarantee he'll have it till the day they drag his fat ass up the hill to the cemetery."

"Porky was the bank guard the day the Green Mountain Trust courier was hit thirty years ago, and he swears that Ben's brother was smiling to beat the band when he made the pick up that morning. Even though we investigated both brothers' backgrounds thoroughly, we found nothing that would lead us to believe there was collusion on the part of either one."

Rooney and Megan sat fascinated as Wilson sipped his dark otter ale and told the story of Southern Vermont's largest bank robbery.

"I was decoyed to the mountain by someone knocking out power at the junction box on White's Corner about a half a mile from here. In those days, there was no substation between here and the next town, so whoever knocked it out killed the power all the way to Stratton Township, eleven miles from here.

The power outage left thousands of pissed off skiers unable to get up the mountain, and in some cases, trapped in lifts, freezing their asses off. By the time I got to Snow Mountain, the place was chaos with fistfights and shoving matches going on all over the place, and no security except the ski patrol, and they had no business getting involved in a riot."

Wilson took a long swallow, and then proceeded with the bizarre tale of the Snow Mountain riot.

"The funny thing was that the Mass. State police had tipped us that a gang out of Somerville was talking of hitting the receipts at the Mountain. We had undercover in there on three occasions. We even had a plan in place to shut down the access roads in and out of the valley. But we never figured they would stop the bus carrying the money to Bratt."

Megan sipped her Perrier and asked, "Has anyone ever figured out what ever happened to Ben's brother?"

"Well, if you believe Porky, the kid is living the good life somewhere with a million dollars of stolen money.

"But you don't believe that, do you?"

"Not now, but at the time I did. I believe now that he never knew what hit him. I've gone over the case a thousand times in my brain. I still have the file sitting in a closet at my parent's lake house, and sometimes I read it just to see what I may have missed."

"Those gangs out of Somerville and Charlestown were vicious," chimed in Rooney. "We had them try and muscle into the North Shore when I was a rookie and they just didn't give a shit who they messed with. We ended up doing a task force with the Feds and State police just to contain them and stop the spread into New Hampshire."

Their lunch came and they reordered drinks. Wilson took his first good look at Megan Dwyer. She had the look of an athlete. Her figure was trim, yet full breasted. He had no trouble envisioning her in shorts and singlet running the twenty-six miles of the Boston Marathon. She looked as good today as she did in the pictures that Dwyer kept all over the house. Her arms were gently freckled and tanned, and her hands were long and well maintained. He was attracted to her deep blue eyes, coal black hair, and Irish smile. She spoke with the same well-educated inflection that he had heard from other Bostonians who hired him for security.

"It was rough on Ben wasn't it?" Megan asked.

Wilson put down his burger and wiped ketchup from his lip, swallowed some ale and said, somewhat defensively, "You have to understand something about police work, Ms. Dwyer. When we got the call from the bus line that day, our first thought was that the driver had an accident, so we dispatched a cruiser out of Rockingham barracks to patrol Route 9 from Brattleboro to Marlboro. I took off from the mountain and headed east toward Bratt from Warrens Mills. When we met in Marlboro and had no sign of the bus, we changed our tactic and called through for backup."

Wilson took another swallow from his ale and continued. "Our dispatcher had received a call in the meantime from the manager of Green Mountain Trust in Brattleboro informing us that the courier was late. So we began to respond as if a crime had been committed."

"Did you have Feds locally in those days?" asked Rooney who found himself listening as if the crime had occurred yesterday.

"There was a one-man office in Bratt at the time. The agent was a fellow named Hanes. We worked together a couple of times. He was much easier to get along with than the agents out of their Albany headquarters." Wilson emptied the glass and went on.

"At that point we had put out a five state alert for the bus. Hanes jumped in with our CID investigator who had come down from D Troop headquarters in Rockingham. That was the most intense day, and probably week, that I will ever live through and believe me, I have had a lot of shit go down in thirty years. There were no clues, no blood in the bus—it was if the brother and the money disappeared into a giant hole."

"But to answer your question, Ms. Dwyer," he nodded slowly when he addressed Megan, "it was a nightmare for Ben, and I was part of that nightmare. He still blames me for his mother's suffering, even though most of the investigation was handled in Massachusetts by the FBI out of Albany."

By the time Wilson finished recapping thirty years of history, he had finished four ales and his audience was sufficiently watered and caffeinated. Rooney decided to check in to the Inn, and Megan had asked Wilson for a ride to the college to hook up with Ben.

"Megan, see you in the morning. How about eight thirty at the little restaurant around the corner, which we spotted coming in?"

"OK, and thanks for the ride, Detective."

She turned to enter Wilson's jeep and began to wonder whether this retired trooper could help her find Johnny's killer.

Chapter 13

July 14, 1997
Marlboro, Vermont

TINY DROPLETS OF moisture ran down Megan Dwyer's lower back as she slowed her pace and started up the long hill that led to Ben's property. The slow build up of good feeling that came with a hard run was just beginning to work its magic as she closed to within a half mile of the farmhouse. The sagging emotional hangover from last night's tears was leaving as she began to smell the apple orchard and newly mown hay that surrounded her. Ben was sitting on the front porch at a table laid out with two steaming mugs of coffee and fresh baked bread.

"I got a *Globe* in case you get homesick." He reached across the table and handed her the *Boston Globe* as well as the breadbasket.

"How was your run?"

"Beautiful. That last mile is like running in a time warp.

It's as if nothing has changed here in a hundred years."

She smelled the coffee, then sipped it cautiously and sat back, breathing slowly as if trying to capture the scent of her new surroundings.

"Do you think I'm crazy to come here?"

"Nope. I think if you didn't come, you would go crazy trying to find out what happened to your brother. Besides, it's a lot cooler here than it is sitting on Beacon Hill."

"Will you come with me today?"

"I may as well. I want to meet the cop who's already managed to piss you off," he said with a grin, raising his hands to protect himself while waiting for a response.

"Latimer, you're an asshole, but I love you anyway. I'm sure the guy is doing the best he can, but I think he's determined to keep me out of it, and I won't put up with that attitude from him or anyone else."

Megan remembered the childhood advice that she and Johnny would get from their grandparents as they sat at Sunday dinner. She mimicked a brogue and laughed as she remembered her grandmother's face after two glasses of Bushmills.

"Remember children, the best way to get ahead in this land is the police and fire. You'll never want for work and there's a pension at the end of your labor. That's what they're looking for, a pension at the end of their labor. Well, I don't care whether he gets one or not, I just want him to do his job and stay out of my way. Enough of my bitterness for now, Latimer. I've got to clean up. Then let's head into Warrens Mills and meet Rooney, then you can judge for yourself what he's all about."

As she began her shower and let the water wash out the road dirt, she could hear the soft plunk of Ben's five-string banjo as he tuned. The water and the music seemed to fuse as she soaped using Ben's long back-washing brush. She felt the bristles hard against her skin. The glow of the run was working and she began to sense hope again. Ben switched melodies and she could hear him pick out the bold Gaelic anthem *"Kelly, the Boy from Kilarn."*

She turned and let the soft spray wash over her face as the music lifted her spirits temporarily, then she thought of her brother and the way he sang it, his voice painting a lyrical picture of a man "who rode like a giant in command." Tears ran down with the shower water and her heart felt like stone, but she knew there was no turning back once she had started this race.

"Do you ever lock your house, Latimer?" she asked, as they walked to the Explorer. She noticed Ben left the porch door wide open and the screen unlocked.

"The day I do, Meggy, will be the day I leave for the last time, or the day they carry me out."

He blew the horn and waved to his neighbor Ann Merrill, who gave him a broad grin and a big wave in return. "Besides, Annie's as nosy as they come. She's my neighborhood watchdog."

"Johnny used to piss me off constantly by not locking the door, especially when he was on the road and his instruments were in the house. She started to speak again and caught the lump growing in her throat. She stopped to wipe the tears that began to fall.

"Oh shit, my eyes must be a mess." She reached in the glove box and pulled out a tissue.

Ben reached across and touched her hand. "I wish I could make it better."

"I know, Ben, I know." She exhaled and tried to catch her breath as the knot in her chest tightened, then passed as the tears came again.

Chapter 14

July 15, 1997
Warrens Mills, Vermont

"**I HEARD YOU** were investigating Johnny's murder."

The waitress spoke with a New York accent and addressed him like an old friend. Rooney was taken off guard for a second until he looked around at the other customers at Dot's Deli. He was the only one wearing a suit, in a restaurant filled with men in green work overalls and boots, John Deere caps atop their heads or placed on the table.

"I'm involved in the investigation. Did you know him well?"

"Yeah, he ate breakfast here most of the time, except when he was messed up from the sauce, and then he went straight to the Colonial."

She brought Brian's omelet and returned to the counter where the officer he had seen in Chief Atkins' office was having coffee. He nodded at Brian and looked a little sheepish for obviously having gossiped to the waitress about Brian's reason for being in town.

"Hi Brian." Rooney turned to see Megan and a tall sandy-haired man enter from the side door just behind his table.

"Ben Latimer." He spoke with a pleasant voice and had a firm handshake.

"Brian Rooney. Nice to meet you," he said, not quite sure if he meant it as he looked at the freshly scrubbed Megan Dwyer. Rooney wondered if there was anything between the two of them.

"Did you sleep OK at the tavern?" Ben asked. "It's usually quiet in the summer."

"Yeah, I took a long walk along the river, then up to the cemetery on the hill. God, this town is so peaceful at night. I think I forgot what it was like to sleep that soundly." As Rooney spoke, Ben continued to look at him.

"This might sound nuts Brian, but were you ever an Olympic boxer?" Ben asked.

"You're either a boxing trivia nut or you've been in my father's restaurant on Nantucket," Rooney said with a laugh.

"I eat breakfast at your father's place at least twice a week. Best pancakes in the world. I'm doing some research for a book and spend a couple of days a week on the Island. You look as though you still keep in shape. Do you still box?"

"Yes, as a matter of fact, I'm going to fight in a charity event in October. After that I'm hanging up the gloves."

"I know it's none of my business, but I would have walked away from Munich, too. I'm sure you've taken heat for that decision over the years."

Rooney silently finished his coffee and looked closely at Ben, not answering the question.

"You're the banjo player who played on Johnny's last album."

Ben smiled, "Last ten albums in fact. I've been recording with Johnny since the sixties."

Megan, sensing some angst between the two, jumped in and asked, "Have you checked with the chief this morning? Can we go in and look around?"

"Anytime you're ready. I assume we don't need keys since I think Wilson is gonna meet us there." Ben looked uncomfortable at the mention of the ex-state policeman's name.

"Is this a hassle for you, Mr. Latimer?"

"Sort of; we had a bad encounter a long time ago, but it's time I worked it out. It's only been thirty years and it's probably time I stopped carrying a grudge." He forced a laugh. "Besides, this isn't about me."

Meggy hugged his arm. They left quietly, leaving Polly Watson a good tip and more grist for the town's gossip mill than it had heard in years.

"That's his jeep in the driveway," said Meggy. They parked next to it and entered the house through a slider into the master bedroom.

The room had been ripped apart. Papers scattered everywhere. Hundreds of books from the wall bookcase were split at the seams and tossed like candy wrappers on a subway floor. The mattress was overturned and slit open, leaving down filler scattered like sooty snowflakes across the wide boards. There was a feeling in the room of personal violation.

"Oh Jesus, who would do this?" Megan gasped.

"Someone very intent on finding something your brother had or they thought he had."

Pete Wilson's voice preceded his entrance, as he emerged from a walk-in closet built to store Johnny's collection of guitars and other instruments.

Megan felt sick, acid from this morning's coffee gnawing at her stomach. She started to walk out and then stopped, resigning herself to the task ahead.

Ben looked warily at Wilson and added, "Meggy, you don't have to do this now."

"It's not gonna get any easier tomorrow, Professor. And I think you and Ms. Dwyer are the only ones who know what might be missing."

"He's right, Ben. If we don't start now, I'm afraid I'll walk out and give in to the bastards who did this."

Wilson went out to his jeep and returned with two yellow-lined pads. He handed one to Megan and said to Ben as he handed him the second, "Why don't Ms. Dwyer and I work together and you and Detective Rooney pair up. We'll work in separate rooms."

"What are we looking for?" asked Ben, feeling puzzled.

"Try and write down any changes that you can notice in each room, no matter how insignificant they may seem."

"When were you here last?" Wilson asked Ben

"Three weeks ago. We rehearsed some music, but Johnny started to get loaded so we split up early."

Ben gave Meggy a nervous look.

"Don't worry, Ben, I hated the 'Whisky Johnny bullshit' too. He was like Dr. Jekyll and Mr. Alcohol. His voice went to shit the minute he crossed over the line. I learned to walk away when it started. It was just too painful to watch him slip." She turned her face to wipe the tears that formed when she spoke. Then, after blowing her nose in a Kleenex, she took a pen from her purse and said to Wilson, "Where do we start?"

She and Wilson walked up the spiral stairs to the second floor and he explained to her that the Salem Police and the Vermont Bureau of Criminal Investigation would coordinate the investigation.

"But would you be willing to take me on as a client?"

"I'm doing this for insurance purposes. It's part of my contract with your brother."

"What will you do with the report?"

"I assumed you knew; his attorney called and asked me to forward to him any claims that would be part of your brother's estate. I guess he's started to get that together for you and the other heirs."

"When you're finished, what then? Will you still provide service, or does your contract end with my brother's death?"

"I've never had this happen. I don't really know, but I'm paid through the end of the year. I guess I'll stay on until you sell the house."

"I won't be selling the house. In fact, as soon as we get cleaned up, I'll be moving in. I'd like to hire you to do more than watch the house. I'd like you to help me find my brother's killer."

Wilson looked at her anxiously. "Look, Ms. Dwyer, I'm no longer a cop, and if you're thinking of getting involved in this somehow, I'd think again. Whoever killed your brother and trashed this house is after something or someone. They're not gonna think twice about hurting you or your family. If this is about drugs and your brother was involved, or if it was owing money for gambling or some other business, then let's hope it dies with your brother. I don't want to have to come here a second time to find you hurt or dead."

Wilson was getting irritated as he spoke. He turned away to calm himself then said, "I'm sorry. Let's just get the missing items report done and talk later. Who knows? Maybe I can be of some help."

Thirty minutes later, as Megan and Wilson were upstairs inspecting the guest bathrooms, Rooney and Ben had come upon boxes of tapes and CDs in the basement. Rooney thought it strange that Dwyer would keep so many tapes around the house.

"Cash," Ben said. "Johnny loved cash when he was drinking. He would take a bunch of tapes and CDs on the road with him, and pay a waitress or bartender a few bucks to sell them when he was performing."

"No taxes, no checks, no credit cards and no records for the IRS to look at," Rooney laughed when he spoke. "Did he spend much time on the road?"

Ben thought for a second. "Six or seven months a year, depending on his time in the studio and how sober he could keep. The last couple of years, his trips were shorter. I think he was burning bridges with the pub owners, and the museum jobs were getting harder to come by with his reputation. The funny thing was, his song research was better than ever, and he was writing good stuff when he wasn't drinking."

"Did you like him?"

"That's a hard question to answer. When he was sober, he was easy to be around, but when he started to drink, he put a ten-foot wall around himself. But I liked him; you'll find most people did."

They looked at each other and neither spoke. An unspoken thought hung in the air like a last minute free throw. *Somebody sure didn't like him very much.*

"What do you know about a group called the Holy Ground Society?"

"Not much, except that Johnny did a lot of concerts for them to raise funds, but other than that, he never really said much about his involvement."

They continued to pick through the basement, but found very little of interest, except memorabilia from various clubs that Johnny collected as he traveled the club circuit. They could hear Megan when they returned upstairs.

"Most of the furniture was my folk's. We moved it up here when he finished converting this place."

Meggy spoke through tears as she looked at the destruction in the living room. The ironstone fireplace in the center of the room stood untouched in the devastation.

"Did your brother keep any big amounts of cash in the house or anything of value besides the guitars?" asked Wilson.

"I don't know, but he always had a lot of cash. I suppose he kept it here in the house. The prewar Martins in the walk-in closet are worth twenty or thirty thousand dollars. He had been collecting them since the early sixties. I don't understand anybody breaking in here and not taking them."

"I don't understand that myself, Ms. Dwyer. Like most people, I'm sure your brother had secrets. Maybe we'll find them, but clearly, robbery does not seem to be the motive here."

She watched as he took video of the damage, going from room to room, slowly running the camcorder over the now-damaged pieces that her parents had lived with for so many years.

Furniture lay strewn about and broken, with no concern for the lives that had touched the pieces in the past. Meggy had never been raped, but now she began to feel that someone had dirtied her and left her empty.

Wilson began to move out of the living room and stopped. "I think that's it for today."

She started to protest and he put his hands up.

"If you want my help, ya gotta listen."

Rooney walked in as Wilson was speaking and echoed the Vermonter's words. "Megan, this process will drain you, and you're not going to be any help to us if you're beat up. Let's get lunch. We can put a game plan together when we've got some food in our stomachs."

Ben gently touched Megan's shoulder and turned her toward the front barn door. Rooney said he'd go with Wilson and agreed to meet them at the tavern.

Chapter 15

THE TAVERN WAS crowded with a collection of Warrens Mills' business people having a luncheon meeting. Their talk was animated but not boisterous. Like "chamber types" everywhere, they seemed genuinely interested in whatever their topic.

After being seated, Wilson asked Ben and Meggy to try and recollect what might be different in Johnny's house.

"I'm afraid the mess still has me rattled." Meggy sipped at her Perrier and tried to recall, but it was clear to the two investigators that it was going to be awhile before she would be ready to make any objective observations that would be helpful.

"Professor, can you give us any help?"

Before Ben could speak, a short olive-skinned man dressed in a blue blazer and light gray slacks left his luncheon group and walked over to their table. He nodded to Wilson and spoke to Megan.

"Ms. Dwyer, I'm Ed Romano. I've been calling the number you left in Marlboro, but you must have been busy with the house inspection. I'm sorry to butt in like this, but I just needed to tell you how upset I am about your brother's death. My services are available whenever you feel up to it."

He touched her shoulder gently as he finished speaking.

"Thanks for coming over, Mr. Romano. I was planning to stop in your office today."

She looked at Rooney. "This is Detective Rooney. He's the investigating officer on my brother's case."

They shook hands and Rooney handed him a business card.

He then turned to Latimer. "Ben, long time no see. I'm sorry it had to be under these circumstances."

Romano spoke with a lawyer's practiced inflection, yet seemed genuinely glad to see Ben.

"You know, Ed, I'm willing to bet the last thing you ever expected to see today was Peter Wilson and me sitting having lunch at the same table. So far, neither one has tried to strangle the other."

The remark brought laughter to the table and Wilson leaned across, and with a mock scowl said, "You're damned right. Let's hope we can keep it that way."

"In that case, you don't need me."

Romano left his card with Rooney and was still laughing when he sat back down to discuss this year's Farmer's Day events with the other members of the group. By now, the group was on its second round of drinks and cajoled him to catch up.

Wilson looked over and mused to himself, "Not hell of a lot of work will get done in Warrens Mills today."

Their grilled vegetable and shrimp plates came, and they talked more about the house as they ate. Meggy seemed to sink inward, but Ben was more animated and obviously more comfortable now that the ice had been broken between him and Wilson.

"The books are gone I think. He kept his song notebooks and the AA books next to his bed," Meggy spoke somewhat tentatively.

"What kind of books?" Wilson and Rooney's words almost drowned each other out as they spoke simultaneously.

"Hardcover writing tablets." Megan spoke as if coming out of a fog.

"How many, and exactly where in the bedroom did he keep them?"

Rooney took out his notebook and began writing.

"Ben, do you remember if they were there the last night you rehearsed together?"

"Absolutely, Detective," said Ben. "We were working on a song he had picked up on his last trip and he was raving about the songwriter. The words were in one of the books and he sang it for me reading the words as he went. In the back of the songbook, he kept a journal of some kind, but he was touchy about people looking at it."

"And you're sure the books weren't on the floor?" Rooney asked, looking at Meggy.

"I'm not sure, but I'll go back and look. They were always on the night stand next to his bed."

"No, I think Brian and I should go back this afternoon and you guys try to take it easy for awhile. We've got to see Chief Atkins after two. Hopefully the crime scene techs will have something for us, but I doubt the people who did this left much behind in the way of evidence."

"Can we meet again tomorrow, same time?" Wilson asked.

Meggy looked at Ben. "Whatever we have to do, that's fine with me," Ben replied.

"We will meet you at the Colonial. They serve breakfast and a lot of Johnny's drinking pals hang around there. Who knows, maybe somebody there will remember something that will help us out. Ms. Dwyer, try to take it easy today."

Wilson signed the bill and pocketed the receipt. He and Rooney walked out first, obviously eager to get back to the house and what might be their first lead.

"You find those books, I guarantee you find his killer," spouted Wilson.

Rooney whacked the bigger Wilson good-naturedly on the arm. "No shit. Is that all you learned in twenty-eight years?"

As they left the building and walked to their cars, Rooney looked across the street to where a man dressed in a tan-colored hooded robe stood silently, waiting to cross Route 100.

"Is that man a local priest?"

Ben laughed. "No, he's a monk. Part of a French order known as the Chartreans. They've lived here in Southern Vermont in a couple of different locations for almost as long as I can remember."

"What do they do?"

"They're a contemplative order, live in small cells and pray. They rarely leave except to come here to the health clinic or over to Marlboro to see their dentist."

The monk looked over at them. His face remained passive as his heart began to race. "God's will be done," he prayed, bowing his head, "God's will be done."

Chapter 16

November 22, 1963
Warrens Mills, Vermont

THE TALL MAN was beginning to sweat, feeling the unusual warmth of a late fall day. He dug deeper into the cesspool trench that ran from the back wall of the foundation. Glad that the frost had not yet set, he found the digging enjoyable.

He piled the dirt neatly to the side of the trench, knowing that the day he finished filling back the dirt would be the last time he would probably ever breathe freely and without fear. Again, with each shovelful he unearthed, more sweat poured from his forehead. Beads of moisture ran across the birthmark below his eye. He paused to wipe his face and drink from the Coleman cooler at his side. He smelled his own scent as he raised the cup and let the chilled spring water cool down his throat.

His thoughts ran to his father's smell in the last days before the old man's death. He hated the smell of fear and toxic sweat that the old man had given off when the end came. He would never lose to those bastards as his father had. He would never again listen to their lies.

A noise startled him and he looked across the tree-stripped lot to a clearing. A white tail deer jumped out and dashed across the lot, stopping to look back at him, then disappearing into the tree line. He watched for a while hoping to see another deer, then returned to his work.

He screwed the cap back on the water jug and surveyed the trench. It would certainly hold the bags and whatever else ended up being buried with them. With an ax that he grabbed from the wooden toolbox in the bed of the truck, he severed the larger roots that could become problems to cesspool pipes as the roots matured. He didn't need this trench dug up because of a broken pipe, not soon, not ever.

As he piled hay across the fresh dirt pile, the smell reminded him of haying Grandfather Willett's farm when he was young. Before the roads turned asphalt and his world so quickly changed, the smell of hay always made him feel more at ease and in touch with a past that he loved.

As quickly as the thought came, it left. He was energized now by the task ahead and what he must get done in order to make it happen. When the dirt pile was covered and protected well from freezing, he collected his tools and replaced them in the pickup. He removed two bags of lime and put them under the tarp where he kept cement.

He looked over his work and thought back to that day on Snow Mountain standing next to his father.

"We're not going to need your crew after November."

"What the fuck are you talking about? You said there'd always be work," his father screamed. "What about my equipment? I'm mortgaged up to my ass. My guys cut every goddam trail on this mountain. We poured every footing for those lifts. You just can't cut me loose after the work we've done."

"You were well paid for the work you did, probably too well paid."

He could still see his father's face when Tim Kane, the mountain manager, cut the old man's heart out. Dressed in his dirt-covered green coveralls and old Dunham work boots, his father was screaming as if his arm was being severed. His face was purplish red with rage. His screaming could be heard throughout the base lodge area, which was empty of skiers and through which every painful appeal was echoed.

"Don't you scream at me, you old bastard, or I'll have a constable throw your ass off this mountain and arrest you for trespassing."

The son started to react. Just then, his father reached across his path and lifted the desk of maple and glass that was the GM's most treasured piece of furniture. He overturned it as if he were raising a framed wall. Kane leaped back, astonished as his papers and mementoes scattered across the office and his face contorted as he looked at the old man whose rage was exploding. Kane raised his arms to protect his face and the old man bellowed.

"I'll get you and every fucking one of the rest of you."

His father dropped the desk that day, doing no more harm. He quieted himself while the office personnel looked on. With a calm dignity, he picked his checkered hunting cap from the floor and spoke to the small crowd that were gathered; they were mostly locals that he had known all his life.

"This ain't about you. It's about them." He pointed with hatred to the cowering Tim Kane who was trying to recover.

His thoughts were interrupted by the car radio. He looked over the scene and was happy with the trench. Picking up the cooler, he placed it in the cab of his truck. As he slid behind the wheel, he heard the radio announcer's voice.

"We are at Parkland Hospital where the president has been rushed, following an assassination attempt. At this time, we have nothing more to report. In the meantime, all we can do is pray for the president and the country."

Chapter 17

Warrens Mills, Vermont
July 15, 1997

"**Halifax, Vermont always** reminded me of Appalachia. It's one of those towns that was overlooked by the second-home crowd and remains a blip on the road between the Massachusetts' state line and the ski areas. You have to understand that I hadn't made a case in Halifax in years, and I hardly expected to even find the guy we were looking for. I was chasing some uncollected bad checks, almost six grand that he had written over a three-week period. We had a tip that he might be hiding out at a buddy's house, way the hell out in West Halifax."

Wilson sat back in the driver's seat of his jeep, unbuckled his seatbelt and related to Rooney the event that hastened his retirement from law enforcement.

"I decided to watch for a while, so I pulled my car up about a quarter mile from the house and walked back. As I approached, it was quiet as hell and I would have bet the ranch that it was a dead end. I remember thinking what a gorgeous fall day it was. That was my first mistake."

Wilson shut off the jeep.

"Because this guy had no history of violence, and the fact that it was a weak lead in the first place, I figured I'd knock and see what happened. As I approached the door, I could see it was open. For some reason, this just relaxed me a little more. Mistake number two."

"I knocked and identified myself to see if anyone was around. When no one answered, I walked off the porch and around the side of the farmhouse because I thought I heard animals in the back. I figured the owner was out there too."

Rooney interrupted him, "Did you let anyone know where you were going that day?"

"That, my friend, was mistake number three. It almost cost me my ass."

Wilson opened his door and gestured at Rooney as they walked around the side of Dwyer's converted barn. "Try to imagine walking around the side of this barn and getting hit full force with an ax handle."

Rooney winced.

"He came from behind the house and knocked me on my ass and kept whacking me. But he didn't get a head shot or I wouldn't be here."

"What about your weapon?"

"I couldn't get to it without leaving myself wide open for a head shot. The next hit damn near took off my hand. I was in deep shit."

He rolled up his sleeve to show Rooney the scar.

"It's funny what goes through your head in those situations. I kept thinking about my wife and her being at my funeral. That did something to me because somehow I grabbed the handle, and hung on with my good hand. He fell back just a little, and I threw myself at him. He went down and I just got my knee up and kicked him in the balls."

Rooney could feel the relief when Wilson spoke.

"Brian, that was the best I've ever felt in my life 'cause I knew the son of a bitch was all done. I knew I was gonna live. He kept looking at me, begging and crying, and I kept kicking him 'til he was senseless. I don't know what stopped me from killing him, 'cause I really wanted to. He was unconscious when I cuffed him. I probably should have called the rescue squad first, but I didn't. I watched him lie there like a trussed pig, and then I called Brattleboro barracks and the local constable. When he came out of it, I Mirandized him. The little prick spent a couple of days in the Brattleboro Hospital before they locked him up."

"This guy attacked a cop on a bad check charge. He had to be nuts or cranked up on something," Rooney said incredulously.

"Angel dust and booze. They said later that he probably would have attacked the postman or anybody else who happened to walk into his paranoid little world at the wrong time."

"Is he still in the can?"

"That's the reason I got out when I did. He tried to bring charges against me for excessive force and almost got away with it, but they finally came to their senses and I was cleared. That episode left me realizing that I'd lost a step. I walked away with an excellent pension and a happy wife. I built a nice little business providing home security and with my wife still a nurse at Bennington Hospital, we do all right."

"What ever happened to the guy?"

"Like all the druggies who get caught, he came to Jesus. He's a drug counselor at a Boston detox. Had the balls to come up here once and try to make things right. But I just can't forget what he almost did to me. I doubt if I'll ever become an organ donor for him, if you know what I mean."

Rooney thought back to his run-in with the state trooper as he traveled to Vermont. "Ya, I'm not too big on forgiveness either," he said, quietly smiling to himself.

Chapter 18

"**This baby lived** only three months. Imagine what it must have been like for her parents to leave her for the winter months in the burial vault."

Ben and Meggy were walking the old section of the Warrens Mills cemetery, looking at the small weathered headstones that were scattered across the hillside overlooking the Deerfield Valley.

Ben pointed to the large wooden vault that was dug to store bodies of those who died in the winter months, when the frost and deep snow made the ground impenetrable and burial impossible.

They had arranged with Paul Harlow, Warrens Mills' only funeral director, to select a site for the interment of Johnny's ashes. Now they wandered in the old section to pass the time waiting for him to arrive.

"The ones who made it through those winters must have been tougher than we are now," Meggy said while kneeling and rubbing dirt off one of the old markers.

"Let's face it, Meggy, they had no choice. But I've often thought that if they could talk, they would tell the same stories we tell today. When I had literary pretensions in my youth, I outlined a play about the people buried here on the hill. I wrote about them talking to new arrivals, and telling stories that all seemed to have the same ending."

"You're kidding, did you finish it?"

"No, in fact until today, I hadn't thought about it much, but who knows, maybe when I finish everything on Nantucket, I'll retreat to the country like Melville and write the great American cemetery play. However, I think I'm condemned to a life of research, teaching, and banjo playing and not cut out for the literary life."

"Are you still seeing your friend on the Island?"

"When I can. She's tied up at the hospital most of the time, and I'm usually at the historical society and the library.

She came to see me when I sat in with some Mystic shanty men at the Brotherhood of Thieves. Some lunches and an occasional coffee are all we seem to be managing right now."

They turned toward the highway as a late model Pontiac entered the long cemetery driveway.

"That's his car, I think. Oh God, I hate this, Ben. These guys always give me the creeps."

Ben said nothing, but reached for her hand and gave it a squeeze as they approached the undertaker.

They walked the new section of the cemetery with Harlow. Meggy couldn't believe that he actually made her feel somewhat comfortable, or maybe it was just the view that stretched across the valley below them.

It was green as far as she could see, and the mountains stood unmoved as they had for centuries. Harlow reminded her of the salesman from Bacon and Company who sold her the Charles Street condo years before. He was on his turf, and like a running back in slow motion, weaving in and out of the various gravesides until he stopped and pronounced what he thought was the right spot.

"That maple will grow and shade his remains over the years to come. It was part of the reason I chose this spot. I hope it's what you had in mind Ms. Dwyer."

The freshly planted four-foot red maple was only a few yards from the site that Meggy approved without really considering whether or not Johnny would be cool enough.

"Well, Johnny, you're gonna have a hell of a view from now on. Enjoy it, brother, enjoy it."

She gave Harlow a check for the lot and the opening costs, and he asked if she would want them to handle the newspaper obituary notices.

"Meggy, I'll write them if you like," offered Ben.

"Thanks, Ben, you probably knew him as well as anyone; maybe we can do it together."

They walked along the car path to the grassy hillside where they had parked, and Ben turned at the sound of his name.

"I thought that was you, Ben. I've just come up to talk to Earl. Hi, I'm Libby Stark." She addressed Meggy who shook her hand and noticed her firm grip and easy patrician smile.

"I knew your brother fairly well. I'm sorry for your loss."

"Thanks. Does Earl work here?" asked Meggy, looking around. Ben and the woman both shared a laugh, and Meggy realized from the markings on the gravestone in front of them that Earl probably hadn't worked here, or anywhere else, since December of 1962.

"Oh God, I'm sorry."

"Don't be. That's the first good laugh I've had all day."

They chatted for a while, and then parted, Meggy noticing that Libby had walked over to another graveside to talk to a woman who appeared to be her mirror image, some thirty or so years younger.

The woman was casually dressed in plain khaki shorts and a golf shirt. She wore no socks and had kicked off her shoes, obviously enjoying the feel of fresh cut cemetery grass beneath her feet.

"That's her daughter Jennifer."

"Her husband must have been a good-looking man."

"They were a handsome couple; it's still hard for me to think of him dead, even after all these years. He was one of the best-natured and likable guys that I've ever known."

"What happened to him? An accident?"

"Let's get coffee and I'll tell you. I don't feel like hanging out here much more, unless you do."

"No, I'm ready to go. Maybe we can catch up with Wilson. He should have spoken to Chief Atkins by now."

They drove down the hill toward Warrens Mills, past Warrens Farm, with its large herd of black and white dairy cows that sat like large Oreo cookies on a hilly landscape. They watched as hay rigs worked the lower fields, bundling and stacking winterfeed.

In the village, they parked in front of a white two-story building that now housed a bookstore, but whose basement once had been Meggy's favorite nightspot, the

Cave. It was where Johnny had sung nightly in ski season and where she had met her pal, Karen Nelson, so many years before.

As they sat and had their coffee in Warrens Mills' only high-test coffee shop, Ben told her the story of the late Earl Stark.

"He was a small town kid who could do anything, fix just about any mechanical object, and play the hell out of the guitar. Earl had a big smile and was friendly as hell. He was the apple of Libby Allen's life. They had known each other since childhood. I remember at the funeral. Libby spoke of her infatuation with him from the time they were kids, even though they came from very different worlds.

He did a lot of odd jobs for the folks on the Handle Road. Earl was one of the local kids who was at ease with the summer people. When Libby graduated from Bennington, she came right back to live in her parent's house, which had been winterized by then and almost immediately, they began to see each other.

Earl left the Valley for a while to go to school in Boston, but hated city life, so he came back and threw himself into working for the mountain. They had a beautiful wedding at her grandparent's house and everything seemed great between them."

Ben paused and pointed to a black-and-white photo, which was blown up and hung on the wall off the Coffee Bean Café.

"That lift you see in the picture was his 'baby'. It was the first of its kind built in this country. It was his pride and joy."

"How long did he work for the mountain?"

"About four years. He loved it according to Libby. But something happened to him, maybe it was booze, but today I'm sure it would be diagnosed as depression."

As Ben spoke, Meggy felt a chill run through her.

"He killed himself, didn't he?"

"Yes. He hung himself from the gondola with a rappelling rope, then started it up. To this day, the old time lift attendants talk about the sight they saw when they came out to start the lifts that morning. It was just as the skiers were getting ready to come out for the day, Christmas Day. Charlie O'Connor told me that he still gets sick when he thinks of it. Earl went all the way up the mountain and then, like a scarecrow, came down and looped past the bull wheel."

Ben paused, picturing the horror.

"By the way, it was your trooper friend Wilson who had to cut his body down and bring the news to his wife."

"My God, that's horrible. Wilson must have been a young kid at the time. Was there any explanation why he did it?"

"It turns out that he had been told that week that he was going to be let go for his drinking or some other infraction. The truth was, the mountain had hired some manufacturer's rep from the lift company who would oversee the next phase of their growth, and the guy thought it would be too much to have Earl around."

"His wife must have been devastated. How old was the little girl?"

"She was only two, thank God. She really never remembered him."

"Did Libby have a lot of family here to support her and the child?"

"Yes, her family goes back a long way here. Her parents had retired to the Handle Road house by then, so she had a lot of support and every available male in the Valley began to look at the widow Stark as a great catch."

"Did she ever remarry?"

"Nope. She laid low for a while, worked as a secretary at a real estate office and did some substitute teaching. Then she decided to run for political office. Even though she got beat the first time out, she got the bug bad, and in the seventies, put a good campaign together and won a state Senate seat that has been like a marriage for her. She seems committed to the office, and has chaired the human service committee for the last few years. She is one of a handful of senators who has built a strong power base statewide. I wouldn't be surprised to see her run for governor one of these years."

Ben waved as he spoke, and Meggy turned to see Rooney entering the coffee shop. He had removed his suit jacket, and the sleeves on his oxford shirt were rolled to below his elbow, revealing a small Marine Corps tattoo on his forearm. He ordered an iced tea and pulled up a chair next to Ben.

"Where's Wilson?" Megan asked.

"His wife called him while we were at your brother's house and he took off. He seemed a little upset, but he said he just had to speak to someone, and we could start again tomorrow. If that's OK with you, guys."

Megan sipped her drink and then spoke. "Did you get any results from the state lab, or did you have any luck finding my brother's books?

"No and no. The chief says the state lab is backed up three or four days because of vacations. We definitely did not find a trace of any notebooks or any other correspondence that your brother may have written. I think it's clear that your brother was hiding something that somebody was willing to kill him for."

"I don't want to believe that," she pleaded.

"I know you don't Megan, and believe me, I don't want to be to keep telling you that, but if I don't, I wouldn't be doing my job. You have been insistent on me keeping you informed, and I will whenever I can, but you have to realize that somewhere down the line, you're going to hear or see something that bothers you."

Chapter 19

July 1997, evening
Marlboro, Vermont

They sat that evening and ate with Ben's mentor and next-door neighbor Dick Barnes. Barnes had retired from active teaching at Frost College, but continued to take over Ben's classes and tutorials when necessary. He reminded Meggy of an aging, but well-muscled Jimmy Cagney. His wife of forty years sat sipping white wine and holding court with Rooney. She admitted to being a fan of the mystery novel and seemed to have an endless curiosity for the details of his work.

"In spite of what you read, the majority of crimes usually don't get solved by fancy scientific methodology."

Rooney sat and finished his grilled chicken and sweet corn. He could feel the tension of the afternoon's discussion with Meggy start to dissipate over the conversation and the ice-cold Sam Adams beer.

"We still rely, in great part, on the criminal making a mistake somewhere along the line."

"What about the crime lab technicians that the state sent down to Johnny's house? Don't they make a difference in these investigations?" Susan Barnes spoke as if the bubble of too many detective novels was beginning to burst.

"To a degree they're a help, especially in sexual crimes and homicides. We couldn't function without them obviously. The majority of crimes still get solved by a lot of legwork and a lot of luck."

Rooney talked easily about Salem and his work. He told them how he happened upon Salem after leaving the Marine Corps. He talked for the first time in a while about his ex-wife and her decision to leave Salem and return to Nantucket. As the cooling New England night came alive with the sounds of crickets and cicada, he began to understand why Megan Dwyer would come here to heal.

This is a safe place and these are gentle people. I wish I could bring Katie here sometime and let her sit out on a porch and swing. Who knows, maybe I can take some vacation when this is over.

"How do you feel about going back to your brother's tomorrow, Megan?"

"I'll be ready to go, after a long morning run and a good breakfast."

"You're pretty tough."

"Well, I'm no kid anymore, and I'm all I've got to work with, so I try as hard as I can."

Rooney watched as her eyes teared. He wanted to reach out and hold her and yet he knew that wasn't going to happen, at least not tonight.

"I'm gonna get back to the tavern," he announced. He spoke to the people at the table as if they were old friends. Susan Barnes got up, and hugged him as he left.

"Be careful driving back. These troopers will stop you at the drop of a hat."

Rooney laughed. *"Let's hope not, Susan. Let's hope not. Troopers aren't exactly my favorite people right now."*

The beer and the long day made him drowsy as he drove the seven miles of twisty mountain roads. When he reached Warrens Mills, he was surprised to find a message from Wilson at the front desk of the tavern. He dialed the number on his cell phone and an angry-sounding voice came on the line.

"Just a minute, I'll get him." Carol Ann Wilson yelled to her husband to pick up the other line.

"Thanks for calling, Brian. I know it's late, but I needed to run something by you."

"What's up, Pete?"

"I had a call today that bothered the shit out of me. It was from a woman who says we might find her prints all over Dwyer's house, and she wants to talk to us tomorrow."

"That's a break. Is it somebody you know?"

There was a long pause and Rooney could hear Wilson walking to another room. His voice lowered and he said, "Her name is Libby Stark and I've known her forever. She's one of the nicest people I know in this town, and she also happens to be our senator from this county. I really can't say anything more. This is a little touchy, ya know what I mean."

"Sure, sure," he said, although he didn't. "I can't believe she called you directly. In Massachusetts, you would have heard from her lawyer."

"That's why I live in Vermont, pal. See you in the morning, Brian."

Chapter 20

July 1997
Marlboro, Vermont

MEGAN DWYER AWOKE at five thirty on the morning of July 15, and tossed the comforter back across Ben's guest room bed. She began to pack her running gear and fresh clothing in her New Balance track bag. She quietly made coffee from Ben's stock of Green Mountain roast and sat peacefully on the front porch while it brewed, reading from her *Alanon* meditation book. She let the quiet of the Vermont morning seep into her as it had so many summers past. She could hear the voice of her sponsor, Margie Walsh, creeping into her meditation. "You didn't cause it, Meggy, and you sure ain't gonna cure it."

Margie had been married to a drunk for forty years; twenty of those years her husband had been sober through the twelve steps. Yet Margie still clung to her Alanon program with tenacity. She latched onto the newcomer Meggy with the same loving care that only a drunk's wife could.

Meggy had watched as this woman wasted away from the breast cancer in her body, yet seemed to grow more loving and accepting as the cells ran out of control through her fair skin and freckled Irish body.

"Stay in the day and trust God as you understand her," she would gently admonish Meggy in their almost daily phone calls.

Meggy could smell the coffee now. She put her books in the duffel and returned from the porch to the kitchen, pouring the rich brew into a large mug. She found a pen on the kitchen table and wrote a note to Ben telling him that she was going to run, shower and change at Johnny's, and that she would see him at the Colonial later on. She started the Explorer and turned on the low beams to combat the dense fog that seemed always to show up in the early morning hours, then break as the warmth of the day set in.

She drove the three miles to Route 9 cautiously, as the dirt roads were slicker than usual because of the wet coating of morning dew. She was glad when she finally hit the pavement on the road to Warrens Mills and could follow the luminous yellow lines that would guide her to town.

At 6:00 AM, there was little sign of life in the village. Opening activity at the Coffee Bean caught her attention as she rounded the corner, but she knew better than to have more coffee or she'd be looking for a bathroom halfway through her run. She didn't feel like stopping to pee in the woods today.

As she made the turn up Town Hill Road and passed the cemetery, the cut grass and monuments made her feel somehow at home. The spot near the top of the hill that she had chosen for her brother's ashes seemed comforting.

She pulled into the circular drive at the barn house and noticed the garish yellow tape had been removed. It seemed for a second that all was normal. She searched her duffel for the keys, and then threw back the sliding barn door that protected the front entrance.

The house was just coming alive with sunlight as she entered. Although the mess of yesterday was still there, it didn't seem to have the same overwhelming effect on her. *Today was today,* she thought as she climbed the spiral staircase to her old room. How strange that her stuff remained untouched in the wake of chaos in the rest of the house. Her pictures were still on the antique bureau that had been her parents. Clean clothes were still piled neatly in the drawers exactly as she had left them in May. She selected blue running shorts, and a tank top, lettered with the logo of the Greater Boston Track Club. She found clean socks and sat on the bed pulling on a pair of New Balance trainers. She then walked back down the spiral to the living room area and pulled back the curtains, flooding the room with light. She began her stretches and felt the tightness begin to leave. Meggy was careful to work each muscle group slowly, and when twenty minutes had passed, she walked out the front entrance, leaving the door wide open.

The road felt good under her feet as she began the descent toward town. She held back on the downhill past the cemetery, then maintained a smooth pace as she reached the bottom and turned onto Route 100 north, checked her watch and saw she was right on a six thirty pace. She could feel the ease of motion that had always been part of her running style. This was her turf, blacktop roads with yellow lines running down the middle. First unbroken, then broken on the straight with skip lines at twenty-five-foot intervals that allowed the cars to pass and gave Meggy a sense of ownership that few people understood. The roads were her ally in life. She had gone to starting lines in twenty-four states and had run on the European track circuit. The minute the gun went off, she felt the asphalt welcome her, whispering to her to watch the lines and follow the angles. It told her when to hold back and when to move on a competitor.

She had raced the streets of Boston and the coastline of Falmouth on Cape Cod. She knew the boroughs of New York and her friend, Fred Lebow's monster marathon that she had won twice. The windy streets of Chicago had buffeted her, but had given her a women's course record as well. Now she was alone again. No crowds, no coach, just asphalt road and painted lines.

She settled into a groove as she turned onto the Cold Brook Road leading to Haystack Mountain, a faint trace of perspiration beginning to trickle under her arm. She was approaching three miles now, her stride was even and she could feel the warm sunshine on her face and shoulders. She began to ascend slightly and decided to turn and head back toward Route 100 at a faster pace. The accumulated miles of the past began to guide her steps and she felt strong as she entered the highway that led to Warrens Mills. She crossed Route 100 and ran facing the traffic that was beginning to flow with pickups carrying large toolboxes in their beds, or an occasional bread or beverage truck making the rounds of convenience stores that served the valley.

Her pace quickened as she left the straightway and ascended the hill toward the barn. Her shoulders squared as she lengthened her stride to accommodate the pitch on the hill next to the cemetery. She strained with a kick that brought her to the final flat stretch off road, leading to the circular driveway and the converted barn that today she would begin to make her home. The breeze from the pasture carried her final steps as she whispered to herself, "You can do it, Meggy, you can do it."

Meggy didn't notice the green pickup parked near the cemetery that had followed her for part of her run. The driver started the truck and drove down the hill toward Warrens Mills and thought, *I hope you are not going to be as much trouble as your brother.* The driver slowly rubbed the wooden handle of the shotgun while turning onto Route 100.

Chapter 21

July 1997
Warrens Mills, Vermont

JACKIE BURNS SAT in the Colonial Inn and sipped black coffee and anisette, enjoying the first buzz of the day from a neatly rolled joint of killer dope that he had scored while he and Johnny Dwyer had been on the road. He checked the balance in his checkbook and tried to figure what he was gonna do without the cash that he and Johnny were bringing home. The fact that Dwyer had about no chance of ever driving legally again had given him a car as well. Now some asshole had "offed" the Golden Goose and Jackie was sitting with his mandolin up his ass, a couple of hundred bucks in his wallet, and a government disability check that was coming up for review by his caseworker at the V.A. Now Dwyer's sister had grabbed the car. *What the fuck else can go wrong?*

The entrance of Porky Atkins and a deputy, as well as two others in plainclothes, whose holstered weapons identified them as cops, added a new dimension to Jackie's paranoia. He decided to go back upstairs to his rented room and enjoy the buzz in peace, but then the munchies kicked in and he said, "Fuck it," and continued to read the sports page of the *New York Post*.

He couldn't help himself, however, from watching his favorite cartoon character, Chief Porky Atkins, salivating over last night's dinner menu that had been left inadvertently on the tables of the Colonial's breakfast and dinner room. Jackie's hemp fantasy ended with the chief blowing up to balloon size and floating toward the sky while desperately trying to eat one last piece of pizza.

"He's got him a nut check from Vietnam." Porky pointed across the room to Burns, who was attempting to hide behind the paper. "Plays the mandolin like a bitch. You're deceased and he traveled all over hell together, and it wouldn't surprise me if he didn't have some information for you. But the son of a bitch is usually too stoned to get a straight answer."

Rooney made a note in his book to interview Burns and sipped at the coffee that had been served almost immediately upon their arrival. They were sitting in a small dining room that faced the main street of the village. The charm of the town reminded him of Nantucket before the new money came.

"This room ain't used in the morning, except by the regulars who rent rooms from Tito on a monthly basis."

Porky had set up a meeting between Rooney and Frank Weldon, who was a detective attached to the Vermont Bureau of Criminal Investigation out of the Brattleboro barracks.

Weldon sipped at his coffee and then said, "Do you think you're going to need much local help with your investigation, Brian? 'Cause if this looks like there is a case here in Vermont, we'll assign an investigator and probably a local trooper to give you a hand."

"Right now, I'm waiting to hear what we've gathered in our investigation; but so far that's been limited to some spent casings and the usual rash of Salem witches who call in tips."

Weldon sat amused at the witch reference and let out a chuckle. He found himself liking Rooney.

"I've got a North Shore detectives' meeting on Tuesday, and I'm hoping to find something we can hang our hats on, but my gut tells me that Dwyer was mixed up in something here in Vermont. It might help if the chief could free up a man to canvas the area around Dwyer's house in case somebody saw or heard anything unusual going on. We should probably keep an eye on the sister at the same time."

"Frank, good to see ya, my boy," said Wilson as he walked up behind the group. "Peter, I heard you were back in the saddle on this one. I hope that means that I can go home and sit it out."

Wilson had come through the Colonial's backdoor unseen by Rooney and gave his former trooper buddy a good-natured whack on the back as he pulled up a seat next to Porky and his patrol officer. The Warrens Mills chief pulled his chair back as if to distance himself from the former trooper.

"I'm strictly working the insurance on this one, Frank. I'm too old and cranky to get involved, and besides, we've got a real cop here from the witch city where they burn 'em first and then see if they're guilty."

"I made you guys a frittata. The voice belonged to Tito Alforno, the proprietor of the Colonial. He came in from the kitchen area bearing an oversized platter of eggs, cheese, and potato blended together into an omelet and topped with a marinara sauce. A waitress who set out toast and small tubs of whipped butter accompanied him.

"Have some more coffee, gentlemen. And I hope you find the basta' that shoot my boy Johnny."

"He must have been a good friend of his," Rooney remarked to Wilson when Tito walked back in the kitchen.

"Two or three hundred a month in bar tabs kind of friend," clarified Wilson and they laughed and ate the omelet with gusto. Rooney and Weldon were exchanging phone numbers as they ate.

"Why don't we talk near the end of the week," Weldon said to Rooney as he rose to go.

"Meantime, I'll check and see if anything unusual showed up through the AFIS system. I'd appreciate you sending me anything you've got on your end especially the photos and whatever ballistics your lab came up with."

"Chief, you will take care of office and phones for Detective Rooney if he needs them, right?" asked Weldon.

"Got it covered, Frank," Porky said, not missing a forkful of food as he spoke. "I can assign Henderson to help him out 'cause you know how people in this town take to cops asking questions, especially flatland cops."

Rooney could sense that the chief was resigned to the fact that there was going to be an ongoing investigation in his town and obviously wanted some of the control of the investigation to come from his office.

As they broke up the meeting, Rooney tried to give Tito his credit card, but the owner refused to take payment, saying it was a gift from Johnny. Rooney felt uncomfortable about the freebie since his department had a standing order of no free goods or services, but Wilson just laughed and said, "Welcome to Vermont."

Meggy was walking through the front door as they finished speaking. She looked fresh, Rooney thought. She was wearing khaki shorts and tank top that highlighted her skin still glowing from the morning exercise.

"Sorry I'm late, but I had to make some calls and try to straighten up some of the mess in the house. I checked every place that my brother kept things and there are no signs of his notebooks anywhere in the house."

Wilson looked upset as she spoke. "I'm not sure you should be poking around the house by yourself."

"Well, I was going to wait for Ben, but he had some things to do at the college, so I figured I'd get a jump on the day. Besides, my clothes and some furnishings are being delivered this week and I want the house to be in decent shape when everything arrives."

"So you're feeling comfortable in the house?" Wilson shook his head in dismay as he listened to this women turn from the weeping female of yesterday to a confident and laughing person about to move in to her dead brother's house. She seemed to have little anxiety about the fact that her brother was recently murdered and his house ransacked by someone who could potentially do harm to her as well.

"I called Johnny's real estate broker and asked for the name of a cleaning service in town, and they are going to help me this afternoon."

"Are you always this organized?" laughed Rooney.

I spent the last fifteen years organizing, to the last detail, the largest women's running event in the country. Try moving ten thousand women through the streets of Boston in a couple of hours and you'll learn quickly what organized means." She grinned, and her smile was the first that Rooney could remember seeing since they had met. Her teeth were model's white, and it was clear that this woman took very good care of herself.

"Pardon me, Ms. Dwyer." She turned to see a pony tailed man wearing a tie-dyed T-shirt and jeans walking toward her from the dining room. "I'm Jackie Burns. I worked with your brother as his back-up musician."

Burns was clearly stoned, his speech was a bit too slow and studied, and he tried to smile, but it didn't quite work.

"I'm real sorry about Johnny and I hate to bug you, but I have some stuff at his house that I'd like to pick up if I could?"

"You'll have to wait a few days, Jackie," Wilson spoke before Meggy could answer.

"We've still got to look through a few things for the insurance company."

"Oh, OK, Pete. Just let Tito know, will ya? See ya later, Ms. Dwyer."

"What was that all about?" Meggy asked Wilson while watching Burns head down the street toward the post office.

"Your brother was his meal ticket and I wouldn't be surprised to see Jackie try to keep that going as long as he can. So let's not let him get too close to the house until those guitars are locked up tight."

"Thanks, Pete, I hadn't really thought of that."

"That's why you hired me, remember?"

They agreed to all meet at Johnny's that afternoon and the two men left in Wilson's jeep, not telling Meggy that they were going to interview someone who might shine some light on the investigation. They drove up Route 100 toward the Snow Mountain Resort, and Rooney remarked how unspoiled the area appeared compared to his childhood home on Nantucket. He was curious about the lack of commercial development along the stretch of highway.

"It looks that way, but don't be fooled. This area has seen a lot of change in just the last thirty years. Christ knows we have seen everything from those monks you saw the other day to a football training camp. Now we got golf courses where farms used to be and development in the middle of forestland. In fact, the developers did such a job on us in the sixties, that the governor came here and decided to get behind legislation that just about stopped development in its tracks."

Wilson pulled to the left lane and slowed to let a car pass him before taking a left onto the Coldbrook Road, which became the Handle Road as it crossed into the town of West Dover. Rooney thought it was like leaving the present, and stepping back in time as they came upon the homes of the "Handlers," the summer colonists who had ventured forth by train from Boston in the eighteen seventies to fish the Cold Brook for trout and whose descendant still inhabited many of these homes today.

Rooney was struck by the contrast between the practical homes and ski chalets of Warrens Mills and the well-preserved mini-mansions that came into view. Wilson explained that these were the homes of the Cambridge and Concord professionals, who came for the long Vermont summers to escape the city. Their lives had intertwined with the local subsistence farmers, to whom they were beholden for everything from milk and eggs for their breakfast tables to transport from the train station to their homes upon arrival and departure.

"How the hell did people get up here seventy or eighty years ago?"

"By rail, up to Hoosic Tunnel and then they switched to a narrow gauge rail that brought them to Warrens Mills. It usually took about eight to ten hours to get up here from Boston."

"Watch out for the bike, Pete," Rooney yelled and gripped the dashboard.

Wilson braked sharply to avoid hitting a woman who had come out of a dirt road without looking. She was dressed in a spandex bike-racing outfit and was riding a European racing bike.

"That's the new rage up here on weekends. They're all over the place. Christ, one weekend they had something like twenty thousand people at the mountain to watch those damn fools race."

Wilson slowed and eased the jeep on to a worn driveway that led up to a long white house, obviously added on to over the years, but still retaining the charm of a colonial grand home that fit the mountain landscape. They parked next to a late model Volkswagen bearing the distinctive plates of the Vermont Senate. Approaching the front porch, Rooney was struck by the view that opened up. He could see expansive fields leading up to maple and white birch woodlands. He could imagine deer grazing near the apple stand, a short distance from the house.

The green screen door opened, and an attractive fiftyish auburn-haired woman came out to greet them. She was carrying a tray that had a glass pitcher filled with iced tea. Her worn jeans had dirt on the knees, and a T-shirt that had the VisionVermont logo hung untucked from her waist. Gardening tools rested on the front steps.

"Morning, Peter, thanks for coming."

She set the tray down on a wicker table and extended a firm handshake to Rooney. I'm Libby Stark, and Pete told me you're Detective Rooney."

"That's right. Pleased to meet you, Senator."

"Call me Libby. If colleagues in Montpelier heard you call me Senator, they'd laugh."

They sat and she poured iced tea for them, and then almost immediately began to tell Rooney the reason why she had called Wilson the day before.

"As a former teacher, the Automated Fingerprint Identification System has my prints on the card file. I know that there is a chance that you will find them on something at Johnny Dwyer's house."

As she spoke, it was clear this woman needed to talk. Rooney took out his notebook and began to write.

"I began to drop in on Johnny about a year ago, because I'd heard he was killing himself with alcohol, and I figured I could at least try and talk to him, and who knows, maybe get him some help. He was a drinking buddy of my late husband, but I hadn't really been that close to him or many other men since I began my work in politics."

"Did you become intimate?"

"No, I told you that I just wanted"—she paused—"oh, damn, yes, we did; and now I'm sorry for that, but believe me, I actually thought that somehow having a relationship might help him to stop drinking."

Her face began to tear up and she took a Kleenex from her pocket and continued her story, "For a while, he actually stopped and began to go to AA. Then two months ago, I went by his house and found him in a stupor. I decided to bail out before I had to live through another disaster like my husband's." She looked over at Wilson and smiled weakly.

"How was he the last time you saw him?"

"He was drinking heavily. He kept calling late at night. I told him to quit and I warned him if my daughter found out about us, that I would never speak to him again."

"When was that?"

"Six weeks ago. The calls stopped and I assumed he was back on the road again. Then I heard what happened, and I couldn't believe it."

"Can you think of any reason why someone would want to kill him?"

"No. He wasn't into drugs as far as I know. He seemed to make a good living. He always had plenty of cash. The record studio is successful. It just doesn't make any sense why anybody would want him dead."

"Did you ever meet any of his friends or hear him talk about anyone that might be angry with him?"

Rooney continued to take notes and observe her closely as she spoke.

"No. The only ones who he mentioned a lot were his sister in Boston, and Ben Latimer over at the College. Occasionally, the creepy mandolin player who backed him up would drop over to rehearse, but I always left when I knew he was coming."

As she spoke, a family of quail paraded across the dirt road in front of the house.

"Look Mrs. Stark, I think we have what we came for, and I will probably have to speak to you again, but there is no reason right now to have your privacy violated. We will try to keep this as quiet as we can, but there are no guarantees that down the road, your relationship with the victim won't come out. If I were you, I'd tell your daughter the truth, rather than have her find out through local gossip."

She wrung her hands, then put them to her face as the tears started to flow. She spoke as though the words were stuck on her tongue.

"I know you're right Detective. I just wish this mess had never happened."

"Imagine that Dwyer feels the same way, don't you think?" Rooney put his notebook in his jacket, then handed her a business card. "If you can think of anything else that might be helpful, please give me a call?"

They walked out to the parked jeep and left her to her gardening.

As they pulled out, Rooney placed his hand across the seat on Wilson's chest. Wilson looked surprised. "OK, what's going on between you and her? If she is involved, then I have to assume you are too."

Wilson pulled over and looked angrily at Rooney. "It was a long time ago and has nothing to do with Dwyer. I was a good cop for twenty eight years. While you were in high school, I was patrolling twelve towns and a major east/west highway, with damn little backup. I never took a bribe or fixed a goddamn parking ticket. You will just have to trust me on this. Anything you detected was over long ago."

He put the jeep back into gear and continued fuming as he drove back to Warrens Mills.

Again, he pulled the jeep over into a ski area parking lot. Rooney watched as Wilson moved his large frame out of the vehicle. He gestured to Rooney to get out of the car. Rooney hesitated; unholstered his weapon, placed it on the seat and walked up to Wilson.

Instead of the angry punch that Rooney thought was coming, Wilson spoke with rage in his voice. He pointed to a silent ski lift a half mile from the road. "In 1962, while my wife was home cooking Christmas dinner for her folks and mine, I was called by Snow Valley to investigate a death. When I got there, I found Libby's husband, Earl Stark, a pretty good buddy of mine, hanging by his neck from a chair lift while skiers gawked and stood around waiting for the skiing to start. He was only hanging about 10 feet from the ground at the point where they had stopped the lift. So I climbed the top of a snowcat and cut the rope from his twisted neck. I carried him from that spot to an area that would leave him protected from the skier's curiosity."

Wilson pointed back up the road. "At eight, on a Christmas morning, I had to knock on that door back there and tell a mother with a two-year-old that her husband had killed himself. And for the second time that morning, I cradled a Stark in my arms. That's how I know the woman, and it is all you need to know now."

Chapter 22

December 1, 1963
Warrens Mills, Vermont

THE TALL MAN had buried his father in the Warrens Mills cemetery. There were few mourners gathered with him as the rain ate away at the freshly dug graveside, old-timers who themselves would be coming here to rest in the next few years. There were a few women from the Congregational Church that graced the main road in the village of Warrens Mills. They were mostly his mother's friends, for she had been a believer, and had spent a lifetime trying, to no avail, to get his father to join her on Sundays. He could remember his father's reply each week that she would ask.

"I choose not to go with you. The boy and I have things to do."

With that, they would spend time hunting or fishing, and there would be a treat for the boy. Just on Sundays, his father would reach deep into his heavy woolen pants as they walked along the Coldbrook Road, or sometimes on the backside of Stratton Mountain *where there were an abundance of black bears. He would produce a piece of maple sugar candy, or a chunk of rock candy that took forever to melt in the boy's mouth.*

They would end the day tired and windburned, with a meal of roasted venison or maybe pork chops from a recent slaughter, and they would plan their next day's labors while drinking cider or coffee before a fire.

He was watching now as the bus pulled into the bank in Warrens Mills. He had been watching for three weeks, and noticed the same young driver behind the wheel on Mondays. The driver spoke briefly with the fat Constable as he loaded the canvas and leather bags into the rear compartment of the eight-passenger Chevrolet van that served to provide local transportation. He eased out into the traffic on Route 9, being careful to follow the bus at a distance that wouldn't arouse suspicion. The driver seemed to be always focused on the road ahead, and rarely did he appear to be looking in his rearview mirror, except when someone would exit the line of traffic and pass. The young man drove slowly as if there might be black ice on the road; the trip to the Marlboro post office took about fifteen minutes. There, the carrier stopped and waited while the postmaster brought out two sacks from behind the counter and placed them in the rear compartment along with the bank transfer bags. The postmaster and the young man bantered back and forth good-naturedly as if they might be acquaintances. The driver, then turned the bus back onto the dirt road that led to Route 9 and Brattleboro.

This pattern didn't seem to change from week to week. The tall man began to question how he was going to get the driver to stop, when suddenly, the driver signaled for a right turn onto a road four miles outside of the town of Brattleboro. The tall man followed from a safe distance as the driver turned again three miles up the road and crossed a wood bridge leading up to a group of buildings that obviously housed a camp of some sort. He was puzzled, until he saw another car parked at the end of the small parking lot, and the mystery was solved. The woman stepped out and ran to meet the driver.

He waited some ten minutes while the couple went inside the first cabin, leaving their vehicles unguarded in the lot. A smile crossed his strawberry birth-marked face for the first time in months. He knew the woman and he understood how he would avenge his father's shame and ultimate death.

The smile lingered as he drove back onto Route 9 and headed over the Auger Hole Road that would take him, unseen, back to his cesspool trench, the final resting place of a young man whose name he didn't know, but was sure he would be finding out soon. He checked to see that no one had disturbed the trench, then, spent the rest of the day at his parents' house, whistling while he cleaned his father's gun and eating a small maple sugar soldier he had bought at the Dover Store.

Chapter 23

July 1997
West Dover, Vermont

THE HEADACHE CONTINUED to pound at her temple. She turned the shower nozzle on full and felt the stream begin to give her some relief. She had taken her headache medication immediately after the detective and her old friend Pete Wilson had left. She hoped the mild narcotic wouldn't cause her to daydream during what could be one of the more important interviews of her public life. She soaped her body to remove the gardening dirt and sweat, then turned and let the water rush over her face and breasts. She shampooed vigorously, as if trying to scrub away the pain in her head.

Libby emerged from the shower ready again to put on the political face she had worn for twenty-three years. She would dress like an aging LL Bean model. The mirror in her bath told her she could still work her old magic. She was beginning to feel confident again after the unsettling meeting with the police. Her reverie was interrupted by her daughter's knock on the door.

"They're out front setting up, Mom."

"OK Jen, tell them to wait just a minute and I'll be right down."

She slipped on fresh panties and a bra, and began to feel some relief from the headache. She selected brown twill shorts and a pink pullover top. She plugged in her hairdryer and faced the mirror, as if it were the interviewer.

"Thanks, Paul, for that kind introduction, and welcome to Vermont," she spoke to the mirror until her hair was dried and brushed out. Then checking herself one last time, she walked out to her closet, selected a pair of sandals, and walked downstairs to face the videotaped interview that would run on Boston's Channel Seven. The show was part of an ongoing series on the political and cultural changes in the landscape of the New England. Her front porch had been transformed into an outdoor studio, and the camera crew and overhead sound operators milled around, drinking coffee and smoking. They had set up two canvas-backed chairs for Libby and Ellen Ansalone to sit in during the interview.

Ansalone was a successful real estate developer who had come to the Valley in the sixties to ski and party after graduation from college. By most standards, she had done well. She had classic Italian features set on a short and firm frame. She was casually but expensively dressed in tailored slacks and a navy blue linen jacket. Her hair was cut short and stylish, accentuating her dark complexion and prominent nose. Her movements were highlighted by the sound of the loose gold bracelets on her right wrist.

"Ellen, good to see you. You know my daughter Jennifer?"

"Of course, I see Jennifer swimming at the lake whenever I can get out of the office to swim, which isn't too often these days."

"How's business at High Mowing?" Libby referred to the large land development that Ellen had almost single handedly built on an eight-hundred-acre property that she had acquired prior to Vermont's passage of *Act 250* (a land preservation bill that was passed in great part, due to the abuses of developers in Southern Vermont). Although Ellen was a constituent of Libby's, she was by no means one of her favorite people. The only reason Libby had agreed to being interviewed on the same show with Ansalone was the fact that the Senator badly needed to raise awareness of her mental health parity bill outside of Vermont.

"We're still as busy as ever. Well, not like the old days certainly, but that kind of boom only happens once in a lifetime."

They were interrupted by a handsome, casually dressed man in navy polo shirt and starched knee-length khaki shorts. He was the producer and on-air host of *Traveling New England*, Paul Abbott.

"Well, Senator, you've had some excitement up here in the last few days, I'm told."

Libby's heart raced as she thought about her interview just an hour ago. She was able to compose herself and casually ask, "What excitement is that, Paul?"

"The murder of the folksinger, Johnny Dwyer, down in Salem. Isn't he a resident of Warrens Mills or did I get it wrong?"

Libby reached over and put down the tea she'd been drinking, then sat back and crossed her legs as she spoke.

"Yes, you're correct. I guess I just try to block that kind of violence. In fact, I met with his sister to express my condolences just the other day."

"I'd I like to tell her what a piece of shit he was," exclaimed Ellen Ansalone, her gold bracelets flying around her wrist as she started to launch into a diatribe on the life and times of the late Johnny Dwyer. As she spoke, Paul Miller's video cam recorded her anger.

"Dwyer was a no good son of a bitch who used people and then brushed them off like dirt. I don't give a shit if he's dead. Good riddance as far as I'm concerned, and shut off the fucking camera, you asshole."

Miller stopped shooting. The assembled crew, as well as Libby and her daughter, didn't speak. They just waited for the rest of Ansalone's speech. Instead, she picked up her car keys from the wicker table and bolted from the porch to the driveway. Her Porsche convertible left a cloud of dirt and gravel as she sped from the house.

"Jesus Christ, what was that all about?"

Abbott was visibly shaken by Ansalone's behavior. The fact that he had just lost half of his scheduled show was also dawning on him.

"Take a break, folks," he spoke to the assembled crew.

"I've always known her as a hothead, but that's incredible." Libby moved to the end of the porch as if to try and run after Ellen.

"Mom, you always said she was crazy. Why act surprised now?"

"Well, for one reason, she is badmouthing a man whose murder has not been solved and she was dumb enough to do it on television.

Fifteen minutes later, Abbott met with the crew. Professional that he was, after twenty years of television, he turned and with boyish charm, he gave the signal to roll the tape. After the camera had panned across the pasture and stone fences, it slowly moved to the porch where a now poised and ready Libby Stark began to unfold her story for the viewers of this widely watched show in the New England market.

"Senator Stark, it's been awhile since we visited, and I'm sure the majority of people watching tonight are wondering how it came about that you have become such a crusader for mental health parity. I know that this is not an issue that I would have guessed you would champion."

He picked up a ceramic half gallon of maple syrup and held it up to the camera "As I remember your past efforts have been mostly involved in protecting the quality of Vermont-made products and the development of new markets for local entrepreneurs through VisionVermont Enterprise activities." Abbot was referring to the truth-in-packaging bill that Libby had been instrumental in getting through the legislature.

"Your bill was the first to make it enforceable under the law that if a product label said "Made in Vermont," then the product had to have been made 100 percent in the state."

She had instigated this legislation at the behest of Lyman Carrier, the chair of VisionVermont Enterprise, whose insight into the preservation of Vermont products had made a huge difference in the economic development of the Green Mountain State. One had only to look at the success of Ben and Jerry's or the Cabot Dairy Co-op to see the fruits of the Stark Bill, as it had come to be known.

"Paul, I'll try to answer that question as best I can by giving you a brief history of my own involvement with mental health and substance abuse issues."

Abbott watched carefully as she spoke and had the momentary feeling that this waspy Vermont legislator was about to out herself as an alcoholic or maybe a depression sufferer. Instead, she raised her tanned slender arm and pointed out the view of the meadow below.

"My family has lived in this house, in some fashion, since the early nineteen hundreds. Most of that period, they came in the summer and stayed till fall. To listen to my grandmother, you would think it was little house on the prairie, but instead of covered wagons, they came by rail. My own childhood summers here were probably the most wonderful period I shall ever spend on this earth. I can never imagine what life would be like without these trees and streams that mark the side of the road." She paused to let the camera pan across the field and nearby stream that ran through her property. She shifted slightly in the canvas-backed chair and sipped at her tea before continuing.

"Part of the reason that we were comfortable here was the treatment we received from the Vermonters who farmed the properties around us. We relied on them for the staples that they grew or farmed, and when work was needed, or a new home was to be built, they did the work using local building materials. It was pretty much a self-contained world."

She looked across the yard to where her daughter sat cross-legged, and she began to smile as she continued.

"But the reason I'm here today is to tell you about a wonderful young man, who was born and raised in this Valley. From the first time I saw him at age ten, I knew that he was the boy I would marry. He was just two years older than I was, but he seemed so grown up as he would deliver ice and do the other chores that my mother needed. He had a deep tan all summer long that illuminated his blue eyes and sandy hair. I would dream about him all winter. When the buggy would pick us up at the train in June, I always knew that my Earl would be driving.

"When I completed college at Bennington, I came back here to live, and within a year, I married that handsome Vermonter right over there in that stand of apple trees."

The camera passed across the porch to the treed area, and as it did, Libby blew her nose and wiped at her eyes as she continued her story.

"My young husband and I lived right here for most of four years, and although I knew my husband drank regularly, I was too young and too in love to see that as a problem. In 1963, he completed his largest project for Snow Mountain, and there was rumor of some layoffs, or at least a rumor that the corporation was going to bring in some hotshot engineer from Europe to replace him as lift foreman."

She stopped and asked to take a break, the cameras stopped, and she once again wiped her eyes, signaled to start again and began to speak in almost a reverent tone.

"He never spoke about it or listened to my suggestion that maybe he should at least look elsewhere for work. Instead, he withdrew into a shell that I now know was depression. He had so much pride in his work that I imagine it was just unthinkable to him that the mountain would just discard him. He had never worked for a large company before, and I suppose if he had, he might have known what to expect."

Once again, she drank from the tall iced tea glass and then said, "On December 25, Christmas morning, he left the house early and went to the mountain before the lifts opened. He had with him a full bottle of Jack Daniel's that we had received for the holidays from my parents. He drank half of it, then tied a rope around the top of the gondola cable and somehow managed to start the lift with the other end of the rope around his neck."

Paul Abbott looked at her in disbelief as she continued. The camera locked on her face.

"I'm not telling you this story today to evoke pity. In fact, I've rarely spoken about that horrible day to anyone. I chose to speak today for the families left behind after a suicide or a death from the ravages of alcoholism. We live today in a state that has the highest suicide rate in the country, a state where 33 percent of kids in our schools have thought about killing themselves in the past year, and 14 percent have tried."

She paused and Abbott spoke for the first time.

"Senator, I'm very sorry for your loss. I've known you now for some fifteen years and have never known the circumstances of your husband's death until today."

She smiled at him and spoke with a little levity, "OK, Paul, now that you've heard my story, let's turn to politics, 'cause after all, that's why you're here."

She went on to give her audience a clearer picture of her proposed parity bill, which in fact was the brainchild of a mental health advocate whom she had known for most of her years in the senate.

"Let's look at an example of health care inequity. Suppose a patient is hospitalized four times in the course of two years for illness due to his or her own mismanagement of adult diabetes. The hospital and attending physician submit a bill to the insurer or managed-care organization. The bill is paid according to the contractual agreement between the provider and the insurer."

Libby spoke with the rehearsed authority of a political pro, pausing just long enough for the viewer to grasp the simplicity of her example, then using her hands to show the other side of the argument.

"Now let's suppose that the same patient suffered from a mental problem that warranted hospitalization. He or she would probably run into a much more difficult time gaining access to treatment since most of the policies issued today have a cap of either dollars or days of treatment. This disparity in service is what our bill is all about. The lack of parity means that insurers and managed-care companies withhold from their customers the essence of health insurance: the security that those serious conditions—life threatening, either physical or mental—will be covered."

"Senator, thank you for that simple explanation." Abbott looked down at his notes and spoke in the neighborly tone that immediately relaxed even the toughest interview. The cameras panned to him as he asked, "What's this we hear about Stark's army? It sounds like revolution in Vermont once again."

She tossed back her hair and smiled broadly at the reference to the coalition of groups she and the Vermont Mental Health Association had managed to put together for a lobbying effort in such a short time. The reference to an army came from a creative tongue-in-cheek reporter from the *Burlington Free Press*. In an editorial, the writer had compared Stark's group to the citizen soldiers who made the march from New Hampshire, under the command of Col. John Stark, to Bennington in August of 1777.

"Well, Paul, as the British learned the hard way, and probably the insurers and HMOs are beginning to learn as well, a coalition of troops, well-organized and utilizing unconventional tactics, can defeat the larger enemy and eventually rue the day."

Her demeanor changed as she finished.

"Stark's Army, as we have been called, is a coalition of groups statewide that have come together as one voice to remove these inequities from our health care system."

She handed him a prepared list of members of the coalition, and then wound down the interview with a general discussion of Vermont politics and a promise by Abbott to return to follow the progress of this one-of-a-kind legislation.

As Abbott watched Libby walk away, he thought to himself, "This woman is running for governor and she may not even know it."

Chapter 24

July 1997
Salem, Massachusetts

KATIE COURIC'S IRRITATINGLY perky voice interrupted Brian Rooney's nightmare in time to save his ass, once more, from the pounding he took when he was seventeen years old. He was glad to wake up in his own bed after three nights in Vermont.

The incident with Wilson was bothersome. He liked the guy, but his involvement with the Senator was gonna be a problem. He let the shower run a few seconds before it became hot. While the water ran, he paused to look in the mirror and take stock at six feet and one hundred ninety pounds; he was still in good shape. His hairline was beginning to recede only slightly, and his belly was still firm. He took his razor from the sink and evened out his sideboards. Then he stepped into the shower to finish his shave, a trick that he had brought home from Marine Corps platoon leaders' school.

He thought back to the summer's day at the end of his senior year in high school. It was late June, the tourists hadn't yet arrived in force, and the Island still belonged to the locals. He had driven to Sconset Beach with his girlfriend Janet Chalmers, whom he later married. The day was hot, with just enough breeze to make it comfortable. The water temperature was still too cold for all but the hardiest to plunge into, and he stood shivering as he good-naturedly taunted her to follow him into the waves that were smashing onto the mostly deserted beachfront.

Brian lathered his face with gel in order to shave in the steaming shower. Even now, in the almost scalding waterfall, a chill came over him as he remembered the three strangers in their late teens who had arrived shortly after the Island couple. They had started to make remarks about Janet's breasts and the way they filled out her two-piece bathing suit. She was embarrassed and threw on a hooded Nantucket Whaler's sweatshirt. The beer-fueled strangers continued their remarks.

"Brian lets get out of here, these guys are trouble."

"No, they're just drunk; they won't bother us."

When he spoke, he didn't see that the largest of the group had walked to within hearing distance.

"You have a problem with us townie, or are you just pussy whipped?" The boy stood in front of him, and Brian could see there was going to be no way out.

"Get in the car," he ordered Janet.

He could sense her fear now as the other two got up and circled behind him, blocking her exit to the parking lot a hundred yards away.

"Look, we're not looking for trouble."

Brian rose from the blanket and stood, hands by his side, staring at the eyes of the stranger, and waiting for the move that he could sense would follow. The broken-nosed boy-man swallowed the last gulp of his beer and with schoolboy bravado, crushed the can in one hand, threw it aside, and charged at Rooney.

The Islander saw it coming and stepped back enough to deflect the brunt of the attack, then grabbed the boy's sweatshirt, pulled it down over his face and began to systematically punish his attacker with short punches to the head.

Ten years of boxing lessons and countless rounds of tournaments at the Boys Club had prepared him well for inclose fighting. His opponent stumbled backward. Rooney felt the power that comes with teenage rage. He landed blow after blow, then stood and kicked with his bare feet at the boy's ribs until he felt someone grab his arms from behind and smash him to the sand.

Janet was screaming hysterically as the two pummeled him from behind, one with an unopened beer bottle, drawing blood from the back of her boyfriend's head.

She tried to drag one of them off when she saw the bleeding, but the one Brian had bested got up and began to kick at Brian's head, and they threw her aside like a doll. Brian lay pinned, trying frantically to cover his head and face as they continued their assault. Janet's screaming only enraged them more.

The shortest of the three hit her across the face, then almost as an afterthought, grabbed at her hooded sweatshirt and yanked it over her shoulders. Her bathing suit top came off in his hands. He tore the sweatshirt off and tried to grab at her exposed breasts. She held her hands across her chest and fell to the sand in fear.

Brian looked across as she lay in the blood-soaked sand, unable to help her while a stranger tore at her innocence. His hands tried to protect his face as the other two continued to kick him.

Then he heard the scream for the first time and saw one of his attackers go down to the sand. Blood running from his forehead, he was screaming in pain. The other looked up in surprise as his eye exploded from a gigantic fist driving with a force of three hundred pounds behind it.

An almost inhuman sound came from a man that Brian knew only as the Whale, as he continued to beat savagely at the larger man. The other two began to run, leaving Janet trembling. Brian turned away as she replaced her top and pulled on the sweatshirt. He could feel her shame and hurt, but felt helpless. She finally came to him and let him hold her. She then began to sob and shake.

The Whale stood over the battered teenager, who now lay motionless on the bloodied sand.

"Go home kid, take your girl home and tell her parents what happened, but don't tell nobody about the Whale."

Rooney turned off the shower and toweled himself dry. He found clean underwear and socks in his travel bag and quickly brushed his hair. He selected a navy golf shirt and a light summer sports coat and slacks from his closet, stepped into tan tassel loafers, and transferred his wallet and notebook to his jacket pockets. His final act of dressing was to strap on his weapon. He checked his appearance in the hall mirror and left for the monthly North Shore Detectives' Meeting.

The conference room at the Swampscott PD was small. Because of vacations, there were less attendees than usual, but still, lively banter filled the room. The towns represented were Salem, Swampscott, Peabody, Marblehead, and Essex. The detectives totaled twelve, including the narcotics squad from neighboring Lynn. They were already passing out bulletins and mug shots. Brian sat and thumbed through the papers in front of him, then went to the front desk to see if a fact sheet on the Dwyer murder had been sent to him that morning as he had requested.

"Fax is right on the desk, Detective. I made you ten copies. I hope that's enough."

"Thanks, Bobby," Rooney spoke absentmindedly to the young desk officer and retrieved the fax copies. He checked to see that they were up-to-date and went back to the conference room.

"This guy has got to be in your nitwit file," Peabody Detective Paul Washington was enjoying sharing his perp of the week with his fellow detectives.

"This clown is hitting houses in the morning and staying long enough to finish whatever booze is lying around. He's bypassing everything in the house, but cash. He then gets his jollies by masturbating all over the women's underwear." The room broke up with laughter as Washington continued.

"To add insult to injury, this guy always takes a shower before he leaves."

Rooney held up his hand to show a palm and got Washington's attention.

"And he never leaves a print, does he, Paulie?" It was clear Rooney knew the MO well.

"We had neighborhoods randomly staked out for three months, trying to catch him in the act until two months ago when the breaks stopped. Now you own him. Good luck."

They swapped mug shots and copies of reports of common concern. Then it was Rooney's turn to bring them up to speed on the Dwyer murder.

"As you can tell by the report in front of you, it looks like this guy was probably involved in something at his Vermont home or at least that's where it seems to be heading. The problem is he was constantly traveling throughout the eastern states and Canada. There seems to be evidence he kept a journal of some kind and the break into his house may be related to something in the journal."

"What's the DA's involvement at this point?" The question came from Lynn Detective Barry Reardon.

"I'm meeting Roche, the investigator from the DA's unit today and bringing him up to speed. We're also involving the Vermont BCI and the locals up there. We may have caught a break on the weapon; it looks like it fires to the right of center by just a hair. So if we can locate the shotgun, we can probably get a match."

"What can we do to help, Brian?" Washington asked.

"Keep your ears open in the drunk community for anybody who might have been drinking with this guy while he was down here. If possible, try to find some of your regular street drunks who might have talked to this guy in the bars. He always carried lots of cash, so I'm sure he had a lot of buddies looking for a free drink wherever the hell he was drinking. And maybe he shot his mouth off about something going down."

"The problem with drunks is they're always shooting their mouths off about some scheme they're involved in, or were involved in, and, of course, the only way to tell if a drunk is lying is to see if his lips are moving." The speaker was Washington.

They laughed whenever Washington spoke about alcohol. He was their authority on the drunken community of the North Shore. He seemed to know every lowlife who walked the streets mumbling to themselves, or panhandling aimlessly from park benches. It was common knowledge, at the table, that he had been a bad drunk who had managed to give up the sauce twelve years before, and often worked with other cops who were having trouble with booze and didn't want to go through their employee assistance unit, or have it show on their fitness reports.

They talked about recent drug activity in their communities for the next twenty minutes, focusing on the changes in drugs on the street and the amount of cash they were uncovering as they raided dealers from Lynn to Gloucester.

Rooney felt himself questioning motive in the Dwyer case.

"Maybe it was just a drug deal gone bad. Dwyer had cash and access to a lot more according to his sister. He traveled into Canada regularly. His driver was stoned most of the time according to the Vermont locals. So why am I having trouble believing this was a drug hit? What about Wilson? Can I trust this guy?"

He pulled out his notebook and found Karen Nelson's work number, and then he made a list to follow up:

1. Call Nelson and set up meeting for today if possible.
2. Call and see if Oak Hill Hospital will meet with him and open Dwyer's records without a subpoena.
3. Whale watch. Call and set up time at the prison.
4. Call Nantucket selectman to arrange next interview.
5. Get birthday present for Kate.

His cell phone went off and a now-familiar voice boomed into his ear. "Brian, my boy, how was your trip home?"

He recognized Wilson's voice and for some reason was suddenly glad to hear it.

"What's up, Peter? Can't stay away from an investigation, or is this a social call?"

"Social call, my ass, just trying to help solve your little mystery for you. By the way, I'm sorry for the blow up before you left."

Rooney let the apology settle and said nothing.

"Last night, while you were enjoying your farewell chat with the deceased's sister, I had a phone call from someone who wouldn't leave their name, but dropped a dime on a tape made yesterday at the senator's house. It must have been sometime after we left."

"A tape? What was on it?"

"Porky sent one of his deputies down with a copy for you. It should be there in an hour or so, and I'm sure you'll enjoy it. See you when you get back."

Wilson hung up and Rooney put the phone away and wondered, "What the hell was that about?"

Leaving the Swampscott Police Station, he drove toward Lynn Beach which had long been a summer retreat for North Shore residents. He pulled the Crown Victoria over to a space vacated by a group of teens in a Dodge Convertible and sat back, letting the sun wash over his face. The view was by no means the same as the one he grew up with on Nantucket. There probably is no view anywhere that could compare to a summer's day on the beaches that surround the shoreline of Nantucket Island. He let himself daydream for a few minutes, but found his thoughts constantly going back to Megan Dwyer.

Last night, before he left Vermont, they had talked until late into the evening, mostly about her life and the discipline it took to maintain her running skills. He talked for the first time in years about his decision to walk away from his last bout at the Munich Olympics. She was a good listener, and seemed to understand the futility he felt when he walked through the blood-spattered bedroom with the wife of one of the butchered Israeli athletes. His coach, a twenty-year marine gunny sergeant, gave him an ultimatum that day: box or go home. Shortly after Munich, he was assigned to a rifle company and lost his athlete's perks.

"I hadn't thought about boxing again until last year, when I decided to see if I still had it in me. Now, I'm not even sure it was worth it, but I promised the chief that I would finish out the season of police charity boxing," he told Meggy.

"It's funny," he added, "since I started again, it sort of brings out a sense of anger that I can't put my finger on. I'm short-tempered and seem to fly off the handle at the slightest things, especially my ex-wife and her new husband, my brother, who used to be my closest friend, and who now I even have a hard time talking to."

Megan spoke fondly of the young athletes that made up the running community of the seventies in Boston. "I can't even imagine the horror of seeing any of them murdered."

She spoke of the runners—Rogers, Salazar, Meyer, and Thomas. They had trained together on the track at Boston College under the Greater Boston Track Club coach Billy Squires. Occasionally, she and another local runner, Patty Lyons, would workout with the men, and she always felt that opportunity was a big piece of her success on the roads.

They were just names from the sports pages to Rooney who had never been serious about running, until he was forced into it as a platoon leader in the corps. She said that they had been the last of the American runners to totally dominate the roads, and she spoke wistfully of the fun they had traveling the road race circuit, making decent money for the first time in their lives, enjoying their short-lived moments in the sun. Most of them were coaching or working for shoe companies now.

"It's all changed and you won't find an American in the top ten at the major races," she commented.

His phone buzzed, bringing him back from the Vermont moonlight to the hot sun of the Lynn beach parking lot.

"Rooney," he said quickly into the phone.

"Brian, there's a deputy from the Warrens Mills Police Department here with a package for you.

"Be there in ten minutes. Thanks, Barbara."

Rooney drove into the new brick station that housed the one hundred and ten members of the Salem Police Department. The building had multiple levels and resembled, in some ways, a fortress. He picked up his pink message slips from the front desk and pocketed them, then slipped the cover off the tape cassette that was waiting for him. It was marked Property of WCVB, Needham, Massachusetts.

"Brian, what was the package from Vermont all about?"

"I don't have a clue, boss, but if you give me five minutes, you can be my guest at the VCR and we'll find out together."

They entered the conference room and Rooney brought his boss up to speed on his trip, including his interview with Libby Stark. He pushed the play button and watched as the senator and another woman began talking back and forth with the commentator. Suddenly, the sound came on and the two detectives were loudly introduced to the hot-tempered real estate developer with the dangling gold bracelets. Her rage at Dwyer blasted through the television screen.

"From what you told me about the senator and now from Ansalone, it appears we have two women involved with this guy. I should be so lucky," Martin joked. Then he thought about his comment. "Well, maybe not that lucky."

The two men reacted to their first lead.

"I'll call Weldon at Vermont BCI and see if he wants to pay a visit to Ms. Ansalone with me. In the meantime, I'll call Wilson and find out what he knows about this woman."

Martin would need to arrange detective coverage for Rooney's absence. As Brian had learned working for Martin for over four years, he loved a plan and just wanted to be kept up to speed.

Brian rewound the tape and retrieved his messages from his jacket pocket.

"As soon as I file some expenses and go through my messages, I'll give you a projection of my activities for the next week or so. Meanwhile, I need everything we've got so far to be sent up to Detective Weldon at this address in Brattleboro."

He handed Martin the card containing the street address for the Vermont State Police D Troop, then walked to his office, stopping long enough to get coffee. Clearing his weapon, he placed it his desk drawer, picked up his daughter's picture, kissed it and thought, "You're the only one I'm not pissed at."

Chapter 25

July 1997
Salem, Massachusetts

"**THESE GODDAM JUNKIES** just love to whine. Where's my bupe? When can we smoke? Do we have any Tylenol? Why don't we use methadone? I need more blankets. What the hell are we running here a Marriott or a detox?"

Carol Sykes was walking in to Karen Nelson's office, mimicking the patients on the detox unit. After twenty years of detox nursing, there was no mannerism she couldn't duplicate. Sykes was a morbidly obese, recovering alcoholic who tended to downplay the physical and emotional pain of heroin withdrawal. Patients were constantly complaining to Nelson about Sykes' condescending attitude when treating opiate addicted clients.

"Other than that, how's your day going, Carol?"

"I'm not through screaming yet, Karen. Don't be nice or I'll cancel the smoke break and tell the inmates you did it."

Karen Nelson loved to listen to Carol Sykes bitch. Sykes had followed Nelson from job to job for over fifteen years, and there was never a problem between them that couldn't be solved by sitting in an office and cranking M&Ms out of Nelson's well-worn candy dispensing machine.

"Your boy Marty is sitting in admissions in tough shape."

"We can't take him this soon again," Nelson remarked casually.

"You tell him that. He keeps insisting that he needs to talk to the cops about Dwyer and that you have to help him."

"What the hell am I, his parole officer?" quipped Nelson.

"I'm just telling you what he's telling the folks in admissions."

"OK, put him in a holding bed until that detective gets here. But don't medicate him till after the interview or the cop will think we're all screwballs."

Sykes grabbed a handful of M&Ms and walked out to the nurse's station to do charts. She called admissions and told them to send Marty O'Brien up to the unit, then pulled his chart for the tenth time this year and checked the date of his last admission.

Marty O'Brien spent the first twenty years of his life waiting for his real parents to come home. He knew the drunks he got stuck with couldn't be his real parents. But whoever they were, they always came home anyway. He then decided to spend the next twenty years searching for the perfect vein in which to shoot heroin.

Having accomplished that with considerable ease, he now found himself with no parents to bitch about and no good veins in which to shoot dope. His latest problem was an out-of-balance T cell count that began to show up on blood tests taken in his last five detoxes.

"I gotta have the bupe, no shit, Carol," he pleaded.

Marty was one of the many street junkies who had been treated by using buprenorphine hydrochloride to aid his withdrawal from opiates. It was a drug that had the properties of both pain relief and symptom relief, especially for the aching and bug-crawling sensation that comes with withdrawal. It had become the detox drug of choice for chronic addicts. The irony of the medication was that unlike traditional pain meds, it was antagonistic to opiates and blocks the euphoria associated with them. Marty had learned the hard way after his first detox with the bupe, as he now called it. He assumed that the lingering affects of the drug and his first hit on the street would be a better ride to euphoria, but quickly found out that he had wasted a hundred bucks on dope. He was bullshit.

"Not till you speak with the cop. Look, Marty, if you don't want to wait, we can cab you over to Boston detox."

Carol knew that O'Brien hated public detox and although it seemed horrible to those around the patient, the withdrawal from heroin was not life threatening.

"Tylenol and extra blankets, Marty, that's the deal."

They charted his vitals and administered a psych-social exam, then put him in a double room near the nurse's station to await the arrival of the Salem detective.

Chapter 26

July 1997
Warrens Mills, Vermont

"THIS GODDAM ROAD is a pain in the ass, Romano. Every time I drive out here, I screw my car up somehow."

Ellen Ansalone was babbling nervously as she and her attorney drove out of Warrens Mills. They drove over the Town Hill Road till it split and took a left toward Raven Lake. The small sandy-bottomed lake had a swimming area at its' northern end, and a boat launching area next to that. They pulled into the boat launching area and parked. Ansalone fidgeted with a pack of Marlboro's and a gold lighter.

Romano had been awakened early by the semi hysterical phone call from his largest real estate client and sometimes lover. He was trying to reassure her that things would work out if she just maintained her cool.

"You cannot tell these cops to fuck off, Ellen. They have a tape of you badmouthing a homicide victim. It's not hearsay, not a rumor, it's documentable proof that you knew and disliked Dwyer."

"No shit Johnny Corcoran. I'm just trying to see if I can avoid talking to them."

Two canoes drifted by and the couples inside waved at them. Ansalone sat back and sighed. She lit her fourth cigarette of the morning from the car lighter and blew the first long puff out toward the passing canoeists.

"Fuck canoes. They're too goddamn quiet. I think the people that own them are all a little weird."

"Did you bring me out this early to talk canoeing or are you going to listen to my advice?"

"Sorry Eddy. It's just that things are good in my life for the first time since I can remember. And now that shithead Dwyer is coming up to mess with me from the grave or wherever the hell he is."

She opened the Mercedes door and flipped the butt into the lake. The pony-tailed women in the canoe looked at her as if she'd just dumped contaminated waste.

She started to say something to them when Romano grabbed her arm and said, "remember, it's your mouth that gets you in trouble."

They walked down the road toward the summer cottages that dotted the lake.

"What exactly did this cop Rooney, say to you?"

"He said he had a copy of the tape and was conducting an investigation into Dwyer's murder, and that I was not a suspect, but he would like to ask me a few questions about my relationship with Johnny."

"Is he bringing the Vermont State Police as well?"

"He said he had spoken to them, but if I'd be more comfortable he could bring Wilson."

"Well, make sure you've got a few beers around if Wilson's coming."

They stepped to the side of the dirt road and let a Warrens Mills police cruiser pass. The uniformed patrolman driving gave them a wave then turned into a lakeside driveway, then pulled back out onto the road and drove toward them. It was clear he was watching them. He gave them a friendly smile and picked up his radio, spoke for a moment, and then drove away.

"Well, they're beginning already."

"What do you mean?"

"Obviously, Porky's got the word to cooperate with the Salem cops and until you speak to them, you gonna find them appearing at odd times and in odd places."

"They can't harass me like that, can they?"

"Did that look like harassment to you?"

"Well, how much can that bother me," she shrugged.

"Put it this way," he turned and looked at her directly. "How would you like to be in the middle of a sales pitch to a young couple and their two kids, and have a marked cruiser like that one stop, and a cop say very loudly, "we would really like you to talk with us about the Dwyer murder, Ms. Ansalone," cupping his hands over his mouth for effect.

"They can't do that shit."

"Wanna bet? When I was with the Bristol county DAs office, we were tracking a suspected serial killer named Nardone, who we caught by involving every hooker working the streets of Fall River. We went out night after night and disrupted the girls and their johns until finally two of them came forward to cooperate."

"But this is Vermont," she protested.

"So what? These guys are investigating a murder. They don't care if it's the Siberian Gulag."

He paused, and then pointed to the cruiser that was sitting in the boat ramp area.

"How long has it been since you talked to Rooney?"

She thought, and then said, "About twelve hours."

The patrolman gave them another smile as he watched Romano and his client look in his direction.

"Oh shit, Eddy, maybe I just oughta quit smoking."

Chapter 27

July 1997
Salem, Massachusetts

THE INTERVIEW WITH Karen Nelson was set for two thirty and Rooney drove out the back lot with a little less speed than he had just a few weeks ago. He would still reach the hospital early. He was puzzled by the message from Captain Martin asking him to speak with the vice president of marketing prior to his meeting with the director of the substance abuse unit.

He parked in a restricted area near the administration building and walked into the air-conditioned suite that held the conference rooms. The secretary he encountered was a brunette with oversized breasts and an unpleasant attitude.

"If you will have a seat, I'm sure Mr. Miles will be right with you."

Rooney walked into the large conference room. This hospital was an uncomfortable place for him since the loss of a premature child three years ago. He never regained any trust in this sterile environment or the people who worked in it.

Rooney took a report from his briefcase and began to read and make notes. The report from Sheila Moreno was based on her activity trying to find information on the Holy Ground Society. It was clear from the notes of her meeting with the director of the group that she was being stonewalled. What was more disturbing to Rooney was the fact that since her meeting, she and Captain Martin had been inundated with subtle and-not so-subtle messages from Irish Catholic politicians and power brokers from Boston's pro-Irish community. There was even a message from the Archdiocese of Boston he began to read but put down when he heard footsteps entering the room.

He watched as a whirling dervish of activity entered the room and came to shake his hand. The man was about five foot five, in his late forties, and carried a folder, which he immediately opened and shoved at Rooney.

Miles pointed to the title on the front cover, *Homicides in Massachusetts, 1996.*

"In 1996, there were two hundred and six murders reported in the Commonwealth. Miles spit the words out like a pedantic, economic geography professor whom Rooney had encountered at Providence College.

"They happened in buses, night clubs and mostly in private residences." Miles stopped, and then, almost screaming, said, "None of them happened at a hospital. What the hell are we going to do about this, Detective?" Rooney sat back in his chair and let his weapon hang slightly out of his jacket.

Before Rooney could answer, the man continued his diatribe. "Whether you know it or not, Detective, this hospital is in the process of merging with the Catholic-run hospitals. We do not need the publicity of some reprobate being killed on our property or any other bad publicity that might, in any way, screw up the negotiations. We need the archdiocese behind us." His forehead was tightly creased and beginning to bead up with perspiration as he spit out the words.

"Did you really call me here to tell me this was your first murder, or do you have information to help me out?" Miles started to speak and Rooney cut him off.

"You," Rooney said with emphasis, "are not going to do anything about Mr. Dwyer's murder, except provide me with information that might help to solve it. The Salem Police Department is. So don't ever bother me again unless you have something relevant to add. And by the way, Mr. Miles, the reprobate, as you described him, managed to raise close to a half-million dollars in the last few years for one of the pet projects of the Archdiocese. Let me show you what they have to say about your reprobate."

Rooney took a pencil and underlined the five-word quote from the cardinal's office. "Johnny Dwyer was a living saint."

Miles read it, looking both stunned and embarrassed at the same time.

Rooney reached across the table and handed his card to the hospital administrator. As he got up, he whipped the homicide report at him.

Rooney shook his head twice as he walked out the door, leaving the administrator sitting in total dismay with an unfinished sentence hanging in the air and the homicide report scattered like trash on Landsdowne Street after a Red Sox game.

He left the building and walked over toward the Dwyer crime scene. As he entered the detox unit, the victim's blood was still visible, even though it had been scrubbed. He felt glad that Megan was in Vermont, away from the hounding of reporters and television cameras.

"How about an M&M, Brian?"

Rooney grabbed a handful and sat in the comfortable chair that Nelson used for patients during counseling. Her office was filled with degrees and certificates of training. He noticed the slogans from the twelve-step programs that adorned her walls and desktop. The room felt comfortable to Rooney and she reminded him a little of the counselor who he and Janet saw before his divorce was final.

"Do you think your patient has anything we can use?"

"Who knows? Right now this guy's got one brain cell holding up the other."

Nelson was all hands as she spoke.

"Marty is a chronic addict who probably will end up doing time after his last bust. My guess is he's looking to do just about anything to keep out of jail."

"Did he know Dwyer?"

"He claims they knew each other from the Harp and Bard, that's a pub in the Quincy market where Marty worked the stick. I know Johnny sang there from time to time, but Johnny hated dope, so I don't see these guys palling up, but stranger things have happened."

"Were they friendly while they were here over the fourth of July weekend?"

"They were both coming down hard, but the counselor on duty says she remembers them sitting together during group therapy.

"What kind of shape is this guy in right now?"

She looked over O'Brien's chart and said, "He's OK, but I think you should talk with him now before he starts whining too loud."

While they waited for O'Brien, they talked about Meggy. Nelson was leaving on vacation to spend some time in Vermont with her, and Rooney was surprised by her frankness as she spoke about her upcoming vacation.

"You know sometimes I think that Meggy will be better off without him around; at least she won't have to live with a lot of broken promises. She's a great person, but she's as naïve as a ten-year-old when it comes to men. I think that this will allow her to sort out how she really feels, and as painful as it is to grieve, it's a lot more painful to live your life with somebody feeding you bullshit from the bottle."

"What do you know about her ex-coach?"

"Cooper Adson is the most self-centered son of a bitch in Boston."

"How did they get along?" Rooney tried to sound professional and not nosey.

"In my opinion, it was a sick relationship. She met him when she was very young. He developed her talent and controlled her every move, both on the track and off."

Rooney took another handful of M&Ms.

"It's none of my business, but between her brother and this guy Adson, it sounds like the men in her life haven't been the best."

"That's the understatement of the week, Detective." She almost laughed as she said it. She spoke with the detachment of a therapist, and Rooney observed her carefully as she walked the line between friendship and clinical reality. There was a knock on Nelson's door and a man entered. He was in his forties and had a weathered face and striking blue eyes. There were gashes on his forehead and lower jaw. He slumped over unnaturally like a hunchback, shoulders wrapped in two gray hospital blankets. His hair was curly, and despite what looked like blood dried on his scalp, he wasn't all that bad looking. He was scratching at his skin and his face and had despair written all over it. He reminded Brian of the bartender at Baxter's boathouse in Hyannis where he often had a beer while waiting for the Nantucket ferry. O'Brien shivered and fidgeted in his chair. He chewed at a nail on his right hand and his face twitched as he spoke.

"Ya gotta cut me some slack on this, pal, if I give ya something on Dwyer. Ya gotta help me out with this shit I got into."

He spoke so fast Rooney didn't get it.

"Slow down, Mr. O'Brien. Let's just take it a step at a time."

"Time, I ain't got a lot of right now. I gotta get straight. He looked at Nelson and she just pointed back to Rooney.

"Give him what you got, Marty, or stop wasting my time. I'm going on vacation and I don't need your aggravation right now."

O'Brien kept crossing his legs, then uncrossing them, and his cuticle was bleeding slightly from having been bitten down. He was making Rooney uncomfortable as hell. Brian took out his notepad to accelerate the process.

"Me and Johnny go back to the Cape in the old days. We worked the Shamrock in Dennisport. I seen him a lot at Oak Hill too. He detoxed twice up there when I still had insurance." Brian cut him off.

"How can you help us, Mr. O'Brien?"

"Johnny spent half his time talking about a big deal and how he was going to get straight when the deal when down."

"A deal?"

"That's what he was babbling about when he came in, then he spent the goddam weekend on the pay phone talking to somebody. Something in Vermont going down, maybe something to do with his music company. When it did, he was gonna get straight with the booze."

"What else did he mention? Any names?"

"No, but he kept calling somebody all weekend from the pay phone. He had them cell cards you buy in 7-Eleven and musta called ten times to somebody"

"Did Dwyer say anything else that you can think of?"

O'Brien's face was twitching now and he was clearly starting to show symptoms of withdrawal. Rooney looked at Karen, wondering if he should stop the questioning.

"One more question, Mr. O'Brien, do you have any idea why Johnny left that morning instead of finishing his detox?"

"Yeah, he said someone was coming to pick him up and he hadda get back to Vermont."

"Did he say who it was?"

"No, he never told me shit like that. The only reason he talked about the deal was he was still blacked out, and he always babbled when he was in blackout. But I'll tell you something weird, after the phone calls, he actually seemed happy. He even sang a few tunes in the shower, you know, shit like that." O'Brien grimaced.

"Shit, Karen, ya gotta stop fuckin' with me and gimme something."

O'Brien was shivering and continued picking at scabs on his arms. "Ya gonna take care of me right, pal?"

"I'll talk to your PO and see what I can do, but in the meantime, I want a place that I can reach you. I might want to talk again."

O'Brien took Rooney's card, dropped it, then picked it up and shoved it in his sandal. As he left, he turned and asked Nelson, "You think we're gonna have turkey again tonight or what?"

Chapter 28

July 1997
Warrens Mills, Vermont

ELLEN ANSALONE STARED at the pictures on her oversized pine desk and thought about her father. Lately, he was never too far from her thoughts. The upcoming meeting with the Salem cop had her rattled and she wondered how Chicky would handle it. She kept reaching for the phone, then putting it down. "Make up your mind, Ellen; either call him or don't, but stop screwing with the phone."

Her intercom buzzed, and Bob Fredericks, her sales manager, let her know that the two gentlemen she was expecting were in the sales room.

"Thanks for your cooperation, Ms. Ansalone. I'm Detective Rooney from the Salem Police Department, and I'm sure you know Peter Wilson who has been kind enough to show me around up here."

"Is there any reason I should have my attorney present?"

"Not unless you feel you need to." Rooney always hated to answer this question, knowing the last thing he needed right now was a lawyer to screw things up.

"First, let me tell you why we wanted to talk to you."

"That's pretty obvious officer, the WASP princess of the Handle Road set this up. I never should have agreed to do an interview with that tree-hugging bitch around." She lit a cigarette and blew the smoke straight up in the air, as if trying not to offend the two nonsmokers.

"Nobody set this up, Ms. Ansalone. I'm responding to videotape I received as part of an ongoing murder investigation. I believe you know the tape I'm discussing. It's clear to me that your opinion of Mr. Dwyer wasn't all that great, and I would appreciate any help you can give us."

"I just plain hated the prick, but I wasn't about to kill him. Christ, I feel the same way about the tree huggers in this town, but I'm not about to whack them 'cause they don't like me cutting up their precious forest.

She looked over at Wilson, then put her hands behind her neck, and rocked back in the captain's chair. "Sorry, Pete, but you know my battle with this town."

Wilson's wife, Carol Ann, was a member of the zoning board and had more than once had gone toe-to-toe with Ansalone on issues surrounding the ongoing development of High Mowing Estates.

"Can you tell us about your relationship with Mr. Dwyer?"

"All I can tell you is that I knew him for a long time, and I couldn't stand the son of a bitch. What the hell, everybody in this town knows each other, or they think they do."

Again, she looked at Wilson for support. Rooney noticed that the ex-trooper held back as if to signal, "you're on your own lady."

"When is the last time you saw him?"

"Probably six months ago, at the tavern. He was drinking club soda and was actually fairly pleasant, but that wasn't unusual if he wasn't on the juice."

"Can you think of any reason why Dwyer might have been killed?"

"Yeah, he was an asshole. But maybe he was doing one of those Irish kids he brought over. Maybe a pissed-off relative."

"Have you been in his house lately?"

"No, I just told you I saw him at the tavern. Are you a little hard of hearing, Detective?"

"Don't be flip, Ellen, the man's just doing his job." Pete Wilson spoke up for the first time, his voice was edgy, and he clearly was not pleased with Ansalone's arrogance.

Ansalone got up and walked over to a small coffee unit. She poured herself a cup. Rooney noticed the printed logo that had the High Mowing design on one side and bold letters that said THE BOSS on the other. She sat down again and it was clear that she wasn't planning to offer them coffee.

"Ms. Ansalone, do you mind telling us where you were on July 5?"

"I do mind, but I'm sure you are going to find out anyway. I was at my father's house in Lynn, Massachusetts."

Were you with anyone who could corroborate that for us?"

"Not without screwing up someone's marriage, and I'm not about to do that."

She got up and made it clear that the interview was over. She rinsed her cup and put it in the small sink next to the coffee machine.

"It's been fun talking officer, but the next time please call my attorney in Boston."

She handed Rooney a card from her desk with the name of one of Boston's most well-known criminal attorneys, a name often associated with organized crime.

"You travel in expensive circles, Ms. Ansalone." Rooney threw the parting jab as he put the attorney's embossed card in his wallet.

"I'm an expensive gal, Detective." With a sweeping motion of her arms, she pointed to the plate glass window and the expansive view of her seven hundred acres of land, still under development, "Or haven't you noticed?"

As she watched the two men drive out of her property, Ellen thought again of Chicky, and wondered how he would have responded.

Chicky "Double Peppers" Ansalone ate breakfast six days a week at the Monument Variety and Deli in Lynn, Massachusetts. He ate a three-egg omelet with two diced green peppers, his regular fare for almost twenty years. He dressed impeccably in a starched white-collared shirt, brown single-breasted suit, and highly polished Bostonian cordovan shoes. His ties were usually conservative, and nine months of the year he wore a fedora purchased from the Empire Men's Shop in Waltham, Massachusetts. When he finished breakfast each day, he would walk ten feet to the phone booth, which he probably should have been paying rent on, and began another day at the office, taking the numbers. His constituents wagered twenty-five or fifty cents, which he then laid off to a group of gentlemen in Somerville. Chicky, was the lottery before there was a lottery. He was the guy you could always get a bet down with, day in, day out. He lived in an unpretentious single-family home near the Swampscott border, and although he had very little to do with his neighbors at Christmas, he saw to it that they enjoyed a gift basket of fruit and nuts.

Chicky had been involved in the use of other people's money since his tenth birthday—when he began selling Boston Record American newspapers at the exit of Boston's Summer Tunnel. The tunnel, for years, had dumped countless horse race fans into east Boston and Suffolk Downs racetrack. Dressed in a sailor's cap, dungarees, and a white undershirt, he would hock the paper in a loud voice, "Get ya Record here, Boston's Daily Record." With every sale, Chicky would give a tip systematically to each buyer, beginning with the number one horse in the first race and ending with the last horse in the last race. By the end of the night, Chicky was at the entrance of the tunnel, hocking the late edition and reaping the rewards of the bettors, who were convinced the kid had given them the winner. Either way, Chicky sold a lot of papers and squirreled away every penny he earned rather than give it to his old man who pissed it away at the Lynn Café.

There was one area that was a problem to Chicky and that was school. He couldn't take the nuns at St. Mary. Not that they didn't like him, since his math skills were the quickest in the class, and his social skills were honed on Boston's streets working for tips. It was the fact that he had chosen his profession at an early age and school had become an unnecessary impediment to reaching his goals. At the age of fifteen, Chicky said goodbye to academia and hello to the 2x2 phone booth that would become his ticket to the betting life.

At the age of twenty-five, he was the numbers bookie for the cops and firemen in Lynn. There wasn't a city employee in Lynn that didn't know how to reach Double Pepper's when it was time to lay down a bet on the Sox or Braves. By now, he had acquired a house and a used car lot where he sold an occasional car and spent his afternoons. Chicky knew nothing about cars, but it was a suggestion from a high-ranking member of the Lynn Police Department that he legitimize his income in case the tax people decided to put pressure on him. Life was comfortable for Chicky until the day he walked into his twelve-car showroom on the Lynn Expressway and saw a woman with dark olive skin, shining white teeth and the garb of an immigrant. Her name was Maria Lombardo. She had come to live with her American cousin and her husband in a rented house in Swampscott. The cousin brought her along when she went to look for a cheap used car and they had ended up at Chicky's lot.

Ellen had heard the story a million times and never tired of her father telling again and again of his short and happy life with this woman from Sicily, with her fiery temper and raven hair. She had also seen him weep openly when he described her birth and the death of his first love in a surgical suite at the Lynn Hospital.

Chicky "Two Peppers" learned child raising as quickly as he learned the bookmaking game. He was the pride of the neighborhood as he walked his beloved Ellen to Sacred Heart School each day. He would be dressed in his usual suit and tie, and his daughter in a blue uniform and crisp, white, short-sleeve shirt. Chicky never remarried.

With the help of a neighborhood widow, he was able to devote his time partially to the needs of his clients and mostly to the needs of a growing daughter.

Ellen Ansalone sat at her desk, a half-smoked cigarette curling toxin in her face, and cried for the first time in years, all the while, cursing the day she'd ever laid eyes on Johnny Dwyer and his Irish blue eyes.

Chapter 29

Late July
Warrens Mills, Vermont

Warrens Mills' Police chief, Porky Atkins, had come to enjoy murder. The investigation into Johnny Dwyer's homicide had the town buzzing with rumors and more media interest than he'd seen in twenty years. The tiny conference room with its police patches stretching along the interior wall was overflowing with Massachusetts and Vermont State Police as well as crime techs from the Massachusetts Crime Scene Service Unit.

It was probably no coincidence that each of the participants in the minitask force brought along some breakfast muffins or donuts for Porky and his staff. Porky was known to throw a barb or two at those who used his conference room without paying homage to the olympic appetite of the Warrens Mills chief.

Atkins had spent the morning giving interviews to the Brattleboro and Bennington papers, as well as trying to keep a nosy reporter with the local weekly from getting too close to the Salem detective.

Rooney had spent the morning outlining the investigation, and now was listening as the crime scene investigators went over what little they had for Weldon and the uniformed trooper he had brought to their joint meeting on the Dwyer homicide.

The officer from the Massachusetts Police Crime Scene Unit wasn't able to offer much information or physical evidence. It was becoming clear that the killer or killers had worn gloves, as there were no fingerprints on the expended casings. The sweepings around the immediate area were mostly cigarette butts and a few candy wrappers. There were no tire marks or footprints that could be captured from the concrete sidewalk. Rooney used an easel and plain paper to diagram their interviews and give reference points for the assembled cops to discuss.

"As far as the O'Brien interview, think it's safe to say from the constant telephone calls that Dwyer placed over the weekend he knew and was waiting for his attacker and may have suspected there was going to be a confrontation. Without any defensive actions, it almost appears that he gave up because he knew he was going to be killed and really didn't care. This rules out stranger murder as far as I'm concerned. According to Dwyer's sister, he'd been acting strange for years, as if he was running from some demon. Maybe that demon caught up with him." Rooney paused before continuing.

"The other person we should be looking at is his traveling buddy, Burns. Rumor is that he collects a disability check from the V.A. We're running an information check on him as we speak."

"We talking PTSD here, Brian?" asked Weldon.

"I'm assuming that's the case Frank, since Chief Atkins refers to it as a 'nut check.'"

The trooper who had been silent and taking notes, choked on his coffee at the description of Burn's disability. He went back to his writing, containing his amusement, and Weldon spoke again.

"What about the connection with the Holy Ground Society you mentioned before Brian?"

"Our investigation is being hampered by lack of cooperation by the leadership of that group, and they are obviously putting the word out to the Irish community in Boston and the North Shore not to talk to us. So we'll continue to dig up what we can."

"Did you and Pete get anything useful from the real estate woman?"

"Ansalone wouldn't give us the time of day. In fact, she points to the Holy Ground Society and says maybe Dwyer was fooling around with one of the kids they brought over from Ireland. Maybe a parent or relative took matters into their own hands."

Rooney sipped on his now-cold coffee and asked, "Anyone know anything about her we should know?"

Rooney looked around the table and saw Warrens Mills patrol officer David Henderson pull a file from his briefcase. He opened it and began to read from his file.

"The last ten years or so, she's been a model citizen except for traffic violations. Prior to that, she had some trouble with drugs, mostly cocaine and pot. She had an assault charge dropped that was for threatening a former employee whom she claims ran off with a couple of customers. It was never prosecuted because the guy refused to testify against her. We think her foreman, "Flip" Morton, may have threatened this guy, but we have no proof of it beyond some hearsay. He protects her like a hawk."

As he finished the sentence, a clipping fell from the file and Swanson handed it to Rooney. "This woman has a hard time keeping her mouth shut, obviously."

Rooney passed the article around the table. It was a color shot from a *Time* magazine article showing a very attractive thirtyish Ellen Ansalone, standing next to a dammed up stream. The caption read, "First we have to kill the goddam beavers."

"It seems she thought the stringer for *Time* was an investor in her project," Swanson interjected.

They continued to pass her file around. Frank Weldon, the BCI investigator, opened a file displaying the logo of the Vermont Attorney General's office.

"We have five of the prints from Dwyer's house identified, and we are sending the rest down to the FBI computer."

"Can you do me a favor, Frank, and fax a copy to the Lynn Police Department?"

Weldon looked at Rooney. "What are ya looking at in Lynn, Brian?"

"She mentioned in our interview that she spent Fourth of July weekend at her father's house in Lynn. That puts her only ten minutes from where Dwyer was killed. Besides, I can't believe that someone with a mouth like hers hasn't had some trouble with the hometown cops."

"What about the recording studio angle, Brian? Anything there, you think?" Henderson asked as he took notes on a portable computer.

"I find it hard to believe anything that I heard from O'Brien is real," Rooney quipped somewhat sarcastically.

"What have we got on the business partners, Brian? Any unusual insurance clauses?" Weldon probed.

Rooney was a little hesitant as he answered.

"I'm interviewing the manager of the studio next Thursday, but I'm waiting to get a peek at the will l before I talk to them. Romano says he should have everything done by Wednesday."

"What about Romano? Any way he could have been screwing with his clients assets?" Weldon sat back and stretched as he spoke, obviously a little edgy from his fourth coffee of the morning.

"Anything is possible with lawyers, but I don't have a feel for Romano one way or the other. You guys have anything I should know?"

"Well for one thing it was your friend Ansalone who made this guy a wealthy man. The way I hear it, he didn't have a pot to piss in until she turned over her real estate contracts to him,"

The speaker was Officer Swanson. "The rumor is she's been servicing this guy or vice versa for a long time, but you can't prove that by me."

As Swanson spoke, Chief Atkins walked in and sat at the head of the table. He selected a chocolate-glazed donut from the box, then as an afterthought, took a honey dipped as well. He savored the donuts as if they were a fine single malt scotch, listening with passing interest. He then dropped the bombshell.

"Don't forget to tell them that that bitch is making some of us here a few bucks too."

Chapter 30

PETER WILSON KNEW the feeling as soon as it started in his chest. Frantically, he searched his glove compartment for the green and black pills while pulling his jeep to the side of Route 100. Labored breathing and tightness began to consume him. The pills weren't there; he remembered leaving them at home. Fear, like an old enemy, crept from his hands, locked on the steering wheel, to his jaw and facial muscles. Panicking, he struggled to remember the technique the therapist had taught him. He tried to control his breathing with simple counting while he inhaled, then holding and counting while he exhaled slowly. Twisted memories consumed him as the panic turned to terror. Ugly scenes, fights with Carol Ann, grotesque scarecrows hanging from ski lifts, crash scenes with blood strewn across the highway. Now he was totally frozen.

The pint was under the seat. He struggled to rip the seal and unscrew the top. He swallowed the vodka and the warmth of liquid in his stomach immediately released the demons that gripped his chest. Vodka did in thirty seconds what it took the medicine a half hour to accomplish. Peter Wilson was fucked and he knew it.

The fear lifted as the essence of the vodka traveled quickly to his brain. He felt relief, pulled again on the half-empty pint, then the relief vanished as he looked in his rearview mirror. The siren of a Warrens Mills patrol car was blaring as it pulled up behind him and a familiar voice bellowed.

"Don't you move a muscle, Mr. Ex-Trooper, and don't even think of hiding the bottle."

Chapter 31

LIBBY STARK SAT in disbelief as she read the letter bearing the official seal of the Vice President of the United States. The letter commended Libby and "Stark's Army" for bringing attention to mental health parity in the New England states. If that were not enough, the letter went on to say that the vice president's wife would be coming to Vermont in November to present Libby and another Vermonter with distinguished achievement awards.

She ran her finger over the stationery. Oh God, if only Earl could share this day. "It's all been worth it Earl, it really has," she spoke aloud to a long dead husband. Then she knew she had to make a call.

Chapter 32

THE GRASS BEHIND the Grange Building sloped downhill forming a natural amphitheater. From there, one could view the celebration of Farmer's Day in Warrens Mills. This day the weather had cooperated. Temperatures stayed in the seventies. As dusk began to fall, sparkling colored lights attached to wooden booths transformed the town's athletic fields into a glittering midway. The smell of Farmer's Day ranged from charcoal-grilled ribs slathered in maple syrup, to fresh-cut hay piled around the agricultural arenas. Everywhere, there was the smell of livestock and sawdust.

Spectators watched the horse pulls and marveled at the strength of the tandem-dray horses as they backed into the wooden sled and were hitched up. They then charged ahead with hundred pound blocks adding to their burden. Their harnesses smelled of polished leather and their droppings steaming on the worn grass created a minefield of horse dung for the fairgoers to dance their way through.

At the baseball diamond just below the Grange Building was a fifty-yard-by-fifty-yard checkerboard made from white lime and divided into squares. It was here that a lucky fairgoer could bet four dollars that a cow, selected from a Warren Farms herd, would make a deposit on a selected square of well-digested grass and feed. The winning square paid off the accumulated bets, minus a fee for the Grange Club, which sponsored the event. This contest was known as the Cow Plop.

The audience for this event was usually bored vacationers and second homeowners, mostly professionals from Manhattan or Connecticut suburbs. They gathered early in the day to pick their squares and try to plot out with citified logic just where the cow would plop. Many of these bettors had advanced degrees in law and medicine or were major players on Wall Street. But today, they were united by the commonality of the bovine digestive system and their affinity for fine cigars, which they brandished like broadswords in the hot August sun.

They dressed as if they were products of a single collective parent. Ralph Lauren pink or lime green polo shirts and khaki shorts, feet shod tastefully but casually in Cole Hahns, or an occasional athletic shoe minus socks. Their children, dressed in the same uniform of affluence, ran helter-skelter through the midway and concession areas, stopping only to eat cotton candy and munch popcorn from the 4-H stand or to wait in line at the porta-potty.

In the midst of the well-groomed crowd sat two men in their seventies whose lives had become entwined in the past month through no more than a chance meeting at Dot's Deli. They were dressed as differently as the seasons of New England. One wore the overalls and blue work shirt of a farmer, his boots told a tale of manure and mud. The other wore a white long-sleeve shirt carefully buttoned at the wrist as if to hide his forearms. His pants were khaki and wrinkled, though clean. His shoes were low cut, black and functional, and his socks were white. He dressed like the immigrant he was, oblivious to the fashion of the day.

"These people pay good money to watch cows shit. I find that hard to believe. As a boy in Poland, I watched cows shit all day and no one would pay me nutting for dat. This Fermont you live in is strange place."

"Ain't likely you'll see too many locals watching. Mostly city people and little kids."

The speaker was Sumner Warren. His family had been the largest dairy owners in Warrens Mills for almost forty years; now he was semi retired, and his two children had carried on the farm and its maple sugar business as well. He met his English-impaired friend Benjamin Wernecki over a cup of tea at the deli. After talking for awhile, they discovered that at one point in their lives, they had been involved in a common nightmare.

In the case of these two men, the nightmare was the death camp at Dachau. Warren was a twenty-year-old Vermont National guardsman assigned to an advance unit that stumbled across the camp on April 29, 1945, only hours after the German guards had deserted their posts in terror. Having been pounded by British and American super fortresses, the guards had opened the gates as they fled, as if this was penance for their collective evil. Warren knew there would be no act of atonement for what transpired under the metal entrance gate with its inscription "*Arbeit macht frei.*"

Wernecki had been a prisoner at Dachau; his job was making sandals for the thousands of Catholic priests who had been arrested and housed in the camp. The two strangers cautiously opened their lives to each other, feeling safe to confide their shared horrors that hot afternoon.

They were also bonded by the love of cribbage. They had begun to spend more and more time together in quiet and serious conversation, occasionally sprinkled with laughter, but mostly straight-faced talk, and on more than one occasion, old men's tears.

"You neffer left this Fermont except to come to fight the war?"

"No reason to go anywhere. I got all I need right here"

They walked through the crowds that evening, and no one took particular notice of the deeply tanned farmer and the ghostly white cobbler. Those who knew the dairyman said hello and made small talk as they passed. They seemed not to even notice the shrunken Polish Jew whose hands were crippled by years of mending shoes.

"Those men are thugs."

Wernecki pointed to a pickup with its tail down, where four men and two women were loudly singing along with a country station and passing around bottles of tequila.

"Shit, Benjamin, those are just good old boys who've been in the woods too long," said Warren, dismissing his friend's concern. Warren pointed to the truck bed and the unclean McCullough saws that were strewn about.

"These guys cut house lots all day long, and today's probably payday, or that Italian woman gave them a bonus for finishing early. If it weren't for boys like them, you wouldn't be living in that chalet your son-in-law bought."

"They are thugs, belief me, Warren, when I tell you. Benjamin Wernecki knows thugs."

* * *

Ben Latimer stood near the infield bandstand of the Warrens Mills Fairground, uncased a Gibson Mastertone five-string banjo worth approximately thirty thousand dollars. The banjo had been in storage in Johnny Dwyer's home, and Meggy had given it to Latimer as a gift that afternoon.

Ben took three picks from a small jewelry bag, and with a pocketknife cut parallel grooves in the light-gauge plastic thumb picks. This simple groove prevented the pick from slipping off during his playing, causing an unbalanced tone.

"That's a beautiful gift, Dwyer," Karen Nelson commented as she stood with Megan and Brian Rooney near the bandstand waiting for the musicians to tune.

"After our talk today, I'm beginning to think I should give all my brother's stuff away. Nelson you know when you said I was clinging to the past, I wanted to kill you. But as usual, you hit the nail on the head. I can't spend the rest of my life wondering who killed my brother. And now, I'm afraid, I realize I don't know half of what was going on in Johnny's life, and I think I don't want to know." She looked at Rooney who sat on the grass and appeared not to be listening. "Besides, it's really police business as someone once told me a long time ago. Right, Brian?"

Rooney caught himself looking at the white lace bra that Megan wore under her tank top. And he could smell her fresh scent as she bent on her knees and faced him. He was becoming strongly attracted to her and he realized for the first time that she was being playful. He reached out and held her hands as if to steady her and said, "That's right, Megan. It's police business.'

The boom of microphones and the sound of bluegrass music jumping from the stage interrupted their warm exchange. They listened as the fiddle, guitar, and mandolin broke into "Rollin in My Sweet Baby's Arms." After two verses, the guitarist welcomed the crowd, introduced the other members and stepped back, letting Ben take the banjo break in the song. As he started to three-finger pick, he placed the banjo head up to the microphone and the entire ball field resonated. At first, it was just a few hands that started to keep the beat. Then, like a wave, the entire audience began to clap and whistle approval. Ben's fingers almost seemed to move in slow motion as they strolled up-and-down the fingerboard, catching each note, and letting it hang in the cool mountain air, all the while, continuing to Scruggs-pick and smile. At the next break in the song, he stepped back and the fiddler jumped in to close out the tune. The audience erupted with applause as they ended.

At the close of the forty-minute set, the four strangers thrown together by Johnny Dwyer's death, walked the fairgrounds. The runner, the cop, the professor, and the nurse, laughing and eating cotton candy as other fairgoers had done forever, were lost in the fleeting moments of sunset and newfound friendship. The women gushed over Ben's performance, and Rooney found himself wishing that he were here on vacation and not investigating how the mysterious life of Johnny Dwyer had led to his bloody death on a Salem street.

The soccer field, with its goals temporarily tipped over, was transformed into a food exhibit put together by VisionVermont. The group, a food producers' marketing consortium, had some two hundred members exhibiting and the tasting had begun. There were cheeses from the large northern dairy co-ops as well as grilled lamb, fresh salsas, and salad dressings—all bearing the distinctive logo of the Vermont trade group.

As they approached the display area, Ben saw Libby Stark talking to a tall, copper-bearded man whose name had become synonymous with Vermont quality. Lyman Carrier was the founder and board chairman of VisionVermont. He had almost single-handedly launched the Vermont logo across store shelves from Massachusetts to Florida. His marketing genius and skill at getting local banks and credit unions to support small business had earned him countless commendations from economic development councils across New England.

Carrier, like Stark, had recently received a similar letter from the vice president's office announcing that VisionVermont had been chosen to receive special commendation from the secretary of commerce, who would be accompanying the wife of the vice president to Vermont in the fall. Both Stark and Carrier's letters had been cleverly blown up to poster size and were being prominently displayed.

"Well, I should probably introduce myself to my new partner," said Meggy. "Let's hope the lawyers can work out the details without a lot of hassle."

Meggy had uncovered the discovery of the relationship between VisionVermont, and her late brother. In going over her brother's will in Romano's office, she learned that 35 percent of Frost Studios belonged to VisionVermont, 30 percent to the managing partner, Brad McGowan, and the balance to her brother. It was also stipulated that the other stockholders, in the event of the death of Dwyer, would purchase all shares at market value to be determined by independent accountants.

Romano had explained that 30 percent of business generated by Frost Studios also had to be performed by Vermont musicians or songwriters and a portion of profits would be used to promote Vermont historical and cultural awareness.

Lyman Carrier seemed to recognize Meggy as she approached the booth area where he stood talking with Libby Stark. He came forward and gently hugged her, expressing condolence for her loss.

"You know, Megan, that your brother's studio was the first business that we invested in that was not food related, and at first we didn't think that it fit our criteria. But God knows, Johnny was persistent and he really proved us shortsighted in developing the total Vermont landscape. Because of Frost Studio's success, we have a great many Vermont artisans in our fold."

Megan felt comfort from this man. Perhaps it was the gentle tone of his clear New England accent, or maybe the sense of tradition that surrounded him, or maybe she just needed comforting from someone who spoke kindly of her brother and his dreams.

When she introduced Rooney to Carrier, she could feel a different flow of energy between them. Rooney handed him a card and made an appointment to see him the following week to go over any possible leads that could be tied to the business relationship between Carrier and Johnny Dwyer.

Rooney was courteous but firm, and when they walked away, Megan realized that Rooney never let his guard down. She wasn't sure she could ever live like that, or even really be attracted to anyone who had that kind of a wall of distrust surrounding him. On the other hand, his slightly broken nose and tight butt were definitely having some effect on her.

When the four friends walked away from the sampling area, Karen Nelson seemed puzzled by the vice president's interest in Libby Stark's bill referenced in the letter and displayed at the VisionVermont tent.

"Well, think about the 2000 elections," Ben said. "The new first lady needs a specific issue to begin her term. What better issue than that of mental health, which she raised in her husband's years in the senate and now as vice president. What Betty Ford did for breast cancer and alcoholism, the new first lady could do for mental health. What better venue to present it than appearing in New Hampshire's neighboring state, eighteen months before the primaries, with a one-of-a kind mental health parity bill in your pocket, and a great campaign issue that is transportable to other states."

"Ben, do you think this Senator Stark will be involved in the national campaign?" Nelson pointed back to where Libby was standing shaking hands.

"She's an absolute natural to carry the flag for at least the New England states, and probably the White House sees her as one of the standard bearers to go up against the large insurers and HMOs when they begin trying to pass a reform bill in the next administration," Ben added.

Megan looked at Ben and said, "Talk about right time, right place. This woman's got it all going for her."

Rooney didn't speak. *If you only knew it all, Meggy. If you only knew it all.*

* * *

Flip Morton was drunk. When Flip got drunk, he thought about making love to his boss Ellen Ansalone. He imagined himself being her number one stud. Pictures of her, taken over the years, adorned the walls of the former monastery chapel where he lived as caretaker. He thought of the men who had had her over the years. The lawyer and the record company asshole. Sooner or later Flip knew she would come around and he would be the man.

Flip loved to drink. Tonight, after completing the better half of a bottle of Cuervo Gold, he felt the anger talk to him. Somebody was taking something away. They took his father's work when he was a kid. Now the redheaded cop was trying to hassle Ellen. Flip drank what was left in the bottle and then snapped.

Brian Rooney and Megan Dwyer began to sense that something good was happening between them, and both began to enjoy the feeling. As they approached the cow plop area, a black-and-white Guernsey was still being led around the checkered squares by his owner, unable perhaps, because of all the attention and noise, to complete that bodily function which every other day came easily and often.

The lights came on at dusk and cool began to set upon the ball field. The crowd was eager for an ending to the event, but few left.

No one anticipated the commotion that broke out near the far end of the cow plop arena. The mildly retarded woodcutter, with an off-the-charts blood alcohol level and hatred in his eyes, let out a piercing and insane yell, then began attacking the off-duty murder investigator.

Rooney caught only a glimpse of Flip Morton. For one second he wanted to believe that someone else was the target of the woodsman's wrath. Instinctively, Rooney managed to shove a startled Meggy to the side, as the tall gorilla-shaped Morton landed a sharp punch to the side of Rooney's head and wrestled him to the grass, smashing his head against the ground, opening a gash above Rooney's right ear.

Both men held onto each other's shirts as they rolled across the wet lime squares, each trying to gain an advantage. Brian felt himself struggling for air and flailed helplessly under the bigger man's weight. Blood flowed as Morton pounded Rooney's head again and again, while still strangling him. Ben Latimer and another man tried to intervene and were immediately pulled off by Morton's drinking buddies who were enjoying watching a cop get beat up. The crowd was screaming for police at this point and deputies came running. Latimer's interference gave Rooney just enough leverage to get out from under.

As the two men squared off in the middle of the field, the excitement must have finally gotten to the prize milk cow, for she let go a mighty blast of steaming manure, just as Flip Morton began to gain his balance for another charge at Rooney. Morton fell backward slipping just long enough on the cow shit to enable Rooney to set himself and change the complexion of the event from mud wrestling to straight out slugging. Rooney paused just long enough to unclip his nine-millimeter from his belt and throw the holstered weapon to a startled Ben Latimer. Then he moved forward, throwing punch after punch into the larger man's stomach. Morton tried to lock Rooney in his massive arms, but Rooney delivered four quick facial punches and felt himself begin to get the edge. He stepped back, allowing Morton to charge blindly, face bleeding and out of breath. Morton missed entirely in his charge, and Rooney sidestepped, kicked Morton's knee and grabbed his T-shirt, shoving his opponent from the back, face-first into the still steaming cowshit. Rooney dropped his knee with full weight behind it, in the middle of Morton's back and felt relief as the pain in Morton's back turned the gorilla man to begging and gasping for air.

Rooney stood and watched, waiting for the man to move, hoping Morton would try to come at him again. The man didn't move. Deputies stood around the crowd, and finally moved to subdue the fighters.

Porky Atkins paused briefly from his sausage sandwich and waved the deputies off Rooney, then told Ward Kinkle to arrest Morton for public disturbance.

"You think Ansalone put that crazy bastard up to this?" asked an excited Porky Atkins.

"I don't know, Chief," responded Rooney, "but that guy had only one target in mind, and if she put him up to it, she's crazier than we thought."

Rooney and Meggy, both shaken by the incident, walked arm in arm from the ball field to the parking lot. There was just the slightest hint of fall in the air. She carefully and gently wrapped a sweatshirt around his now aching shoulders and her lips lightly brushed his forehead. "Let's go home and I'll make you a cup of tea and tell you about my grandmother."

Overhead, the PA system announced that Dr. Kenneth Stiles of Darien, Connecticut, was the winner of this year's Cow Plop event.

Chapter 33

August 1997
Dublin, New Hampshire

OAK HILL HOSPITAL was the first, and in many cases, the last hope of the people who drove into its tree-shaded and cigarette-littered parking lot. The hospital was the oldest freestanding treatment facility for alcoholics and drug addicts in the eastern United States. It was clear to Brian Rooney as he parked the Crown Victoria at the admissions entrance that this place had seen better days. The white guesthouse buildings, with carved oak-leafed shutters, seemed in disrepair, and the paved parking lot was gutted with potholes. However, the view of the four-mile lake that abutted the property was spectacular. He could see pajama-clad patients sitting on Adirondack chairs near the dock area smoking and talking to staff members.

He reviewed the questions that he had written last evening. He realized from his initial conversation with the administrator that his trip might be a dead-end, shrouded in confidential records and other bureaucratic crap that he wasn't in the mood to hear.

His notebook was becoming crammed with information surrounding the three-week-old homicide, and yet it seemed that at every turn he stumbled on someone who could benefit either emotionally or financially from Dwyer's death. His list read like a mystery novel:

- Senator Stark, no real motive, but was involved with Dwyer.
- Ellen Ansalone hated the deceased, but won't let on why. Crime of passion? What could Dwyer have done to her? Background check with Lynn police, as well as fingerprints should be completed this week.
- Jackie Burns, closest person to Dwyer on the road. Did his driving, could have flipped out. VA records showed he had been hospitalized on four occasions and was clinically unstable without psychotropic medication. His records showed that he was capable and qualified in small arms. Was at one time assigned a sawed-off shotgun for use in the tunnels surrounding his base camp at Cu-Chi. Documented use of pot and alcohol since discharge. Was currently being considered for removal from disability pension if his attitude toward long-term treatment for PTSD didn't change.
- McGowan, Frost Studios. Had major financial dealings with the deceased and rumor has it that McGowan considered Dwyer a pain in the ass. Interview next week.
- Megan Dwyer. Had financial motive, but seems genuinely devastated by sibling loss.
- Follow up with Vermont BCI and check on fingerprints not identified.

Rooney closed the notebook, and stepped out of the air-conditioned Ford into the hot New Hampshire sun. He entered the admissions building and immediately was struck by the huge slogans hanging from the walls of a large room that must have been used as a lecture hall.

"One day at a time, easy does it, keep it simple." He remembered seeing these same slogans in Karen Nelson's office.

"Detective, the doctor is waiting in the conference room for you." An extremely attractive, solidly built strawberry blond woman in her thirties had come in from the adjoining office.

"Can I bring you some iced tea or lemonade? I know it's hot out there and our air conditioning isn't the greatest."

"Thanks, I could use some iced tea with a little sugar if you've got it?" He walked down a narrow hallway and into a small conference room and was surprised to see a familiar face.

"What's happening, Brian?"

"Washington, what the hell are you doing here?"

"I invited him. I hope you don't mind." A short, light-skinned African American came around from behind his desk, shook hands and extended a business card to Rooney.

"I'm Paul Wellman. Welcome to Oak Hill. Detective Washington is an old friend, and when we set this meeting up, I figured it might be helpful to both of us to have him here since he's the one who told me of John's murder." Wellman spoke with a Boston accent and dressed the part of a well-groomed professor, wearing a blue, oxford-cloth shirt and a paisley bow tie. His slacks were cotton twill, and he wore a casual, tassel loafer. His glasses perched above his forehead. Rooney mentally pictured this man lecturing in a small prep school or college.

"I'm sort of caught between a rock and a hard place, Detective. I can't let you look at a patient's record without a warrant, and at the same time, I want to see Johnny's murderer brought to justice. So I suggested to Paul that he referee our discussion, and I also want to add that this meeting never took place."

Rooney was caught off guard, but he trusted Washington.

"All right, Dr. Wellman. We'll try and play it down the middle for now, since I don't feel like trying to get a search order for records in New Hampshire, but let me be clear. If I think something important is being withheld, I will be in a judge's chambers in a heartbeat."

"Fair enough, Detective. Where do you want to start?"

"Dwyer, according to what we can gather, has been in your hospital at least twenty times over the last decade. Isn't that a bit unusual?"

"It's not the Oak Hill record, but it's more than usual."

"Any reason you can think of why he kept coming to treatment?"

"Let me answer that with a question and maybe that will help you. Do you know much about alcoholism or substance abuse?"

"Very little and most of that I've learned in the last few weeks." Rooney got the feeling that he was about to be lectured by Wellman, and he was right.

"Alcoholism is basically a neurobiological disorder that is probably caused by an imbalance of two neurotransmitters called dopamine and serotonin. As best we can figure out, this imbalance is in an area of the brain known as the nucleus accumbens. It sets off an insatiable craving response in certain individuals, probably due to some genetic precursor, which I can assure you we haven't figured out yet."

Rooney sat back in his seat and threw his pencil up in the air, as if to signal a halt in the conversation. "Give me a break, Doctor. Explain this in language a cop can understand."

Washington laughed, as did Wellman.

"OK, Detective, put it this way, when ya got it, it doesn't go away, no matter how hard you want it to. Friend Johnny never wanted to believe that message and so he kept ending up here time after time, begging for help. He also paid cash up front for his treatment, and believe me, in this day and age that made him a hero in my eyes."

Again, Wellman finished with a comedic flourish and Brian began to sense that a door was being left open. Before Rooney could ask another question, Wellman spoke again.

"Johnny Dwyer was running from some ghost. As hard as we tried in a therapeutic setting to exorcise that demon, we could never get by his wall of shame and fear long enough to help him gain insight into a solution."

"Could this demon be something he did, while in what his sister calls a blackout or gray out?"

"Possibly, but we just don't know enough about the blackout process to say definitively if that was the case with Johnny. Whatever else was going on with him, I guarantee he suffered from some form of PTSD."

"He wasn't in Vietnam."

"I'm afraid that particular war did much to familiarize the public with the term, but its general use by professionals refers to some traumatic incident in a patient's life that forever transforms the landscape of the patient's mind."

"Is there anything in his records that would tell us what the trauma might have been or if it might be connected to his murder in some way?"

"The answer is not in our records, and you would have to subpoena them to get a look, but I assure you that I spent last night studying his charts. Starting from his first detox in sixty-seven, right up to his last treatment in ninety-six, there is no evidence of any criminal culpability, or evidence of particular deviant behavior that would justify someone taking his life."

"In other words, there was no child molester or rapist hiding behind the booze?" Rooney asked.

"Correct. It seems that whatever the horror of John's life was, it's gone to the grave with him, or it's written in his journals."

"You know about his notebooks?"

Wellman sat back and removed his glasses from his forehead. "The notebooks were part of a contract that we made with Dwyer. He committed to writing out in detail, drunk or sober, his everyday thoughts and his fears that led him to a drink. They were to remain anonymous, unless he chose to share them with us. The tragic part of this is that he called one of our counselors two weeks before he was killed and said he thought he was ready to share some of the writing with us."

"Did he ever show up?"

"No, he said he had to deal with something first, and then he would come in and begin the process."

"Do you think the information in those books was enough to get him killed, Doctor?"

"Jesus, Detective, I can't speculate on that. But it's safe to say that somebody hated this man deeply or he was a threat to someone's well-being. If I were honestly keeping a journal, I sure as hell would know whose path I crossed that caused these feelings."

"Well, somebody got their hands on those books when they went through his house, and if it was the murderer, then I guess this investigation is going to hit a wall unless we can put together this information from another source. Is there's anybody that Dwyer was close to that you know of?"

"Other than his sister, there's no one he ever spoke about, and he wouldn't even sign a release form for information to be released to her. Dwyer was a solitary man, and yet in his own way, I think he wanted out of the isolation, but didn't trust anyone to help him. I'm sorry to be so vague, Detective, but as much as I liked Johnny, he would only let me get so far." Wellman paused, then added, "Have you spoken to his sister?"

"Yes. She spent a lot of time trying to help me sort out some of this."

"Well give her my condolences and tell her that Oak Hill is here for her as well if she feels a need for someone to talk to."

"I will, and thanks for this discussion that never happened." Rooney smiled as he said it.

"What discussion?" Wellman smiled back.

As Brian left, Washington walked along the hallway toward the front entrance with him.

"I'll buy you a cup of coffee in the cafeteria, Brian. Just let me say hello to the cop they're bringing into detox. I always try to grab 'em cop-to-cop when I'm up here. It seems to make it a little easier."

"No problem, I'll wait in the parking lot."

Rooney walked toward the door then stopped. He caught a glimpse of the man being led through the admissions office. At first, he didn't believe his own eyes, but there, staring at him and looking more afraid than drunk, was Peter Wilson.

Chapter 34

August 1997
Salem, Massachusetts

"**Get your coffees** and let's get started folks; we haven't got all day." Captain Martin called the morning meeting to order with more than the usual sense of immediacy. He was getting ready to go on vacation and God forbid the person or issue that would keep him from his beloved Nova Scotia.

"First, let me introduce the new boxing champion of small town Vermont, our own Brian Rooney."

The Salem detectives stood and applauded as an embarrassed Rooney sunk down in his chair.

"What's the chance that your suspect Ansalone put this gorilla up to trying to clean your clock, Brian?"

"I can't imagine that she's that stupid Cap, but the guy works for her, and he has gone after people in the past who have screwed around with his boss, so who knows."

"What about the administrator at the hospital in New Hampshire? Anything there we can grab on to?"

Rooney shrugged his shoulders, and sipped at his coffee, and began to read from his notebook. He covered the highlights of his meeting with Wellman and the conclusion that was reached. The key to finding Dwyer's killer probably was in the missing notebooks.

"Brian, what are the chances that the break-in at the house and Dwyer's murder were unrelated?"

Rooney looked over at Red Nolan, puzzled at the question.

"What do you have in mind, Red?"

"Suppose that somebody had something to hide and was suspicious that Dwyer was writing it all down somewhere. Let's suppose that the same person knew this guy had a habit of never locking his doors. If I was that person and wanted to protect myself, I would just grab the books whenever the opportunity presented itself. That doesn't make me a killer, just a person trying to protect himself from being potentially humiliated by the drunken babbling of Dwyer."

Rooney paused, as if clearing his brain. "OK Red, let's suppose you're right, I hadn't separated the events, but why hasn't the person come forth if they know they're clean?"

"Because they've already lied about their relationship with Dwyer in some way or other, and now they're not gonna further incriminate themselves by getting involved."

"What about the unidentified prints? Have we heard from the FBI computer?"

Martin walked to the chalkboard as he spoke and pointed to the names on the board.

"The senator acknowledges her prints, and we got Burns' prints matched through his military records. We still have two missing prints to deal with, besides the sister's and the professor's."

Red Nolan sat back with a grin and spoke. "Here's a present for ya, Brian. Now, we only have one missing print."

Nolan passed over a fax to the Rooney. It was a copy of the Vermont BCI request for Ellen Ansalone's fingerprints. They matched the ones taken from Dwyer's house. The document also pointed out that Ellen Ansalone had a sealed juvenile file.

"Red, don't you have a buddy in the Lynn PD?"

"I already called him, Brian. He's due back from vacation on Monday."

"I need everything we can get on Ansalone; 'cause I don't like people bullshittng me."

"Brian, take a couple days off before you head back to Vermont, but get me a murder suspect while I'm on vacation 'cause I'm sick of taking heat from the hospital administration and the members of this Irish fundraising group."

Rooney stumbled from bed at six thirty and could still feel the ache gnawing at him even after three days of anti-inflammatory medication and a couple of long hot soaks in the tub. He was feeling good in spite of his pain and was looking forward to getting back to Vermont and a second interview with Ansalone.

As he made coffee, he checked his dry cleaning bag and decided Martin was right when he told him to take a few days off. It was time to get his personal life squared away. At least his house was immaculate, thanks to a Colombian cleaning woman that Janet found just before she moved back to Nantucket and her new husband.

He reviewed the last week and his progress on the case. Clearly, Ansalone was lying, but why? Could she have caused the destruction to the house? Possibly, but what about Red's theory of two different people being involved? What the hell is Ansalone so angry at? What about McGowan and the VisionVermont guy, Carrier? Is there a connection at the music studio? Have Weldon come along on this interview. Interview Carrier separately. Check him out through Weldon. Check on Pete Wilson. Call Washington and see if he can get any information on Wilson. Jesus, he looked like shit. Should he call Wilson's wife? What do you say to people like her?

He finished his notes and dressed in slacks and blue polo shirt, then strapped his holster on, grabbed his keys, selected a blue blazer from the closet, and headed for the car and an overdue trip to see the Whale.

The maximum security prison in Massachusetts is located in Walpole, about one hour from his house in Salem. The imposing structure held a couple of thousand of the state's most evil people and one overweight whale. Rooney had been coming for six years to visit the man whom he befriended after that fateful day on the Nantucket beach. Rooney's superiors had at first viewed this friendship skeptically, but as time passed, and bosses went the way of the political winds, the relationship was just taken for granted by his fellow cops. None of them had ever gotten close enough to him to hear the story of Brian and the Whale.

The Whale, whose real name was Domingo Pyres, was a born-and-bred Nantucket legend who could easily have been a harpooner on the whaling ship *Essex* one hundred and fifty years ago. His football prowess had led the tiny island team to three consecutive championships and the Whale to Boston College on a scholarship. The Whale loved Boston, especially the area known as Kenmore Square where he became a bouncer at a college hangout that was principally owned by two brothers from Somerville who made their fortune the old fashioned way. They stole it.

It was a marriage of Nantucket brawn and Somerville balls that made the Whale a legend in Boston. He became a numbers enforcer for the two Solomon brothers and his quick hands and total lack of conscience soon moved him to the top of the pecking order in Boston crime circles and out of his dormitory at Chestnut Hill. The years in Boston had treated the Whale with respect and he might have spent his later years drinking coffee and Sambucca with the old men on Winter Hill had he not been videotaped smashing a temporary no parking sign with a concrete base over the head of a Vietnamese street punk who had tried to muscle into a Solomon brother's porn and good times shop in Boston's downtown. Unfortunately, for the Whale, the tape ran that evening on the Channel Five news. Six witnesses came forth at the trial to attest to his sterling character, but manslaughter is manslaughter and the Whale ended up doing a twenty-year sentence in maximum security at MCI Walpole.

Rooney checked his nine-millimeter at the front desk of the prison, and was ushered through to a private room usually reserved for attorney and incarcerated clients.

"Hey Roons, how they hanging?"

The man who greeted Rooney was a throwback to Neanderthal. He walked slightly tipped forward, and his shoulders were hunched over his huge chest. His arms were enormous and hairier than Rooney could ever remember seeing outside of a zoo. The Whale had always looked like this; he was dressed in prison denim jeans and a clean white T-shirt.

"Nice greeting ,Whale. Did you practice that in the yard today?"

"Fuck you, Roons; you ain't been up to see the Whale in awhile."

This banter was always the way their visits began the Whale in mock self-pity and Rooney keeping it as light as he could when talking to a three hundred pound man who thrived on beating people to death.

"You seen that scumbag brother of mine?" the Whale spit out the question.

"Over Fourth of July weekend I saw him long enough to give him the message about the property."

"What did that shit fuck have to say?"

"What did you expect him to say after you threatened to whack him if he tried to sell?"

"Good, how's my mother doing? Is that shitbum taking care of her?"

"That shitbum is a Catholic priest, and I guarantee you he's doing the best he can taking care of a ninety-one-year-old demented Portagee widow."

"Don't call my mother a *dement*."

"That's how the doctor at Cottage Hospital refers to her condition: as dementia."

"Fuck him too. You banging that chick in New Hampshire yet?" The Whale cracked his knuckles as he spoke.

"Vermont, and no I'm not bangin' her. I'm trying to find out who offed her brother."

"Wasn't the Whale." The Whale broke up with laughter at his own joke.

The Whale then did something he had never done in six years; he leaned forward looking out the glass wall at the guard in the next room and quietly said, "That wasn't local."

"Are you sure?"

"What the fuck do you think?"

They talked for almost an hour about Nantucket. Rooney said no more about Dwyer's murder. The Whale never volunteered information and Rooney knew enough not to pry. Rooney checked his watch and the look from the attending guard's face and knew it was time to leave.

As Rooney was almost to the door, the Whale again spoke quietly.

"Remember the story about the heist your state police buddy in the boonies told you belonged to us?"

Rooney was puzzled, and then remembered telling the Whale about the missing bus with the cash that had disappeared in Vermont and how the brother never got over it.

"That wasn't us."

Rooney started to speak and the Whale turned his back to him. The visit was over.

Chapter 35

August 1997
Marlboro, Vermont

FRANK WELDON WAS Rooney's kind of cop. A uniformed trooper on the Vermont State Police for twelve years, he had a knack for getting past bullshit. His manner was friendly and nonconfrontational, yet he missed nothing when it came to interviewing a potential suspect or witness. It was clear after fifteen minutes of conversation with Frost Records executive Brad McGowan, Weldon wasn't buying into McGowan's version of life with Johnny Dwyer as a business partner.

"Do you know a sound engineer who lives in Grafton named Meyer Lang?"

"Everybody in the business knows Lang, Detective. He's one of the best sound guys outside of Manhattan."

"He worked on Dwyer's sessions, isn't that true?"

"He works all our important sessions. As I said, he's the best around."

"Do you remember an incident between you and Dwyer that happened about a year ago involving studio time?"

Rooney sat back and watched as McGowan squirmed in his seat. Weldon had obviously done his homework on the relationship between the Frost partners and was moving toward something that McGowan clearly wasn't comfortable discussing.

"Lang had no business taking that discussion out of this studio, Detective."

"I don't call threatening your partner's reputation or his livelihood just a conversation."

"It wasn't like that at all. I was just pissed off at the way Johnny thought he could come and use the studio as his plaything when we had more important things going on."

"How did Dwyer feel about that, Mr. McGowan?"

"He was a little hurt but he always got over it."

Weldon reached in his leather case, produced a tape player, and inserted a tape.

"Why don't we listen to Lang's take on that?"

"Bullshit, Detective, you have no goddamn right to pull this shit with me. I told you what happened and that's that."

Rooney spoke. "I haven't heard the tape, so why don't we all just sit back and enjoy it."

As the tape began to play, McGowan sat straight up in his chair then leaned forward in his seat.

"Shut it off. Alright, you want to hear my side of the story?"

He stood up and motioned to the two detectives to walk with him. They left his office and walked down a corridor lined with pictures and jacket covers of various groups and individuals. Rooney was surprised to see some pictures of well-known contemporary artists that for some reason, he hadn't put together with Meggy's description of Frost Records. They entered a large room with a glassed-in area set back on the far wall and overhead microphones and equipment carefully covered over with leather cases and cloth mike covers.

"When I came to Frost, they were operating reel-to-reel tape and making demos for every clown with a guitar who tried to sound like Dylan. Or the place was loaded with Dwyer's drunken Irish buddies trying to fight the Easter rebellion for the two hundredth time. My deal with the VisionVermont group was to make the place run smoothly in spite of Dwyer's influence."

"You're saying they hired you to watchdog Dwyer."

"Yeah, in the beginning that was it. But I realized that the times were changing, and I managed to make this studio what it is today. We record and own the publishing rights to a whole new group of artists, people who are steadily making the changeover to the semipop stuff, what the industry calls contemporary folk."

"Dwyer had a problem with the way things were happening?" Rooney took notes as he asked the question.

"Johnny wanted to cling to the past. He would have been happy to keep bringing in the locals to sing about the Battle of Bennington."

"Isn't there something in your agreement with VisionVermont that says you have to produce a certain percentage of Vermont music or performers?" Rooney remembered the stipulation in the agreement between Dwyer and VisionVermont that Meggy had mentioned after reading Johnny's will.

"There is, but that's no reason that he had to get so goddam protective about the business."

"Are you happy to see Johnny dead, Mr. McGowan?"

"What the hell am I supposed to say to that, Detective? Why don't you ask me if I still beat my wife?"

"OK, Mr. McGowan, I heard that you use this studio to enhance your sex life with the young performers. Any truth to that?"

"This interview is over, Detective, and I assure you that Lyman Carrier and I will make it clear to Montpelier that your style is anything but professional."

"I'm sure you will, Mr. McGowan, and I assure you that I will be just as clear with Mr. Dwyer's family about your attitude when it comes time for you to purchase his interests from the estate."

As Rooney and Weldon walked out of the entrance to Frost Studio, they entered the small common area in the middle of Frost College campus. They ran head on into Ben Latimer and two students headed for the library. Rooney introduced Weldon to Latimer and started to say something about the Whale's reference to the old crime involving Ben's brother, then stopped. This was not the time or place.

"What brings you to Frost, Brian?"

"Interviewing Brad McGowan. You work for him as a musician, don't you?"

"No longer. After Johnny's death I really don't like going in the studio."

"What do you think of McGowan?"

"Not much. He spends half his life on his radio show trying to convince people that he built Frost Studios from the ground up."

"It appears the guy made a lot of changes that Johnny didn't like."

"How so?"

"All the young artists he attracted to the studio."

Ben looked perplexed.

"Brian, you don't read the scandal sheets enough. Those young kids recording at Frost are mostly recovering addicts and alcoholics that Johnny brought in to give them a safe place to record."

"Are you sure?"

"God, yes. The studio owns more publishing rights than you can shake a stick at, and that's because Frost bought them up early in their careers when things were shaky."

Weldon and Rooney looked at each other and realized at once that for whatever reasons Brad McGowan had, he just fed them a line of shit and neither one of them was happy about it.

"What was on the tape you got from Lang?"

Weldon smiled. "Not as much as McGowan thought there would be."

Chapter 36

August 1997
Lynn, Massachusetts

"LYNN, LYNN, THE city of sin. You never go out the way you went in." Marty Doyle hummed the old street song. His return from vacation and the note from his pal Nolan brought back memories of his forty years as the juvenile officer for the city of Lynn. He had seen the changes to the streets more than most cops ever would. Sometimes he longed for the old days when the crime scene belonged to the Irish, the Guineas, and the Jews. You could at least talk to the parents in those days; even the immigrants had some respect for his badge and knew he was at least trying to do the right thing for their kids. He decided to call Nolan and was surprised to get him on the first ring. "Nolan, you old fart, what can I do you for?"

"I sure as hell don't want fried dough. How ya been, Marty?"

Marty Doyle had spent the last twenty years, from June until Labor Day, making fried dough on the boardwalk at Hampton Beach, New Hampshire.

The resort still drew families to spend their week's vacation swimming in frigid water, exercising in front of a huge bandstand, and strolling in the evening to big band sounds emanating from the casino ballroom. Hampton was one of the last resorts to serve liquor, and even now, it was rare to see a drunk on the street. Marty had put three kids through school and taken half the population of Lynn juvenile offenders off the street by putting them to work at Doyle's Dough.

"I need a line on a juvenile case that got sealed."

"What's it about, Red? You know I need something to unseal a juvie record."

"Does the name Ansalone mean anything to you?"

"Chicky Ansalone was my bookie for years, you mean that Ansalone?"

"Did he have a daughter that now would be in her forties?"

"Would her name be Ellen, Red?"

"You know her?"

"I don't need to unseal the case, Red. I took the original call and handled her case personally."

"What was she involved in?"

"Jesus, Red, you got bananas for memory. It was in every paper on the North Shore. She took a shotgun to Walter Carvella."

"No shit. She was the one who supposedly saved her father's life."

"The one and only. That dumb bastard Carvella couldn't get the safety off a military forty-five and stood, pointing the goddam thing at the kid in her own backyard. She was as cool as a cucumber, walked in the house, and brought out Chicky's shotgun and unloaded on the Guinea buffoon."

"She killed him?"

"No, but he's been in a nursing home for the past twenty years. She really did him good."

"So tell me, Red, why the interest in Chicky's kid after all these years?"

"We think she could be involved in the homicide we had at the hospital in July."

"The Irish guy, Dwyer? Wasn't that a drug deal?" Doyle probed.

"No, at least at this point we don't think so."

"You oughta talk to the old man; maybe you could squeeze him a little."

"He's still alive?"

"Ya, he's in the big nursing home on the Lynnway."

"Have you still got a psychiatric profile on the daughter?"

"Somewhere in my files. It might take me an hour or so, but I can tell you something about her without looking at the shrink's report."

"What's that, Marty?"

"That kid at fourteen years old had more balls than most people get in a lifetime. The day after the shooting, she went back to school as if nothing had happened."

"You gotta be kidding."

"No, and the next thing I know is she graduates top of her class two years later. Saw the shrink only four times and never missed a session with her probation officer. I tell you this, Red, this broad could kill you and never miss a hair appointment."

"Can you send over what you got today? I'd appreciate it."

"Have it over this afternoon and Red, be careful around this woman."

Nolan dialed Rooney's cell phone and Brian answered on the first ring. He proceeded to fill him in on the information on Ansalone. Rooney was pleased to hear it, but was still having a hard time picturing the diminutive real estate broker opening up on someone with a shotgun. "Jesus, Meggy's living in the same town with this woman. Maybe I should ask Atkins or Henderson to watch Johnny's house for a while. What if this woman's crazier than we think? He picked up the phone and dialed Wilson's number, then hung up. For Christ's sake, Pete, you said you'd watch her."

Chapter 37

September 1997
Warrens Mills, Vermont

As much as Benjamin Wernecki hated trenches, Porky Atkins loved them. Wernicki watched the police chief unload his backhoe from the trailer. The feeling came over him as it had that day when he was marched to the *SS* shooting range in 1942. They were marched to Hebertshausen, near Dachau, to what he was sure was going to be his death. Instead, he was forced to witness the mass executions of the weaker prisoners. The older crematoria at the camp, built in 1940, could no longer keep up with the significantly increased death rate in the camp, so the prisoners were forced to help bury them. Benjamin did not die that spring day. However, a piece of his soul was ground away by the machinery that dug the long trenches in which he was forced to bury his fellow Jews as well as Catholics, homosexuals, and political prisoners. Benjamin never understood why he was marched back alive to the barracks that day. Maybe it was the prayers of the priests whose sandals he mended. They always joked with him about "saving their soles while they saved souls."

Porky had a large thermos of coffee and more than a dozen mixed donuts sitting on the recessed seat of the backhoe. Ward Kinkle bent with a shovel and a pick trying to find a place to start digging in order to unearth the cesspool pipe that had been laid here over thirty years before.

This section was the oldest of Ellen Ansalone's development. Porky and Kinkle had managed to turn their excavating business to a tidy profit at her expense. They had a contract to convert the old cesspools to more modern septic treatments, and every trench dug was another dollar in their vacation kitty. Porky dug for fifteen minutes and then raised the bucket. Ward Kinkle climbed down in the trench to check for pipe. Porky kept eyeing the old man who watched them from the back deck. "Nice day. This your place?"

"It's my son-in-law's place. I live here now."

"You foreign?" Porky liked to get right to the heart of things.

"I'm from New York. Is that foreign?"

"Might as well be." Porky laughed at his little joke.

"Vat is that trench?"

"We're gonna put in a new septic system. Should have it dug up today."

Porky had climbed back on the bucket seat when Kinkle shouted. Porky had started to dig again and paid no attention.

"Shut it down Pork. Shut the fuckin' machine down." Kinkle was raising his arms up and down and shouting with a strange look on his face.

"What the Jesus holy Christ are you yelling at Kinkle?"

"Come down here Pork."

Like an overweight bull, Porky charged off the side of the machine and slid into the trench ready to carve Kinkle a new asshole. Then he stopped, and saw the object in Kinkle's hand.

"That's a cow bone you dumb shit. Ain't you ever seen a cow bone?" shouted Porky.

"It don't look like a cow bone, or a deer bone for that matter, Pork."

Kinkle put the piece of bone aside and started to probe with his pick, loosening some dirt.

Above them, the old man looked with terror at the trench and the bone that had been put aside. He then began to shriek at the moonlighting Warrens Mills police chief and his pick wielding patrolman.

"That's person, that's person, that's human person." Wernecki screamed at them, letting go a rage that he thought he had lost in the trenches of Germany. It came from some primordial place, long buried and now erupted at the two men in the trench. They turned to look at this demon above them. He pointed to the end of the pick in Kinkle's hand.

"Oh Jesus, Pork, this ain't right."

He dropped the pick and backed away, horrified by the human skull that was attached to the sharpened end of his tool. Porky stared at the face that looked up at them from this foul smelling old grave.

Kinkle had climbed out of the trench and stood beside the now silent, shivering old man. Slowly, very slowly, and cautiously Porky took the skull and removed it from the pick head. He placed it, almost lovingly, on the dirt pile. Kinkle extended his hand to the obese lawman, and Porky, as gingerly as he was capable of, stepped out of the hole and sat next to the two men. Each in their own way, tried to process what they had unearthed.

Chapter 38

"**SWEET MOTHER OF** Jesus. This cannot be happening to me all in one day." Ellen Ansalone was standing in her office, looking out to her deck. In one hand, she held her telephone, now silenced, but seemingly burning in her hand. She had just finished a call from the Salem police detective, Rooney, who insisted that they meet again, either alone or with her attorney.

She couldn't figure out what the hell was going on in her own development. There were State and local cops all over the old section of High Mowing, and an ambulance from the rescue squad had just passed her window with their sirens screaming. As if this wasn't bad enough, she was due to lead a presentation to thirty-five real estate brokers from across New England who were considering the brokerage of her next subdivision. She lit Marlboro after Marlboro, took a few puffs, and put them out. Finally, she grabbed her car keys and headed out the door. Her secretary, a born-and-raised Warrens Mills High School graduate, started to say something to her, but Ansalone just said, "Handle it dimwit," and walked out the office doorway to the parking lot and her dark green pickup truck with the High Mowing logo on the driver's side door. "What is going on?" She screamed at the now subdued police chief who was standing talking to a uniformed state trooper.

"We dug up something on that septic site."

"What the hell was it? The Lindbergh baby?"

"Can't tell you right now, it's police business."

She started to walk toward the area that was being secured by Patrolman Henderson and a uniformed state trooper.

"That's as far as you can go Ms. Ansalone." Henderson stood in front of her and blocked her view of the trench site. She put her hand on his chest as if to move him and as quickly as she did, he grabbed her gently but very firmly and said, "None of your bullshit today, lady. Take one more step and you're going out of here in handcuffs." Ansalone knew the tone of voice that cops have when they're not in the mood to be hassled, so she dropped her hands to her side and turned back toward the road.

The ambulance driver was parked across the street, and she could see old Mr. Wernecki arguing with the paramedic about the blood pressure cuff they were attempting to place on his arm.

"Leaf me alone, just leaf me alone." He pulled away and quickly pulled his sleeve back down to cover the tattoo of numbers that were fading but legible on his forearm. The police chief walked over and quietly told the overzealous paramedic to back off, and then for the second time that day laid a hand on Wernicki's shoulder and assured him that everything would be all right. He looked across the street to the barricade and told the trooper to let the old farmer in to comfort his friend.

"This Fermont is evil, Sumner."

"No Benjamin, people are evil."

"Today was all over again Dachau. Sumner, am I crazy?"

Warren looked around at the crowd of police and bystanders who were already forming to witness the rumored gravesite that had been unearthed.

"Maybe we're all crazy Benjamin. Maybe we're all crazy." They sat on the wooded roadside and talked quietly, then were interrupted for just a second by Porky offering the old man his box of donuts. Warren looked at the chief, then laughed and said, "Now Benjamin, I know we're all crazy."

Chapter 39

THE VAN WITH the state of Vermont forensic laboratory markings was parked at such an angle as to block the vision of the curious townspeople of Warrens Mills. The technical crew from the laboratory in Waterbury, Vermont, was participating in a tedious grid search in the backyard property of Benjamin Wernecki's son-in-law, whose recent purchase of the property was the catalyst for opening of the cesspool system and the discovery of the skeletal remains. "Forensics is simply the application of science to law," and the way the two groups, technicians and cops, worked together on this site reminded David Henderson of why he had become a cop in the first place. There was no bickering between state and local police on this crime scene; egos hadn't entered into the investigation as yet, probably because there was a great deal of curiosity at this point as to what they may have uncovered.

The unlikely star of this event was kneeling in the septic trench with a small brush in her hand meticulously trying to gather evidence from the site. She had assembled, as best she could, all but two bones from the deceased. She had carefully videotaped and still-photographed each piece of evidence that had surfaced. Dr.

Janet Dixon was a forensic anthropologist from UVM who had been called in by State police to work the crime scene. She was a product of the forensic anthropology program at the University of Tennessee. Her primary function was to determine the sex, height, weight, and ethnic group of the deceased from an incomplete body. She was a team player and had worked well with pathologists and homicide investigators throughout the State.

Janet loved to dig in dirt. She had been a curious kid and had become a curious adult. Right now she was digging, knowing that if her patience prevailed, she would find the slugs that had done the massive damage to the skull.

The scene had yielded enough to point to foul play. The canvas and leather bags were in remarkably good shape and the metal stamped zipper tag clearly showed the Green Mountain Trust logo. Each piece of evidence she unearthed was placed in evidence bags and marked, then placed in the van.

"Yes, yes, Paul, I got it."

She smiled like a kid with a new toy as she held the .70-caliber, twelve-gauge slug that had been buried just beneath where the cranium had been found. She thought about the pressure of a slug at close range and thought of brain tissue being violently forced against the internal walls of the cranium, the kinetic energy of the slug propelling the fragile brain tissue laterally away from the wound track and eventually blowing off the top of the victim's head.

"This bastard was vicious."

"Who you talking about, Janet?" Trooper Paul Miller asked.

"Whoever did this was a fuckin' executioner."

"Look at this, Miller. It looks as if this person was forced to bend over, or maybe he was shot putting the bags in the hole."

"Hey, Janet, what's that next to your knee?" She turned to where Miller was pointing and, with tweezers, picked up a small diamond ring.

"Jesus, Paul, it's an engagement ring." She bagged the ring carefully and handed it to him.

She stepped out of the trench and walked over to the van where there was coffee for the crew provided by one of the neighbors.

"We're going to need lights in about an hour."

She spoke to the tech who was dressed in black coveralls bearing the Vermont forensic laboratory logo. "I guess we're here for a while, huh, Doc?"

Chapter 40

September 1997
Nantucket Ferry

"How are the cannibals this week, Professor?"

"Still getting enough to eat I suppose, Joseph."

Ben Latimer stood with able-bodied seaman Joseph Sears on the forward deck of the *Nantucket* ferry. As a regular passenger on the Steamship Authority's vessels, he had come to share stories of his research with the crew of the island ferries. He was always amused that the cannibalism performed by the shipwrecked members of the whaling vessel *Essex* in 1821 was their favorite topic. His research into Nantucket's dirty little secret often had some of the old timers on the island looking at him as the enemy from Vermont, but he knew that a major piece was going to be written sooner or later by some researcher and he figured it might as well be him.

"Looks like the bubble boys are meeting the boat today."

Sears pointed at the dock area where a blue and gray Massachusetts State Police cruiser stood near the entrance to the docking area. As they felt the engines reverse and the glide to the dock approach, Ben thought he recognized the man sitting with the trooper. It looked like Brian Rooney. He thought it strange that the Salem cop would be on the dock, then remembered that he was a Nantucket native. Maybe he was going home to visit, Ben thought. They landed harder than usual against the bulkhead and Ben had to grab the railing in order to stabilize himself.

"Nice landing, Skipper, you asshole." Sears had very little love for what he thought were highly overpaid ferry captains.

The trooper and what now Ben could see was clearly the Salem detective were approaching him on the departure ramp. He waved at Rooney.

"Brian, what's going on? Are you going home?"

"Ben, this is Bob Azarian."

Ben shook hands with the trooper and still was puzzled by what Rooney was doing at the dock.

"What's going on, Brian? Is Meggy OK?"

"She's fine, Ben. I need to ask you a couple of questions."

"Sure, Brian. Is this about Johnny?"

"No, it's about your brother."

Ben couldn't speak for a second. He flashed on that day years ago when another trooper had entered his life and asked the same question. He put his duffel bag down on the seashell-strewn pavement.

"Ben, was your father's name Samuel Latimer?"

"Yes. How do you know that?" As he answered the question, he started to weep. He knew, without another word being said, they had found his brother.

"My father's watch. Billy was wearing my father's watch the day he disappeared."

"We don't know for sure, Ben, but we think we've found your brother."

Chapter 41

September 1997
Cape Cod to Warrens Mills, Vermont

"I CAN'T BELIEVE that Porky Atkins had the courtesy to send you to tell me about this, Brian."

Ben Latimer and Brian Rooney were driving back from Hyannis, by way of Route 495 to the Massachusetts Turnpike, then to Springfield and up Route 95 to Vermont. They made good time as the September highways were uncrowded, until they would fill again with leaf peepers later in the month.

The drive had developed a different feeling between the two men. Ben spent most of the time telling of his and his brother's childhood summers at the lake outside the small college town of Castleton. Rooney had been stunned that morning by the news from Meggy that a body had been found in Ellen Ansalone's development. The fact that Porky had called her in his attempt to reach Ben seemed out of character for the Warrens Mills chief. "Meggy said Porky seemed like a different person," Brian told Ben.

Brian couldn't bring himself to talk to Ben about the condition of the skull that Porky had found. He tried to keep Ben focused on the good times that he and his brother had as kids, rather than the potentially grotesque period that he was bound to face as police reopened his brother's disappearance. Rooney had seen old wounds reopened in victim's families over the years, and he wished he could insulate his new friend from the media and police agencies.

"You know something, Brian, as strange as it may sound, I'm somehow ready to deal with this now. I think I've always known that someday the knock would come again, and someone would bring this news. Now I can at least say to people my brother was a victim and not some punk who ran off with a couple of million dollars."

"Do you think you really knew your brother very well?"

"I thought so, but who knows. He was just out of college and having a good time skiing and partying. I knew he would start grad school in the fall, so I never gave it much thought as to what he did with his time."

"How did he end up driving a bus?"

"The owner of the bus company had a son at Williams with Billy and the son got him the job part-time to earn spending money. When he graduated, he kept it part-time to earn his rent and skiing money."

As they drove into Warrens Mill and parked near the town hall and municipal building, they were both taken aback by the media vans and relay satellite trucks that had assembled in the small town parking area.

"Jesus, Ben, this is turning into a circus. Can't believe that the press is turning out like this."

"Fortunately, not many people know me. Maybe we can get into Porky's office without a lot of hassle from the press." As they approached the door of the police station, they were met by Porky and Frank Weldon, and ushered quickly into the building.

"Professor, I'm sorry to have to see this day come. Do you mind taking a look at some items we found?" asked Porky.

"No, Chief, let's have a look." Porky brought out two small evidence bags and opened them carefully. He took the watch from the first and handed it to Ben.

Without any hesitation Ben said, "That's my father's watch. Look at the engraving. The watchcase had the name Samuel Latimer engraved in script and the date 1961. It was a retirement gift from his company. Billy took it from him the night of his heart attack and rarely took it off."

"As soon as we process this stuff, I'll make sure you get it back."

Porky then removed a belt buckle. It was wide and had a carved scrimshaw whale on the front. Ben held it and laughed. The men in the room looked at him with curiosity.

"I've been looking for this buckle for thirty years. Damn, Billy, I told him not to borrow it."

He turned it over and on the back was a quote from *Moby Dick*. "A whaling ship was my Harvard and my Yale."

"You know, Brian, somehow I'm glad he had it with him all these years."

Suddenly, Ben sat and sobbed. The men in the room shut the door to the outer office and, unable to comfort him, they just sat and said nothing. Then Porky, who had never been much for soft talk, walked over to Ben and said, "Let me tell you about the smile on your brother's face that day. It sure was something. He was a good-lookin' boy."

Outside the press was waiting for someone to give them something. They were surprised when Ben Latimer walked into the street, eyes red but smiling and said,

"I can't talk about this crime. That's the job of the law enforcement team assembled here. But just so you get it right . . ."

He proceeded to tell of his brother's life and love for Vermont. He talked of their childhood and the lake where they learned to fish. He spoke of icehouses and dirt roads and hot summer days, of sunburned kids and maple sugar treats. He spoke without bitterness. It was as if this speech had been lying dormant for a long time. The assembled TV and print reporters, many from nearby Vermont and Massachusetts towns, listened intently as he spoke. When he was through, he concluded by saying there would be no questions and he would not speak to them again, and he thanked them.

Frank Weldon stepped up and let them know there would be a press briefing the following morning.

Chapter 42

September 1997
Warrens Mills, Vermont

THE LARGE BEDROOM that overlooked the pasture and east toward the mountains was bathed in morning sunlight. Meggy Dwyer awoke, pleased with her world. For the first time in a long time, she felt good about sharing herself and her home with a man. The memories of the room were no longer just her brother's. She had brought her own furniture up from Boston, as well those pieces that had belonged to her parents and grandparents. Now they seemed to be settled as if there were a plan somewhere in time for this mingling of generations. She watched Rooney as he slept. They had talked late into the night with Ben who was sleeping in the guestroom upstairs. Rooney had been gentle with Ben just drawing him out enough to ease his feelings and give him comfort. It was late when they finished talking. For Meggy, it seemed natural to invite Brian to her bed. Their lovemaking had been tentative and a little rushed at the same time. There was a sense of comfort when they finally began to give in to sleep, still embracing early in the morning.

She looked at the leather-holstered handgun that was on the bureau with its extra clips stacked next to it; his wallet hung open with his badge pinned to the leather. It all seemed to be natural now, part of her life today. And yet she knew that he was here to catch a killer, and when that was finished, what then?

"How are you feeling, Megan Dwyer?"

"Like taking a long run, Brian Rooney."

"Is that always gonna be your answer, Megan Dwyer?"

"That's how I've dealt with feelings since I was fourteen years old, Brian Rooney. Do you think I can change that overnight?"

"You can change anything if it's worth it, Megan Dwyer."

"Are you worth it, Detective Rooney?"

"There's only one way to find out, Megan Dwyer; stop running and start feeling."

Megan Dwyer said nothing. She removed her UVM sleeping shirt and rolled across the king-size bed to a bemused and excited Rooney.

Chapter 43

September 1997
Manchester, Vermont

SALSA, BARBECUE SAUCE, and salad dressing made a violent mosaic across the wall of Lyman Carrier's office in Manchester Center, Vermont. He stood shaking as he tried to remove the mess with paper towels and water. The person or persons who had committed the break-in to VisionVermont's headquarters had cut a path of destruction through the offices, not unlike a hurricane cutting its path through a southern coastal trailer park. Carrier had arrived in to the office early to await his meeting with Brian Rooney. His files were scattered and his computer smashed. The break-in seemed to have no pattern in its randomness, as if the intruders were raging as they searched.

Carrier kept no money on hand so he could not find a reason for the break-in. Throwing his chairs through the windows had left them broken, and each wall was defaced by some food sample that had been smashed, and then lathered on the conference room walls.

"Fuck you, you bastard," was scrawled on the wall.

Carrier's collection of Vermont literature and old journals was ripped item-by-item at their bindings and scattered across the floor. Lyman Carrier was scared; his world of Vermont antiquities and homemade food products was in shambles at his feet. He began to shake, as if freezing on this warm September day. He could feel this violation all the way to his soul. Since returning to Vermont in the sixties, he had worked with a single purpose: to build his state into the symbol of New England at its best. He had worked side-by-side with small food producers and dairymen to stick to the old ways and produce quality. His small group of believers had petitioned the legislature to make Vermont purity laws stricter and enforceable. He had found money for start up businesses and found ways to cooperatively bring products to market across the region.

His Vermont was now crumbled around him, and he felt powerless and overwhelmed.

"Could this break-in have anything to do with the murder of your partner, Mr. Dwyer?"

"I doubt it, Detective, since I spent almost no time with Johnny, and almost all of our business was conducted through Brad."

"Can you think of any reason that someone would want Dwyer dead?"

"No, although he could be abrasive when he drank; that would not be a reason to wish him dead."

"How did you meet Dwyer?"

"Through a Southern Vermont folksinger and folk historian named Margaret Macarthur. She was playing at Putney School one night and I went to hear her. Dwyer was on the same bill and he talked my ear off about his idea for building a recording studio in Marlboro."

"Did Johnny strike you as a man afraid or running from his past?"

"No, not really, but how much do we really know about our associates? Don't forget, we have over two hundred participants in VisionVermont's program. So I hardly have time anymore to know them well. As long as they are fulfilling their mission of spreading Vermont quality and uniqueness through their products and services, we tend to let them be independent."

"How did you happen to start this business?" Rooney asked while taking notes.

"When I came out of the Navy and returned here, I found a lot of small businesses trying to get off the ground, and nobody willing to go to bat for them. So with the help of Senator Stark and some other legislators, we got some grants and borrowed what we could to bring better production methods and packaging, as well as a cooperative marketing effort. At the same time, the ice cream boys had some success and the large dairy co-ops were breaking new territory in the regional markets. The rest was a matter of local banks and credit unions getting behind us rather than loaning strictly to the out of state developers who, by then, were destroying some of our natural resources.

"Speaking of developers, do you know a woman named Ansalone?"

Carrier rankled a bit then spoke with bitterness. "Don't dishonor womanhood by including her in the mix. She's everything I detest. Had they not passed good legislation in the seventies, we would be buried under the dregs of her idea of Vermont progress." Carrier stroked nervously at his full copper brown beard and then said, "Sorry, Detective, but this isn't the day to talk to me about people like that."

"Can I get a list of your membership?"

"Certainly, but what do you need it for?"

"I want to ask some questions to anyone who might have known Dwyer; your members may be helpful."

As Carrier made a copy for the detective, Rooney began to look over the destruction. *"Why, does this look like Dwyer's mess? Same person? Is Carrier on someone's hit list? Somebody was very pissed off who did this. Check on McGowan's background."*

"Here you go, Detective, but try not to upset these members. Remember, people in Vermont really don't like a lot of police intrusion in their lives, if you know what I mean."

"I'm not sure I do, Mr. Carrier."

"Well, I heard you were a little rough on Brad when you met at the studio."

"We asked some questions he didn't like, if that's what you mean."

"That's exactly what I do mean, Detective. We don't like people prying into things that are none of their business."

"Is McGowan using the studio for anything but making records, Mr. Carrier?"

"This interview is over, Detective, and again I'll ask you to not give my members a hard time, and I will go to the commissioner of public safety if need be to make sure you stay in line."

Rooney started to walk out and then thought he might take a jug of maple syrup from the display to give to Red Nolan. He thought better of it and walked out to the parking lot and the screaming, hate-filled graffiti that was painted in red on the paved surface and against the front wall of the building.

Rooney left VisionVermont's parking lot and headed toward the village of Manchester. He noticed a small, crowd gathered near the exit of a retail shopping area. The crowd was lined up at a hot dog cart.

He pulled over and parked near a jewelry shop, and as he approached the friendly looking vendors, he watched two women interact with the crowd as if they were all old friends. He could tell by the license plates that many were not local, but tourists. The two women handled the orders quickly, but still left you feeling as if they had known you forever.

He ordered two steamed dogs with homemade coleslaw and diet Coke. When he got his food, he sat with his back on the tailgate of a nearby pickup truck to take in his lunch and the sites. The lines at the cart continued to grow larger; people ate on the grass and in their cars, and didn't seem to be in any hurry.

He thought about what it was that attracted people to this tiny oasis. It was a feeling that these two women conveyed without having to say it; they respected their customers. He walked back to his car and thought about what made his father's donut shop so successful. Respect was the key, no matter who you are serving, proving that the taste of respect along with good food can be a powerful attraction.

He laughed to himself. Respect is great, but he had also just eaten the best hot dog he had had in years.

Chapter 44

September 1997
Warrens Mill, Vermont

SOFT SEPTEMBER RAIN laid a blanket of fog across the lake. Wilson awoke to waterfowl screech and the sound of the rain as it landed on the metal roof of his parent's summerhouse. *This is the way I remember it.* He tossed the blanket back across his parent's brass bed and threw on shorts and an old T-shirt with ARMY printed on the front. The running shoes were new. *Replace the booze with something else.* He hit the switch on the Mr. Coffee, then laced on the Adidas trainers and walked out to the lakefront road. This was his fourth day of trying to run. His efforts had been less than Olympian as he gasped for air after a quarter mile. *Walk for two minutes.* He could hear Abenaki John, his counselor at Oak Hill, as he talked about the native way. *Listen to the woods as you run.*

"Fuck off, John, I'm having a hard enough time just breathing," he moaned to himself as the intrusive voice kept repeating its mantra over and over. He began to jog slowly, repeating his old military cadence. This technique seemed to help, and he pushed a little harder on the dirt-packed road that ran around the perimeter of the lake. The new shoes reminded him of childhood races that used to be so important to win.

John had told him what the first week out of treatment would be like.

It's all about memories. Don't let them destroy you, Peter. Learn from them and welcome them as you would an old friend. Wilson felt the sweat across his face and the salt as it hit his eyes. He wiped his forehead and slowed to a walk again. He had been isolated since his return from New Hampshire, and the peace of his surroundings was slowly beginning to relax his anxiety, even better than the pills. Carol Ann was as distant and angry as he thought she would be. However, she was smart enough to know that the business still had to operate, and she had the billing done and the phone transfer arrangements completed when he arrived back at the lake house. His pace was slow, but even now, he felt a sense of accomplishment for having completed the two-and-a-half-mile loop that led him back to the house and his first cup of coffee. The answering machine was blinking; he paused for just a second then retrieved his messages. The first was Rooney, just wishing him well and wondering what he thought about the gravesite being unearthed. *What gravesite? What the hell was he talking about?* The second message was from Frank Weldon saying he was going to take a ride out his way and needed to talk to him. He rewound the tape and poured himself a cup of coffee, sat down on an old wooden rocker his parents had left him, and took off his wet running shoes and socks. The lake was still, the summer people gone, and the locals who owned cottages wouldn't be back until the weekend.

I'm fifty-eight years old and back where I started. Maybe I could just have a beer.

He picked up his phone to call Rooney, and then heard a car pull up in front of the house. Phone in hand, he walked to the kitchen and saw two men standing just outside on the porch.

"Hey, Brian, Frank, what the hell brings you two out here?"

Rooney said, "Didn't you get my message?"

"Just now is the first time I've picked up messages in a couple of days. What is this about a gravesite?"

"Let's sit down, Peter, 'cause you aren't going to believe what turned up after all these years."

"Let me get some more coffee; you guys take it black? I'm sort of batching it for a while till things get straightened out at home."

"Don't worry about it, Pete, black's fine with us."

They sat on the porch and watched as the sun spread across the lake. Weldon produced a file and began to read the information on the site at High Mowing Lot 12. They spent an hour going over details with a stunned Wilson.

"Jesus, I can't believe this was local. You know there was just no evidence to point us in that direction."

"We still can't rule out that the people who did this were from out of state and just hid the body and left."

Weldon looked over the file with frustration on his face.

"Peter, I was five years old when this took place. I'm also up to my ass in work at the moment, so here is the million-dollar question." Weldon paused and looked straight at Wilson, "Will you help us reopen this case?"

Wilson said nothing for what seemed like an eternity. "Frank, I'm five days out of alcohol rehab. My marriage is headed for God knows where, and I haven't been involved in a serious investigation in years. What possible good could I do?"

Chapter 45

Libby Stark had seen it coming, but refused to believe it. For almost two weeks, her daughter Jen had been slipping out at odd hours and had been totally uncommunicative. Every encounter was testy. And her room stunk of pot residue. All the signs were pointing to her decomposition, and Libby knew the downhill slide of her depression was always trouble. This was not the time for that ungrateful kid to fuck up. She caught herself feeling out of control. *Put a plan together, Libby,* she thought. She could usually rely on Peter Wilson for help, but he hadn't returned the message that Libby had given to his wife.

"I'm going to Bratt, Mom."

"OK. Anybody going with you?"

"Jackie Burns is going down to the VA and I'm going to drive him."

Libby started to react and then said nothing. She knew that making an issue of Jackie Burns would just start a battle she couldn't win. "What time will you be back?"

"I don't know, we'll probably hit a movie or maybe just have dinner. Don't worry, I'll be fine."

"Jen?"

"What, Mom?"

"Are you taking your medication on schedule?"

"Don't start, Mom. I'm a big girl, remember?"

"I know that but—"

"Don't but me, Mom. It's my life and I'll live it my way."

"I just don't want—"

"You just don't want to see me swinging from the Quad lift by my neck."

"Jesus, don't say that."

Her daughter walked out the screen door and started her Honda. Libby picked up the brown plastic bottle of pain medication, swallowed two and began to cry softly.

Help me out, Earl. She's your kid too.

Chapter 46

THE FILE WAS stuck in a closet along with fifteen or so others that Peter Wilson had kept when he retired from the State Police. He looked over the notes he had written in 1964 and was surprised at his total focus on the missing driver. He remembered well the rush to investigate the Latimer family, especially the brother, and the owners of the People's Bus Line and its employees.

He could track the inevitable closing of the active file almost a year later. The Massachusetts State Police couldn't come up with anything to substantiate their beliefs that a Somerville gang had set up the driver and removed the money. Yet that seemed to be the direction that each law enforcement agency ended up heading toward.

The FBI report was as inconclusive as was his. The feds still believed that Billy Latimer had managed to pull this off himself. They were relentless in tracking down the most obscure friends and relatives, and yet they came away with no evidence that he had committed the crime except for the fact that he and the money were missing.

There were no prints, no blood, and no signs of a struggle. The snow had obliterated all tracks by the time they found the bus. *How many involved, two or* three? How did they get back to Warrens Mills? Back up Route 9 or Auger Hole Road? Who cut the power? Where did they stop the bus? Marlboro town road? Why choose the Boy Scout camp to hide the bus?*

The coffee was moving his thinking along at a rapid clip. He realized that he was glad that Weldon had asked him to help. There was a feeling starting to come back that had been lost since his retirement. He noted that Billy's dentist in Newton, Massachusetts had faxed the dental work to Waterbury, and that was being evaluated along with the evidence found at the gravesite. Wilson heard the phone ring. He was totally unprepared for the voice on the other end.

"Pete, it's Ben Latimer."

"Ben, I'm sorry for—"

"Don't worry, Pete, I know you are. What's been between us is over and done. I'm told you're going to help on the investigation."

"News travels fast."

"Rooney stopped by to see how I was doing. He told me."

"I'm going to try to help, but I've had my own problems lately, and I don't honestly know what I can do."

"Pete, I want to help; maybe there's something we missed years ago."

Wilson started to refuse. He could do this alone. Abenaki John's voice crept into his head.

"Remember, Peter, learn to ask for help if you don't want to drink again."

"OK, Ben, what do you have in mind?"

"I'm a researcher, Peter, let me go over the original information with you and see if we can't sort it out differently; in the meantime, I'll go through Billy's stuff again and maybe there is something in his mail or his personal stuff that would help."

"All right, Ben, but let's keep this between us."

"That's not a problem for me."

Wilson hung up and began to write on a yellow pad: Title search on lot 12, who owned in 1963. Talk to Ansalone. Get report on crime scene evidence from Weldon. Don't drink.

Chapter 47

ELLEN ANSALONE ENTERED the Warrens Mills Police office with a determined look on her face and no lawyer on her tail. She had decided to look at the tape, answer a few questions about Dwyer's death, and get all the bullshit behind her. The body in the cesspool had rattled her, and now she began to hope that the good-looking Salem cop could help her out with a little information. *Chicky would have told them to shove it, but that wasn't gonna work.*

"Did your buddy finish drying out yet?"

"Who's that, Ms. Ansalone?"

"Wilson. I heard he was in detox somewhere, and that his old lady had thrown him out."

"That's really not my business, Ms. Ansalone, and I'm sure it's not yours either."

"Sorry, I was just curious; besides, everybody in town knows it."

Rooney flipped the switch on the portable VCR and watched as Johnny Dwyer, now sitting on a stool tuned, and talked to the sixty or so people assembled in the Essex Peabody Museum auditorium.

"Bullshit, this isn't the tape; what the hell are you trying to pull, Detective?"

The camera slowly panned out into the audience and paused for a split second on a couple that was arguing back-and-forth. The woman was Ellen Ansalone, and it was clear, as Rooney froze the frame, that the man was Dwyer's business partner, McGowan.

"Is that you, Ms. Ansalone?"

"What do you think?"

The tape of Ansalone and McGowan together had been discovered by Red Nolan as he was reviewing evidence and decided to watch all of Dwyer's concerts. Having just minutes before watched the interview with the real estate developer, he called Rooney, who asked him to overnight the tape.

Rooney turned to his notebook and read: "'I haven't seen Dwyer for a couple of months.'" "Do you remember telling me that in your office, Ms. Ansalone?"

"Up your ass. I told you that I wouldn't talk about someone who was married."

"Why did you lie to me about being in Dwyer's house?"

"I wasn't in that bastard's house."

Rooney placed the fingerprint report in front of Ansalone and she looked at it, not quite sure how to read it.

"I need a cigarette. Can I go outside?"

"You're free to go wherever you want. You walked in here voluntarily and nothing's changed, unless you want to talk to me about all of this."

As she walked out the front door, Rooney fired a mild salvo and let it sail over her head.

"Have you ever fired a shotgun, Ms. Ansalone?"

Ellen Ansalone lost the color in her face, olive skin turned sickly white. "You are a no good prick. That bastard was going to kill my father. What would you have done, Detective?"

"I don't know, Ellen, probably the same thing."

He watched through the window as Ansalone drew deeply on the Marlboro, as if it was an oxygen tank. He knew she was ready to break and didn't want her to spook and call for a lawyer. *Good cop time, Brian*

"It was Brad's idea to go to the concert. He said that he and Johnny had some business to discuss."

Ansalone was composed now; she reentered the conference room with a new attitude, as if the cigarette had emboldened her.

"How long have you been seeing McGowan?"

"Off and on for a couple of years, but always out of town. He's happily married."

"Happily?"

"You know what I mean, he's got two kids and his lady is a leftover from the seventies."

"Does she know about you?"

"I hope not. I don't want to screw up their marriage."

"That's considerate, Ms. Ansalone."

"I'm a considerate person, Detective. You ought to loosen up enough to find out."

"Did McGowan have reason to kill Dwyer?"

"No more than anybody else who spent time with him."

"Were you with McGowan all weekend at your father's house?"

"Mostly, except when I left to see my father on Monday."

"What time was that?"

"Six in the morning."

"Isn't that early for a visit?"

"Not with Chicky double peppers, it isn't. He's up at five and God forbid I don't bring him his omelet."

"I'm going to want to talk to McGowan and then you again at some point, Ms. Ansalone."

"Am I a suspect?"

"Everybody who knew Johnny is a suspect right now."

"OK. By the way, I'm sorry that goon Morton tried to rough you up at the fair."

"I'm sure you are, Ms. Ansalone. Because you're a considerate woman, right?"

"You're a shit, Detective."

"Thank you, Ms. Ansalone. We'll talk."

Chapter 48

September 1997
Rutland, Vermont

RUTLAND HIGH SCHOOL was alive with the expectancy of the coming year, and at the same time dying in the recognition that one of its students had taken his own life. Student assistance coordinator, Lorraine Barnes, sat in her office and cried as she stared at the yearbook picture of Porter Hughes, a seventeen-year-old senior. Hughes, just three days before, had taken an overdose of prescription sleeping pills washed down with a quart of vodka. Attempts by his mother and the local rescue squad had failed to resuscitate him.

"Those bastards at Horizon had the balls to tell this kid's therapist that he was in no danger."

"How long had he been in trouble?" Libby Stark asked the same question over and over whenever she spoke with the school crisis teams, and she knew the answer.

"He had been drinking out of control since he was fifteen, and the depression started shortly afterward."

"His insurer wouldn't allow in-patient treatment?"

"His insurer recommended outpatient counseling and an antidepressant."

"You're telling me that in spite of a history of suicide in the family, they wouldn't change their policies."

"Ask them yourself when they come to the hearings."

The tiny office next to the school cafeteria seemed to close in on Libby as she looked at the picture of the young man in Janet's yearbook.

He had the look of a farmer, which he was. A third generation dairy farmer whose parents were still trying to squeak out a livelihood from the industry that had dwindled to almost nothing despite the fact that this state had once bragged of having more cows than people.

Libby Stark left the meeting with Janet Barnes and did the same thing she had done twenty-seven times before, and the thing she hated more than anything. She drove out of town on Route 7, then took a side road to where the road became dirt, and a small sign led to a red farmhouse. The sign read A VERMONT DAIRY FARM OF DISTINCTION.

Jerseys sat across the pasture, and watched as she parked her car. She saw a woman in her forties approach her, no words passed between them, just the wailing sobs of two people who had lost their young Vermonters to an unkind God.

"Will you be willing to testify before a Senate committee?"

"Will it bring Porter back?"

"No, but it might just save some other mother or wife from having to go through what you and I have had to."

"Maybe. Give me some time, I'm raw right now."

"Thank you."

Libby drove out and wrote a memo to herself as she entered the highway south toward Manchester: *Call Horizon Mental Health and make sure they are there the day Mrs. Hughes testifies.*

She drove to her next meeting with an irritable feeling toward insurance companies, HMOs and especially Jackie Burns. Jen had been spending nights at the dump that Burns was renting in the Colonial. Libby was beginning to let the stress of trying to control a mentally ill adult get to her. She knew all the clichés she had learned in therapy weren't working at the moment, and she figured it was time to get back in therapy on a weekly basis herself. She pulled to the side of the road, got out, and stretched, then uncapped a bottle of Poland Springs and hesitantly took a pill. For now, she thought to herself, a percocet would have to suffice.

Chapter 49

"**I NEVER MUCH MADE** a go of the business after that day, Mr. Wilson. In fact, within six months I stopped all the routes and retired."

Peter Wilson had found the owner of the former People's Bus Lines in a small but well-maintained colonial home on a side street in old Bennington. Paul Martin was in his seventies and had the look of a man who enjoyed a daily round of golf and an afternoon cocktail at the club. He had a charming manner and clearly wanted to help in any way he could.

"Your phone call really caught me off guard. It's been a time since I've spoken about that day to anyone except my son. You know, he always blamed himself for Billy's being missing."

"They were good friends as I remember."

"Roommates for two years at Williams."

"Can you think back to that day and remember anything we might have missed?"

"Between my insurance company and the FBI, I'm sure we covered everything."

"Did Billy ever seem afraid of anything? Did he seem particularly nervous that day?"

"He didn't have a nervous bone in his body. Did you ever see him race?"

"No, I really didn't know him at all."

"My son and I used to follow the ski team to meets. Billy would attack the downhill like a pro. He had confidence. He was steady, never panicked. That's the reason I gave him the job in the first place. He never bitched about the weather, or the hours, and he was a courteous kid. The customers loved him, especially the regulars."

"Did you have a lot of regulars in those days?"

"Oh God, yes. They were a big part of our business."

"Was Billy friendly with any of them?"

"Hard to say. I never really knew if he had any contact with them outside the bus. The FBI asked me that same question."

"Were there any particular people that rode the bus to Warrens Mills on a regular basis?"

"There was one guy from Boston I told the FBI about. He was like clockwork every week. He came to see his daughter who was working in real estate at that office near the town hall. He always wore a suit and tie and tipped very well. Talk your ears off if you let him."

"Remember his name?"

"Not really, but the daughter still might be working over in your neck of the woods. She was a real knockout."

Wilson tried to remember who worked real estate in those days, but he remembered mostly men. He made a note to speak to Jonathan Poole who had recently retired and sold out to a Brattleboro firm.

"Did you see Billy's remains, Mr. Wilson?"

"No, I wasn't in town when they found the body. Why do you ask?"

"It's hard to believe it's over after all these years. I guess I never thought it would be."

"Tell you the truth, Mr. Martin, I think it's just beginning."

Chapter 50

THE SOUND EMANATING from the studio was pleasant to the ear. The voice was rich yet gentle, and Rooney couldn't place it until he saw the performer. She was a striking black woman whose twelve-string guitar seemed dwarfed by her rotund presence. Brian had seen her picture in countless photos of demonstrations along with Jackson, Farmer, and other leaders of the civil rights movement. Rooney recalled that her picture had been taken by an AP photographer as she lay on the ground being kicked by a small town deputy, his face not visible, just the American flag stitched on his shoulder. Her song told the pain of long-suffering black women, but her gold jewelry spoke louder than her history.

"Oh freedom. Oh, oh freedom over me." The studio resonated with her voice. Rooney listened for ten minutes as she completed two songs then took a break. As McGowan walked out of the sound booth, Rooney was surprised to hear the woman's voice. "You got a man here who reeks of cop Bradley."

Rooney laughed.

"It isn't nothin' personal officer. I'm just not too big on white cops."

"You sounded wonderful. You sang that same song twenty years ago at the Fourth of July celebration in Boston."

"Jesus, Brad, a cop with a memory. You better watch out for this man." She laughed through gleaming white teeth.

McGowan wasn't amused by the singer's remark.

"Can we talk in my office, Detective?" As they walked back along the corridor of pictures and album covers, Rooney could hear the licorice-skinned woman as she started her next song.

"She's good."

"Bread and butter for us, Detective. She's never been with any other label." McGowan sat behind his desk. Rooney took a comfortable captain's chair from the small conference table and faced it directly toward of McGowan.

"Did you enjoy your holiday in Lynn? I hear the fireworks were spectacular."

"I can't believe that bitch told you we were there."

"What were you doing at a museum in Salem the day before your business partner was killed?"

"Discussing what I hoped was going to be a buyout of Johnny's share of the business."

"With him drunk?"

"Believe it or not, Detective, he called me two days before and said to meet him that day. The strange part of it was that for the first time in years he sounded sober and actually agreed to a buyout."

"Why bring Ms. Ansalone?"

McGowan sat quietly for a minute then spoke hesitantly, "She was going to finance the buyout."

"What did Mr. Carrier think of her money coming into his studio?"

"He didn't know. I figured I would deal with that later."

Rooney took notes and wrote very slowly, allowing McGowan to stew a bit.

"What did your wife think of your relationship with Ms. Ansalone?"

"My wife was fine with it."

"You don't mind me asking her then?"

"She's got nothing to do with this. Leave her out of it."

"That's not possible, but the business between you and Ansalone is up to you to work out with your family. I'm not in the habit of screwing up marriages." *Except maybe my own, Rooney thought.*

"Are you willing to take a lie detector test about your activities with Dwyer?"

"No, I'm not. I don't believe in them."

"That's funny."

"What's funny?"

"Ms. Ansalone seems to have no problem taking one."

Chapter 51

THE LAST TIME that Peter Wilson had been in the small lecture hall was the day that he'd met Ben Latimer for the first time. It was snowing that day. He was twenty pounds lighter then. His hair had been full. He had also been in the middle of a full-blown sexual affair with the widow of a man, who, a short time before, had taken his own life. The long-time web of deceit that followed him seemed easier to live with. The first lie had compounded and multiplied like laundered money. *You're as sick as your secrets, Pete.* The blackboard in the lecture hall was divided into segments. Ben and Wilson drew a timeline of that December day, and next to it, they drew a rough map of the Warrens Mills / Marlboro area.

"Three weeks? We can't get the results back for three weeks?" Ben Latimer was agitated that the Waterbury forensic lab said there would be no results of the evidence from the crime scene until their vacationing employees came back.

Wilson knew this crime would not take precedence over current work at the lab. One of the reasons he liked working alone was the fact that years of investigate work had taught him patience.

"We work with what we have in front of us Ben."

"Sorry."

"Let's look at how many people were probably involved and start from there."

"At least two."

"Why?" Wilson felt he had to question each assumption.

"The first person had to kill the power. They couldn't have done that at eleven in Warrens Mills, then got to Marlboro in time to stop the bus, could they?"

"I doubt it."

"They were men," Ben said.

"Why do you think so?"

"The electric power thing just seems like a man thing. Plus, the witness from Connecticut says they thought they saw someone in a workman's outfit at the pole that morning." Wilson picked up the yellowed case file and showed Ben the section that showed the witness' statement he had taken in 1963.

"Consider that it was snowing to beat the band, and the statement from the witness says the person they saw had a long canvas coat and a ski mask on, but seemed to be of an average height and weight. So let's not rule out a woman at this point."

"What about the trench at the lot at High Mowing? That seems to be more like something that a man might plan."

"I think you're right, unless there were two people involved."

"Who owned the lot in '63?"

Wilson pulled a copy of the town clerk's title search from the assembled paperwork and files.

"The title was conveyed from Green Mountain Trust to a family named Rougere."

"Has anyone spoken to them?"

"Basically it's him, not them. The house was a gift to Father Rougere. He was the priest at Our Lady of the Mountains. He's retired and lives in a home for clergy in Greenfield. He has no family left, and I don't see him as fitting our suspect's profile. Weldon's gonna talk to him."

"So you think this house was randomly chosen to bury the evidence?"

"I don't know, but considering how isolated the area was before it was developed by Ansalone, it wouldn't surprise me at all."

"What else was around there in '63, any neighbors?"

"Nothing within a half mile."

"Was it plowed?"

"Up to where the town road ended. I think it's safe to say our killer had weight in his vehicle and probably chains on."

"Killer," stuck in Ben's head. He sat and put his head in his hands.

"How did you deal with this kind of stuff all those years?" Ben's voice trailed off and he put his hand up to his mouth.

"Not too good, buddy, just enough to get by and grab a pension."

Ben took a step, then grabbed a metal wastebasket and vomited. "A lot of times, I puked."

Wilson closed the files and stared at Ben for a minute. A student walked in, looked at the two men, turned and walked out.

"Ben, you're a teacher not a cop. You're too close to help right now. If this bastard's alive, I'll find him."

Ben didn't speak, just sat and buried his head.

Wilson got to the door and turned, "Ben, go home, take time off, and then deal with this however you can."

Chapter 52

*T*HWACK, THWACK, THWACK.

Rooney could hear the sound, but was clueless as to its source. He walked behind the rambling mountaintop contemporary, drinking a diet Coke and wishing he could go back to Meggy's and spend the afternoon. The morning had started with them showering together and making love. She seemed relaxed and happy, but after coffee, she seemed detached, so he got dressed and left while she stretched for her morning run.

He could make out the sound even clearer in the mountain stillness.

Thwack, thwack.

He followed the sound down a short path and came to a twelve-foot windscreened fence and the source of the mysterious *thwack*.

A blond, tanned beauty dressed in a T-shirt, tennis shorts, and an old pair of Adidas tennis shoes was taking strokes at the arching yellow tennis ball as it landed near the baseline of a red-clay tennis court. She was taking the ball as it began its bounce and making shots crosscourt to a set of tennis ball containers that were placed at various intervals. She shut down the ball machine when she saw him approach and laid her racket on the table where Rooney had seated himself.

"Regina McGowan. Brad said you might be coming by. Can I get you another Coke or an iced tea?"

She shook his hand with the authority of a weightlifter. Rooney handed her a card.

"Brian Rooney, thanks for seeing me on such short notice."

As he spoke, a ball bounced off the back of his head and landed on the table spilling his drink. He turned and saw a four- or five-year-old child of oriental extraction getting ready to line up another shot at his head with an obviously modified tennis racket. Regina grabbed the racket and calmly told the child to sit. The child looked like an angry dog.

"I'm sorry, she can be a little hard to control sometimes, especially around strangers."

"No problem."

Rooney wiped at the spill with a tennis towel she'd pulled from a bag at her feet. "She's from an orphanage in Byelorussia. We adopted her last year, and sometimes I'm afraid we made a mistake." When she spoke, she moved closer to him and spoke softly.

"I'm sure that adoption is hard. I admire you and your husband for having the courage to—"

She shut him off in mid-sentence. "My husband wouldn't go across the street for a child. I went myself."

Rooney sipped a fresh Coke and pulled his notebook from his blazer. "How well did you know Johnny Dwyer?"

"Hardly at all, but enough to realize that he was screwing up the company and Brad wanted him out."

"Did you socialize?"

She twirled her racket around in her hand as she answered, "Never. Even if we wanted to, its was impossible. You never knew if he would show up drunk or sober, and in this town, it's hard enough making friends."

"You knew your husband was borrowing money to buy him out?"

"Yes."

She twirled the racket faster, then held it in both hands like a club, and put it close to Rooney's face. Before speaking, she looked over at the now quiet child and spoke softly. "Detective, I know my husband has been fucking that woman for a long time. I'm not an idiot." Her face reddened as she spoke, but she still looked like a fashion model. Sweat broke through her shirtfront, accentuating her breasts and the nipples that stood out through her sports bra.

"I didn't mean to say that you were, and to tell you the truth, I think your husband is nuts to fool around with her." *Rooney, get out of here or you'll be asking her out.*

"Thanks. Look, Detective, I don't have a clue about who might have killed Dwyer. I just know that we have a great chance to sell out, and when we do, I'm gone. He can have that hawk-nosed bitch and all her property."

"What do you know aboutCed Lyman Carrier?"

"Saint Lyman, 'the Savior of Vermont'? Not a lot. We socialize occasionally at studio functions, but to tell you the truth, I don't know much about him except that without Dwyer's stock, he can't block us from selling."

"Can you think why anybody would hate him?"

"You mean the deal with his office. No, but his and Starks' purity regulations pissed off a lot of serious money."

"How?"

"There were a couple of companies that had large shares of the maple syrup business that were using Canadian producers."

"Anybody local that might have any reason to dislike him?"

"There were a few small business types who he may have hurt, but I don't honestly know."

"Do he and Brad get along?"

"Yes, except for the one issue of selling the company."

"Would Brad kill to get his own way?'

"Ten years ago I would have slapped your face for asking that question, but since he's become involved with her, I don't even know him anymore. Isn't that sad? I sit up here and look at the world, play tennis to keep my sanity, and I don't even care if my husband's a killer."

Rooney put down the notebook and stared at the mountains.

"Go home to your woman if you have one, Detective; otherwise, I might make a fool of myself."

She packed the tennis racket into the red oversized duffel, threw it over her shoulder, then bent and picked up the now sleeping child and walked into the house. Rooney watched as she walked away, then picked up her still-moist drinking glass and carefully carried it to the car.

Chapter 53

"Weldon got no business asking him to get involved. Where'd you get that shit anyway?"

"He's helping Pork. That's all I know."

Porky Atkins had indigestion. News that former trooper Peter Wilson was conducting an investigation into the murder of Billy Latimer was adding, by the minute, tiny stomach acids into his already-beleaguered and bloated digestive system.

"I want to know what the hell he's doing, and who he's talking to."

"Why don't you ask him, Pork?"

"Up your ass, Henderson. Just do as I tell you."

They were driving north along Route 100, headed for Snow Mountain to meet with Vermont State Police and Federal Secret Service agents. Porky was eating a breakfast cake, the frosting sticking to his hands and the seat of the cruiser. Porky read the document issued as standard policy from the Secret Service to local police when the president or vice president or their families were going to be in the area.

"We're gonna need everybody working. Shit, we're gonna have to control traffic and a bunch of other stuff."

"I wouldn't sweat it, Pork. The state boys will be all over this like a new suit." They drove up a winding hill toward a large Adirondack-style hotel that housed some three hundred rooms and had just recently opened to mixed reviews by the locals.

"You remember what this was?"

"Shit, no, Pork. I ain't as old as you."

"It was a farm, sat up on the hillside, pretty as a picture."

"Did you know the people?"

"Friends of my folks, they raised sheep and pigs. When they slaughtered, we used to come up and trade for meat with the old man."

"It's always been just Snow Mountain to me. We used to ski for nothing on Wednesdays when I was in school."

"I never figured you were a skier, Henderson."

"Mostly I played soccer, I don't ski anymore, can't afford it."

They parked next to a small fleet of state police vehicles. Porky wiped the frosting on his pants.

"Jesus, Pork, use a napkin." Henderson handed the chief a napkin from the pastry bag, but Porky continued to wipe the frosting on the bottom of his pants.

"Gotta take a leak; I'll see you inside."

Henderson watched as the police chief of Warrens Mills urinated on the grass next to a chairlift that abutted the hotel. When he finished, he zipped up with some effort and with a grin said, "Some days I just like to piss all over these bastards."

Chapter 54

"MOVING TO WHERE?"

"Jackie and I are thinking of moving to the Northeast Kingdom."

"Jackie who?"

"For Christ's sake, Mom, don't treat me like I'm fifteen. I've got to get the hell out of this town. I can't do anything or go anywhere that people don't compare me to you." The argument with her daughter had been raging all morning, and Libby was feeling the urge to strangle her. It was clear to Libby that Jen had slipped on her medication regimen and was beginning the slide.

"What does Dr. Barront think about you being involved with a loser like Burns, or have you even said anything to her?"

Jen sat in the restored summer home smoking a cigarette and drinking her third cup of coffee. She had been up most of the night and looked disheveled and older than her years. The smell of marijuana clung to her clothes.

Libby Stark tried to remain calm in the wake of her daughter's revelation. "How would you support yourself if you moved North; are you planning to live on his disability check?"

"Fuck you, Mother. I can get a job up there, and Jackie's got his music."

Libby sat back in a wooden captain's chair and laughed. "Forgive me Jen, but do you want to talk about the last time you struck out on your own, or how about the time before when you and the playwright moved to Provincetown? Why don't we talk about how I felt bailing you out of that hellhole you were living in?"

Libby picked up two bottles of pills that were standing on the wet sink. She removed the childproof plastic lid from one bottle and held a pill out to her daughter.

"Let's talk about your herpes; does your new lover know you live on medication to keep the virus in check? You are an ungrateful little shit who always waits for me to pick up your trash after you're finished playing games with people, and I'm sick of it. I'm sick of the Retreat and McLean's. I'm sick of not knowing where the hell you are half the time. I'm sick of the phone calls in the middle of the night. I'm sick to death of shrinks and social workers working their ass off so you and Jackie fucking Burns can move to the Northeast Kingdom and start making the doctors there work overtime."

Jen Stark stood up and grabbed the pills from her mother. She threw the bottles across the kitchen and blue and white capsules flew everywhere. Her rage filled the room and Libby backed off.

"You're a fucking whore; don't you think I don't know about you and Dwyer? Don't you think I know you were screwing Wilson just after my father killed himself, you selfish bitch? And I don't know what's with that weirdo Carrier, but I'm sure you're using him to get what you want. Ever since I can remember that creep has been calling here and you talk secretly for hours about who knows what."

"You don't have any idea what goes on in my life, Jen, and you have no goddam right to judge me."

"Then you get this straight, bitch. I'm not sick and I don't need the goddam medication." Jen grabbed her car keys from the kitchen table and walked out, slamming the screen door. Libby listened to her car start, and feeling once again she had screwed up, the headache aura began—first, the brightness and the squiggly white dots. While she could function, she grabbed her medication, swallowed, and then cried and cried and cried.

Chapter 55

September 1997
Bennington, Vermont

SPIDERS RAN DOWN her back, stopping just as they reached her panty line. The back of her neck and her shoulder had a coiled snake angrily looking at her listeners, daring them to question her serenity.

The tattooed speaker represented a colorful but unwanted break in Peter Wilson's day. She sat just in front of him at the noon AA meeting on the third floor of Bennington's Baptist Church. Wilson fidgeted in his metal seat and tried to pay attention as she spoke. The crowded meeting was Indian John's idea.

"You feel like drinking, Peter cop?"

"No, I just can't stand all the God stuff; besides, I've got things to do and driving here is a pain in the ass. Don't call me a cop in here, John; I'm sure that at least one of these people has walked in front of a judge because of me." Wilson kept looking over his shoulder, unable to relax.

"You want to drink, Pete?"

"No, I don't want to drink. I've been busy with this old case and haven't had time to get to a meeting."

"When did you drink, Peter?"

"Yesterday."

"Keep going to meetings, Peter, and it will eventually get you. Maybe you should drive up to East Dorset and talk to another Wilson who's buried there."

"That's all?" Wilson thought his counselor was putting him on for a second.

"That's all. Just stand at his grave, maybe tell him you would like to stop drinking."

"Maybe I will, John, but I'm too busy today."

"You're always too busy, Peter."

Wilson stood with the others and held hands to say the Serenity Prayer. When it was time to leave, a sixteen-year-old well-dressed girl with deep blue eyes and short red hair spoke to him as if she knew him.

"Thanks again for the quarter, mister"

"Do I know you?"

"The day I got to Oak Hill, you gave me a quarter to call my boyfriend to get a ride out of the place. Then you told me to give it a couple of days. I just got out. Thanks again."

He left the church hall feeling good. He stopped at a grocery store, looked at the beer display for a second, then, instead, bought a can of Coke.

He drove and tried at the same time to read his old case notes. When he almost hit a side rail, he pulled the Jeep over to a roadside rest area. The view overlooked two hundred miles of multi-colored forest that eventually would wander into Massachusetts. He sorted through piece after piece of notepaper until he found the first report with the December 27, 1963, date in the corner.

The bus had been reported to be at the scout camp by a neighbor who thought it odd that people were making stops on this semi-deserted stretch of back road. He had always assumed the bus was dumped after having been wiped clean. He sketched from memory that section of highway leading to Brattleboro and drew arrows to mark possible points where the bus might have been stopped. He thought about the weather on that day. *Could the driver have purposely stopped at the camp? Was it plowed? Was he meeting someone? Who had keys to the camp?*

He drove carefully out of the rest area and fell into the long line of leaf peepers making their way across to Warrens Mills or Brattleboro, seeking shelter in the overcrowded motels and inns that lined the highways of Southern Vermont. Those who were shut out headed back from their trip with Vermont trinkets and syrup packed in their trunks, and the promise to make early reservations for next year.

"What was the kid thinking that day? Why the hell would he stop so far off the highway? Did he know his killers?"

He pulled into the parking lot of the sealed-up camp that now belonged to a church group from Massachusetts. They used it for retreats and summer camping for city kids. He read the dedication plaque that adorned the chapel; it was dedicated in 1964. Wilson walked the grounds as if waiting for some past clue to magically appear. Instead a blue pick-up appeared and a man in his seventies or maybe even older got out and confronted him.

"What you doing here mister? This is private, can't you read the sign?"

"I'm trying to help the police with an old case." Wilson looked at the case file and surprised the man.

"You're Ed Haven, aren't you?"

"I was when I got up today. Do I know you?"

"Remember the trooper who interviewed you the day they found the bus in here?"

"You were a lot younger and had a lot more hair. What the hell are you doing here now?"

Wilson explained that he was just trying to recall that day thirty years before. The old man and he walked and talked about the camp.

Haven explained some of the changes over the years. "Now it's blacks mostly, scared of the woods and the animals when they get here, but you see them change after a week or two. Pretty good kids when you get to know them. Some of the ones that come at the end of the summer are sick; they got AIDS, and the place changes. Doctors and nurses come with them from Boston. It's like a regular little hospital."

Wilson hardly paid attention to the old man. As they talked, he kept reading the old file.

"Tell me something, Ed, do you remember if you plowed in here the winter the bus got dropped off?

"It's funny you ask, 'cause that was the only winter I ever did plow."

"How come?"

"The only reason I plowed was so them real estate people could get in here to show the place."

"What real estate people?"

"Company from Warrens Mills, don't remember the name. Shit, Trooper, I'm lucky to remember my own name some days."

"Ed, this may sound funny, but how come you never told us that the place was for sale thirty years ago?"

"You never asked, and besides, you were a nasty bastard. I felt like maybe you thought I had something to do with the robbery."

Wilson sat on a picnic bench and read the interview from 1963 and couldn't believe his own notes. Nowhere had the caretaker been asked about the plowing.

"I'll bet you only plowed once a day."

"Seven in the morning, and then I went to work at the Retreat Hospital. I've been there for thirty years."

Wilson realized that at 4:00 PM, when they found the car, there was no sign of plowing. *Of course not, Pete, there was half a foot of new snow on the ground; so we assumed that the camp had been closed up. We were in too much of a rush to nail Billy Latimer.*

Chapter 56

September 1997
Salem, Massachusetts

PROJECTILE VOMITING SENT Mickey Furtado to his knees. Retching and flushed, his mouth tasting of bile, he hugged the dirt-encrusted toilet bowl that sat in the corner of his tiny room at the Salem mission. An empty bottle of vanilla extract and a quart of orange juice sat next to the carton of cigarettes on the cluttered nightstand. Brian Rooney stood looking uncomfortable next to the urine-stained cot.

"Washington. I'm finding it hard to believe I left Vermont to watch this guy puke"

"Good part's coming now, Brian"

"I can hardly wait. What's he do next, shit himself?

"Just hang on a second and you can watch the miracle of alcohol at work."

Furtado slumped over the bowl his face covered with sweat, and his nose dripping vomit. Washington handed him a yellow-labeled pint of Caldwell's Vodka.

"Oh Christ, Paul, you're not giving him another drink?"

"Show time, Brian. Just bear with me for a second."

Furtado drank a third of the clear liquid, then paused, nodded his head to Washington. "Thanks, Paulie."

"Tell my friend here about Fourth of July weekend, Mickey." Rooney watched as the man sat back and smiled, eager to talk.

"The guy Paulie asked me about, the guy who got popped at the detox, he was in the Wharf Bar about four thirty in the afternoon." He stopped and drank slowly from the bottle.

"How do you know it was him?" Rooney was skeptical. *I could be lying in bed with Meggy right now.*

"The son of a bitch took the place over, bought rounds, then sat on a stool and sang chanteys and Irish songs. Big voice, easy to listen to, it was the guy; I'm sure of that."

"Was he with anybody?"

"Tall guy and a good-looking woman, that's why I called Paulie."

"What's why?"

"The tall guy and this singer got into a screaming match and the broad was just as bad. She kept calling him all sorts of shit and the tall guy shoved him into the jukebox. The bartender shut 'em off and they left, but the singer stayed, then took a cab to the hospital. I think he did anyway, but I'm not sure"

"Can you describe the woman any better?

"Guinea or Greek, flashy bracelets, nice tits, nice clothes. She had a mouth like a longshoreman. I wouldn't mess with her, the kind of chick that could cut your nuts off."

Rooney was taking notes furiously as the man spoke. "Could you identify her from some photos?"

"Maybe, but I'm feeling like shit right now."

"Are you willing to go to detox when we're ready for you to take a look at this woman?

"Someplace nice, not the city shit hole."

"I'll put you up at Oak Hill. How's that, Mickey?

Washington produced another bottle of vodka as he spoke and put it on the table.

"Ya, Paulie. I like the Hill, food's good. Who knows? Maybe I can get it this time."

Rooney and Washington walked out of the room and sat in the empty television lounge at the Salem Seaman's Bethel.

"Thanks, Paul. How did you find this guy?

"I knew him when he still had a job. He's a bright guy, but he can't stop drinking right now."

"He looks familiar as hell."

"He should. He used to be the superintendent of schools in Gloucester. Dr. Michael Furtado."

"What happened to him?

"Like he says, one day he took drunk and never came back."

Chapter 57

September 1997
Bennington, Vermont

THE CLUB HIT the top of the ball and it skidded twenty feet, landing in the woods to the right of the tee.

"Look what you did to my shot, Pete."

"Take up bowling, Jonathan; you'll have a better chance of not hurting yourself or someone else."

"Your ass, this is why I retired." Jonathan Poole bent and put another ball on his tee. "How about these clubs, Pete, titanium. Remember when we used to have those wooden shafted poles and played in bare feet?" Poole hit another shot, this time straight up in the air and thirty yards out.

"You never could play golf."

Wilson and Poole had known each other since grammar school. They grew up in the shadow of the Bennington Battle monument, and for the most part had never lived more than a hundred miles from it.

"Did you ever think we would both be living alone again, Pete?"

"No, I figured, somehow, that life worked out; but I didn't figure the curveballs."

"How pissed is Carol Ann?"

"Very, but I don't think it's just the Libby Stark thing. I think she's just reacting to being a cop's wife and I don't blame her."

Later that afternoon, the two old friends sat and talked at Poole's house and office.

"Tell me about a piece of property that you had listed in the sixties."

"You mean the property where you found the abandoned bus in Marlboro?"

"Yeah. I talked to the caretaker and he said he only plowed the year you sold the property." Wilson opened his notebook as he began to speak.

Poole walked to his mini bar fridge and opened a beer for himself and a Coke for Wilson. "We kept a rotating staff out there."

"Who was out there the most?

"Guy named Bill Hamilton, then me, and occasionally Ellen Ansalone."

"Ansalone worked for you?" Wilson appeared surprised.

"She worked for me when she moved into the valley. She was damn good."

"Did you ever know her father?

"Shit yeah. Old Chicky was a character straight out of the movies. He used to take the bus up from Massachusetts, and then the People's Bus Line to our office on Fridays to see Ellen."

"You think she got the money for her development from him?"

"I always thought she did. Why?"

"Just trying to tie up loose ends on that case, and she always seems to be in the picture. Any other staff to speak of?"

"No, not really. Part time secretary and myself," replied Poole.

As he started to ask another question Wilson's cell phone rang and Trooper Weldon's voice at the other end said, "You sitting down, Pete? The lab reports just got faxed from Waterbury, and the body that was found on Ansalone's property wasn't the Latimer kid."

Chapter 58

"Where the hell is the Latimer kid?"

"We know where he isn't, that's for damn sure, Pork."

The Warrens Mills Police Department conference room was littered with stale coffee cups and pastry wrappers. The officers surrounding the table had been meeting since 6:00 AM, and it was clear that there was more confusion than clarity in the caffeine-charged room.

"I still don't see why the hell that Pete has to be involved in this anyway. Ain't you got enough help sitting on their ass in Montpelier? God knows he frigged up the first time around, so what the hell good is he going to do us this time?"

Wilson had been silent for most of the meeting, sipping coffee and listening as Weldon laid out the forensic report for Warrens Mills police and members of the county sheriff's department.

Weldon started to answer Porky's retort when Wilson stopped him midsentence. "Porky, let's get something straight. You're pissed off at me for something that happened years ago. You know damn well that I had to take you to Redstone. You know goddamn well I had to take your sister. You were the last two people to see this driver alive. The only other person was Lionel Howard at the Marlboro post office and you know I took him for a polygraph. It wasn't personal, Pork. It was all we had at the time." Atkins chewed slowly on a jelly donut and then sat back from the table.

"You got no business being involved now."

"He's involved, Pork, that's all there is to it," Weldon spoke firmly to the red-faced police chief. "Peter, give us what you got so far."

As Weldon spoke, Porky Atkins pushed back from the table and walked out of the room. The others watched as he walked back to his own office and slammed the door.

Wilson had two files in front of him and opened the smaller of the two. "The person who fits the skeletal profile could be a ski bum who was here in the valley in the early sixties. His name was Tommy Birdsong, and he had a string of arrests out of state. Before moving here, he was dishonorably discharged from the army for assaulting a superior officer, and his juvenile record has the usual profile of assault, breaking and entering, and car theft. He has not been heard from since 1963."

"How the hell did you come up with that file, Pete?" asked Weldon.

"I had a call from the Pima Arizona sheriff in 1965. It seems that nobody on the reservation ever heard from this guy again. They had traced him to Vermont and wanted to reach him to tell him about his mother's death. I hadn't really thought of it until this all came up."

"How long had this guy been in town before the robbery?"

"Eight months, maybe ten, but no more than that. I arrested him for assault in July of that year. It's funny how you remember incidents. This guy wore glasses and was maybe five feet eight inches, but he had a punch like a sledge."

"Who did he assault?" Ward Kinkle spoke for the first time.

"He punched the shit out of Flip Morton and a biker from Greenfield. They were a mess by the time I got there."

"Did Morton start it?"

"I'm sure he did, but since I didn't know this guy, I figured I'd run him anyway. It turns out he had about twenty-seven amateur fights out West. I spoke to a deputy on the Pima Maricopa reservation who knew him and said he was basically a quick-tempered kid who hated to be hassled. He and I never had another run-in, but I kept hearing his name anytime there was a brawl."

"Whom did he work for in the valley, Pete? Anybody that might remember him or know what might have happened to him?"

"The last place he worked was the cave. He was the bouncer or doorman or whatever else Dwyer wanted him to be."

"Pete, why don't you check him out further to see if anybody remembers anything unusual or any reason he might have skipped town in a hurry. In the meantime there is a ton of evidence from the cesspool site to look at." Weldon produced a report from the state forensic lab and passed around copies.

"We have positive identification of Latimer with the wallet and belt as well as his watch. The glasses that we found probably belonged to Birdsong, if in fact it's his remains. What might help is the ring that was found. It's initialed, and it looks like it also belonged to Latimer. WJL and EA 1963 was engraved inside the tiny silver band.

"Did the Latimer kid have a serious girlfriend, Pete?"

"Ben has never mentioned that he did, but I'll go back over it with him."

"If we can find out who EA is maybe we can put the pieces together."

"I'll start nosing around to see how many people in town had those initials. In the meantime, I need to find out more about the sale of the camp property and who might have been out there the day this all happened."

Weldon made notes in his notebook and then spoke with a grin, "Pete, what if Porky was right all along and Latimer killed Birdsong and took off with the money?"

"I just don't believe the kid was capable of it. I think somebody local put it together."

"You want to tell the brother about the body not being Billy or you want me to call?"

"No, Frank, I want to talk to him anyway, and I might as well bring him more bad news. It seems to be all I have ever brought him."

Chapter 59

At four fifteen in the afternoon after their first argument, Brian was trying to get Megan's clothes off. She had been angry with Rooney since his flip remark that morning, and Rooney was feeling horny and guilty since his encounter with Regina McGowan earlier in the day.

"It's not gonna happen, Brian."

"Why?"

"It just can't be about sex."

"Can't we talk later?" Rooney knew this was a no-win. He sat up in the king-size bed and watched as Megan reached over to his side of the bed and opened his notebook. "What are you doing?"

She read from his notes taken at Oak Hill. Rooney listened as she read the notation about Megan still being a possible suspect.

"Jesus Christ, Brian, you still have me lumped in with these people as a suspect?"

"Of course I don't."

She opened the notebook and showed him the notation.

"That's not what it seems to be; it's just the way I take case notes."

She took his hand and held it. "Do you have any idea what I'm going through right now? Do you have any idea what it is like to watch you talk to people about my brother like he was a statistic?"

Rooney tried to pull her closer.

"No, no, no. Don't try to hold me and make it better."

"Investigating your brother's death is my job."

"I'm really having a hard time imagining someone wanting Johnny dead." Her face paled as she spoke. "Brian, he was my big brother. He took me to beaches, he kept the bullies away, and he made me laugh more than anybody else could. Johnny was all I had after my parents were killed. Sometimes he used to sleep off his drunks on my couch. I would watch him for hours. Even drunk, I knew he would be there for me and now he's gone. I feel alone and afraid."

He had never seen anyone sob so intensely, almost losing her breath as the racking sounds of grief filled the bedroom.

"Do you want me to call Nelson for you?"

"No. I just want you to be here for me right now."

The last time someone had said these words, Brian Rooney had made every excuse he could to leave. It was on the night of his wife's miscarriage. He pled an ongoing investigation as the reason for walking out. Less than one month later, she told him their marriage was over and she was returning to Nantucket.

"I don't know how to help you, Meggy."

"Have you ever dealt with a rape victim, Brian?"

"Yes."

"Do you walk away from them and say you don't know what to do?"

"No, of course, it's just that I—"

"Shut up and listen," she screamed at him, grabbed his face in her hands, and turned it roughly toward her. "I feel like a rape victim. I've lost all the good things, all the little joys, all the stuff that families get as part of life. I can't let myself start to care about you without worrying when you're going to walk out. Make up your mind, Rooney, or get out of my life, because I can't take another emotional beating, not now."

Rooney stood up as if to leave. Megan watched as he walked to the bureau and picked up his wallet. He took a picture from an inside compartment, walked to the bed and put it in her hand.

"That's my father; he bakes the best donuts on Nantucket. I think your gonna like him."

Chapter 60

"**WORM, WORM, WORM.** You are a worm, McGowan. I can't believe you're letting some small-town cop scare the shit of you. He's got nothing on either one of us, and I never said I'd take a polygraph. So stop being an asshole and make sure that we can get Carrier out of the picture and sell the goddam studio." Ellen Ansalone blew Marlboro smoke at the phone as she ranted.

Brad McGowan listened fretfully as Ellen screamed at him through the phone.

"Ellen, this guy thinks we were somehow involved in Johnny's murder. Christ, he's talked to Regina and got her all pissed off at me. I'm not sure that we should go ahead. What if anybody finds out what's going on?"

"You dumb hayseed. Just shut the fuck up and make sure this deal happens. I'm too far invested now to pull out because off that stupid Irish drunk getting whacked."

Chapter 61

PETER WILSON WAS slowly making his way around the lake. His size twelves were taking a beating as he turned the corner from the wooded lakeside trail and headed on to the dirt stretch that led to his parents' cottage. He dreaded making the inevitable call to Ben Latimer, and yet he knew he would have to eventually. He was finding a rhythm with his daily running and he found himself having to walk only a short part of the two-and-a-half-mile loop around the lake. For just a few minutes every day, he could forget Carol Ann and forget Billy Latimer's death. Somewhere in the back of his mind, he was finding a calm place. Sometimes it was as simple as sitting at the end of his run with a cup of coffee and watching the lake.

Lately, he found himself wanting to spend more time in his father's old boat with the five-horse *Evinrude,* trolling a bass lure behind him and cruising at a snail's pace on the tiny sandy-bottomed pond.

He walked onto the front porch, saw his favorite rocker and thought how good a beer would taste. He picked up the old rotary phone and dialed Ben's number.

His stomach churned from the black coffee and the anticipation of laying more bad news on the already bruised professor.

"Hello, Pete, what's up?"

Wilson hesitated and said, "Ben, the skeletal remains aren't your brother's."

"What do you mean? Of course, they are his. You saw the watch and the buckle."

"The bones were those of a forty-or-so-year-old man with a busted nose and some other physical characteristics that lead us to think they're remains are of a drifter who lived here for a short time in the sixties. This guy could have been involved in your brother's disappearance, but that's all I know for now."

"Was this guy involved with a gang?" Ben sounded desperate for an explanation.

"I doubt it. Ben, can you remember Billy ever buying an engagement ring?"

"Of course not. I don't even remember him talking about going out with anybody. Why do you ask, Pete?"

"They found a ring in the trench with his initials and the initials EA. Have you got any idea who those initials might belong to?"

"No, I don't remember anyone with those initials, but it was a long time ago, and besides what has a ring got to do with the robbery?"

"We don't know, and maybe we're way off, but maybe the grin on your brother's face that day was because he was going to ask someone to marry him."

"That's crazy, he would have told me."

"Maybe he was going to surprise you Ben, or maybe it had to be kept a secret. I don't know the answer. Do me a favor, Ben, go through his stuff one more time and see if there is anything that might connect to those initials."

"All right, Pete. I'll call you if I find anything."

"Thanks, Ben."

Wilson spent the morning cataloging his information and comparing it to old cases. There seemed to be no pattern to Latimer's disappearance.

The whole town knew the money was transferred on Mondays, but only a local would know that there was no immediate backup for the resident trooper. Whoever pulled the power box shut and smashed the cover plate must have known that the Green MT power crews didn't work on snowy days. Someone local knew that the Boy Scout camp was plowed. Someone found a way to have the driver turn off at the camp road. How? How did Birdsong get involved? Could Ansalone's old man have set it up with her help?

Wilson thrived on self-questioning. He looked at his old case files and took comfort in his methodology. Ask the questions and answers until it makes sense, then ask it again. The technique came from a master sergeant he had served under in the military police. Follow the evidence. "If it looks like a mule, it's a mule you dumb bastard, it ain't a zebra."

The knock on the screen door caught Wilson off guard, and he jumped to answer the door. Immediately he knew they were federal agents.

"Brian Leary. United States Secret Service; this is Agent Mansey. May we come in and talk for a minute?"

Leary was halfway in the door before Wilson could answer.

"Frank Weldon gave us your name. He thought you might be able to help with our survey of the upcoming visit of the vice president's wife. He said that you knew one of the recipients of the award fairly well."

"Senator Stark?"

"Right, it seems that you have information that points to her being involved with a recent homicide victim."

"Look, gentlemen, any information I gathered was while I was riding along with an out-of-state police officer. Anything she said was to him. I'm retired." Wilson got up and poured coffee into a mug. He was feeling uncomfortable being questioned in his own home.

"We are going to speak to Detective Rooney, but Frank thought that you may be able to help us."

"What do need to know?

As they spoke, a deer walked across the road from the woods and began to drink from the lake. Wilson signaled with his hand, and the two dark-suited agents sat quietly as the deer finished drinking. The deer snapped his head toward the cottage as if hearing a sound, and bounded back into the orange and yellow forest that surrounded the lake.

Leary was edgy when he spoke, "What are the chances that Dwyer's murder was politically motivated, and that the upcoming visit of Mrs. Palmer might be used to the advantage of some fringe group?"

"Gentlemen, all I know about Dwyer was that he paid his bills in cash and on time. As far As Libby is concerned, I think she genuinely was trying to help Dwyer stop his drinking and that he charmed her into bed. Dwyer was dirty somewhere in his life, but I doubt that it was anything to do with politics or Libby Stark. The guy was too sloppy and usually too drunk to be involved politically."

"Are you familiar with any radical groups that could be a threat to Mrs. Palmer?"

"In Vermont? The whole state is a radical group. You just pick and choose the cause, and you'll have protesters coming out the windows. As far as violence, I doubt if you have a safer place for her to visit. The majority of radicals here are probably on her side politically and the gun nuts aren't that verbal."

"Is there any chance that you could help us sort out some of the nitwits who might show up at this thing?'

"Look, right now is not a great time for me to be taking on any more stuff," said Wilson.

The agent responded as he picked up a file from a leather briefcase. "Don't be surprised, Mr. Wilson. We know about the booze, and we suspect that you had your own history with the senator. We also know that Frank Weldon went out on a limb to get you involved in a thirty-year-old case and in doing so, he might have ruffled a few feathers with the locals."

"What the hell don't you know?"

The agents smiled. "We don't know how you did the trick with the deer."

Chapter 62

MEGAN DWYER FOUND the pictures inside a Martin guitar case. They were bound by an elastic band in a small flap that her brother used to hold extra picks and his capo. The photos were of a cross-country race she had won in her junior year at UVM. They seemed to have been taken from a distance as if the photographer wanted to shoot without being seen. The background was the Middlebury College cross-country trail.

"Why do you think there is something wrong with these pictures? Probably some friend of Johnny's sent them to him." Rooney was looking through the photos and drinking a beer while Meggy cooked pasta, marinara sauce, and fresh mushrooms at the stove.

"Look at the back of each one."

He flipped the picture in his hand over and looked at the word written boldly in red marker across the back. REMEMBER. He flipped each photo over and the effect was striking. Twenty-four pictures lay like a deck of tarot cards on the table. Each one contained the same block-printed word.

"How did you find these?"

"They were in the guitar that I had picked out to use for lessons. I knew it was his working guitar; the sound is incredible. It's a prewar Double O18. When I went to find a flat pick in the case, these pictures were in the compartment."

"They look like stalker photos. Are you sure that your brother never mentioned anything that might explain these?'

"Never. Brian, what the hell was going on with my brother?"

"Meggy, I would tell you if I knew, but the more I know, the more questions I have."

They sat before the first fire of October and ate pasta. The house echoed with fiddle music from a tape labeled *The Donegal Fiddlers*. The view from the house was magnificent as the change of seasons drew out all the best in Vermont.

"Are you afraid of these pictures?"

"Should I be?"

"Yes. I want to talk to Wilson about being around while I'm in Salem."

"No argument from me."

"Do you want to move back to Boston?"

"No, this is where I live now and that's not going to change. Besides, I think this business was between Johnny and somebody who has no reason to harm me."

They spent the evening watching the fire and making love under a large quilt that Meggy bought at the Artists Guild in Bennington. The phone rang at 10:15.

"We gotta talk, Brian."

"How about 'Hello, how ya doing, Brian,' or 'How's Meggy doing?' Didn't they teach you manners at the academy, Peter?"

"Sorry. Brian, you know how us ex-drunks are."

"It's OK. I was just about to call you."

They met an hour later in Wilson's cottage. Wood smoke from the pot bellied stove and the smell of fresh brewed coffee made the old summerhouse comfortable. Rooney listened and shook his head as the former trooper outlined a possible scenario for the Green MT Trust robbery.

"Ansalone was here in the sixties?" Rooney seemed surprised.

"Not only that, but I've tried for two days to find out how she financed her development and the records don't lead me anywhere but back to a lot of cash coming her way a year or so after the money disappeared. Her old man rode the bus from Bratt on Fridays, and I'm sure that he knew that the money got moved on Monday by People's."

"Do you think she's dumb enough to bury the bags and the body on her own property?"

"What better place if you're in a hurry? Don't forget the property wasn't hers in '63. She took it over as part of a deal with the town to maintain the roads."

"You think she and her old man hit the bus?"

"I think there were four or five people involved, and I think some of them are still around."

Wilson drank coffee and held an unlit cigarette in his mouth.

"Look at the initials on the ring."

Rooney read the file and continued to shake his head.

"Do you have any idea who else might have been involved?"

"I have a couple of people to talk to in town before I can make up my mind. Otherwise, it's just a guess. The Indian kid was fiercely loyal to Johnny Dwyer."

"Do you think Megan's brother was involved?"

"Shit, Brian. There are no coincidences in this work. There is a good chance he knew about it."

Chapter 63

Stratton Mountain Resort sits beneath the highest peak in Southern Vermont. Several hundred miles of woods and meandering streams surround it. The base of its south-facing ski area is reminiscent of a village idiot's dream of a Swiss town, complete with stylized condos, bell towers, and shop complexes.

The tall copper-bearded president of Vision Vermont was pleased as he exited the conference area and headed for the hotel parking lot. The conference on economic development had gone well. He was carrying a small plaque that recognized his work in improving the Vermont economy and the creation of some two hundred new jobs. His pickup looked a poor cousin to the garden of affluence that sprouted from the asphalt lot; Mercedes after Mercedes, row upon row, with an occasional Ford or Chevrolet thrown in like dandelions in a flowerbed.

He was parked next to a Range Rover. These suburban Goliaths formerly used in the African bush now provided their condo-dwelling owners the means to lug their children between tennis or snowboarding lessons or to make the trek to Manchester a few miles away to shop at the Gap and Ralph Lauren outlets. Taking care not to scrape the paint off the Range Rover, he settled himself in the Ford truck, buckled his seatbelt, and pulled out into the downhill roadway that descended steeply for six miles to the town of Bondville. He drove past the golf course on the right and waved casually at the cars turning into the country club. For October, the day was warm, and he opened his window and breathed the fall mountain air, his spirit soaring with the thought of his upcoming award.

A bee sting caused him to pull his arm inside the cab as blood began to flow from his skin. He hit the brakes as another sting entered his shoulder, and the truck slowed as he fell forward. His pulse and blood pressure rose in response to the assault as a third sting entered just below his neck. For one split second, he remained calm then blacked out, causing the vehicle to careen down the hill out of control. To the New Jersey couple who were hiking nearby, it seemed as though the truck had wings as it left the road and smashed its way through the trees and rolled over to land in the boulder-strewn streambed.

"He's dead, I guarantee it," Harper Hyde spoke to fellow first responder and ski patrolman Russ Nardone as they scrambled down the embankment to the steaming Ford pickup. They had been dispatched by emergency rescue just ten minutes before and were getting ready to go home. In the distance, they could hear the Winhall Vermont Fire and Rescue Squad making its way, sirens blasting, up the mountain access road.

Carrier was slumped against the steering wheel, deflated air bag drooping like a giant condom on his lap.

Hyde checked his pulse and was surprised to feel a relatively strong, but rapidly beating heart muscle.

As his hand professionally checked over Carrier's limp body, he discovered a twenty-two bullet hole in Carrier's neck.

"Get on the horn to the sheriff's office, Russ. This son of a bitch has been shot!"

Twilight leaguers swung their clubs aimlessly or sat on the greens as the Medivac helicopter from Dartmouth Hitchcock Medical Center came in over the trees and began its hovering descent to the fairway below. Carrier, strapped firmly in the backboard and neck brace, an IV line running in to his wrist, had almost no color. He was mumbling incoherently about a bee sting, then lapsed into unconsciousness.

The Windham County Sheriff's department cruisers were parked at the crash scene; deputies walked the road, carefully trying to determine the site of the shooting.

"That was fucking beautiful, just beautiful," the driver said aloud while heading away from the scene. The driver steered carefully over the winding and hilly road that led out of the backside of the mountain through the tiny town of Stratton, and eventually to Route 100 South and the town of West Dover.

Chapter 64

WILSON HELD THE phone in one hand and a sandwich in the other.

"Somebody tried to kill who?"

"Carrier, the guy who is getting the other award from Mrs. Palmer and the Secretary of Agriculture." Agent Brian Leary sounded exasperated as he spoke. "I hate coincidences and I've got nobody in Vermont to sort out what the hell is going on with the locals. Tell me something, was this guy connected to Dwyer in any way?"

"They were business partners." Wilson bit the sandwich and took a long drink of Coke.

"Swell. Look, Wilson, have you got any idea who might be behind this shit?"

"Have you spoken to Detective Rooney? He's been interviewing people involved in Dwyer's murder."

"No, I haven't been able to reach him since we got the call about Carrier."

"Who notified you?"

"Windham County Sheriff's Department. They were at our survey meeting and called us immediately when they realized that Carrier was on the list of people receiving recognition."

"Is Carrier going to make it?"

"Touch and go, we'll know better in a couple of hours."

"You want me to find Rooney?"

"That would help."

"Give me your number and I'll get back to you in a few minutes."

CHAPTER 65

SMOKE CURLED OUT of the hospital stacks. White smoke spread into the Salem morning and caused Brian Rooney to pause as he looked out his third floor office window. He thought about the day a few months before when he had raced out the door and into the life and death of Johnny Dwyer. He had been in Salem for eighteen years. Having come from the military, not wanting to be a Nantucket cop, he took the Salem civil service test and made the Academy on his first try. He had watched the changes with amusement as the town became the witch capital of the United States. Condemnation of the innocent in 1692 had stimulated a growth industry in tourism—the mercantile and maritime history of the town being glossed over by the ever-present broomstick-riding witches that dominated the roadside signage and even the masthead of the local paper. Now the witches were riding him. The papers were pressing for an answer to the Dwyer killing. He was fielding more and more heat from the hospital; political types in town wanted to find a suspect.

"I think we ought to run the new information by the witnesses that were coming to work that day, Brian."

"What kind of stuff, Red?"

"Let's run Ansalone's vehicles and numbers; let's face it, a woman driving a pickup with out-of-state plates might just jog something in one of the morning shift employees."

"I suppose you already have that information handy."

Nolan grinned and pulled a copy of State of Vermont Department of Motor Vehicles information on the Ford pickup as well as information on Ansalone's Porsche convertible. "Sheila and I will start this afternoon."

"Meanwhile, Red, I think it's time we put some heat on the old man. Where did you say he was living?"

"Meadowbrook Nursing Home on the Lynnway."

"Thanks. I'll go out there this afternoon and check him out." Rooney's phone buzzed and he picked up his coffee and answered, hoping it wasn't the Salem newspaper reporter that had been leaving messages nonstop.

Wilson greeted Rooney with "Brian Leary says hello."

"How did you meet Leary?"

"He's the lead guy out of the Boston office. He's doing the survey on Janet Palmer's trip to Vermont and I think right now he'd rather be wearing a funny hat and working at McDonalds."

Rooney listened as Wilson went through the attempt on Lyman Carrier's life.

"Who wants Carrier dead?" asked Rooney.

"You tell me. From what you told me, McGowan would be a prime candidate. If it ain't him, then I guarantee you that Ansalone's involved."

"Leary must be off the wall. Do you think they will cancel her trip?"

"Not gonna happen, according to my sources."

"Your sources being the recipient who so far, hasn't got shot. Right?"

"None of your business," Wilson replied good-naturedly.

"When does Leary want to meet?"

"ASAP."

"I'll be back tomorrow. Set it up for tomorrow night and see if you can get any information on Carrier for me."

"All right. By the way, I dropped by on Meggy. She's fine. I'll cruise by when I make my house inspection later today."

"Thanks, Pete. I may be able to help you on the other matter. I'm going to see Chicky Ansalone today and see if I can't rattle him a bit."

"Good luck, but if he's like his kid, you'll be lucky to get out with your nuts intact."

"Thanks for your vote of confidence. See you later."

Rooney spent the rest of the morning returning phone calls and refusing interviews. At 12:15, he ate a quick lunch at the deli near the station and headed for the Meadowbrook Nursing and Assisted Living Community.

"Mr. Ansalone's been with us almost six years. He came after a fall to rehab his hip and ended up staying." The administrator, Aubrey Bilger, was a bespectacled man in his mid-sixties whose face had a slight twitch as he talked. His brown suit and wing-tipped shoes looked more like a banker's garb than a heath care professional's.

"Do you know his daughter?"

"Of course. She's a regular visitor. I wish that the rest of the children of our guests could be as attentive as Ms. Ansalone."

"Was she here on the fifth of July?"

"Let me check."

When he left, Rooney looked over the room. It was void of personal mementos or photos. Instead, it contained row after row of wall-mounted plaques that attested to Bilger's ability to keep a full census. Brian thought it strange to keep score by how many, rather than how well.

"Ms. Ansalone was here that day." He handed Brian the sign-in book for July 5. Ellen's signature was clearly legible on the line marked visitor.

"There's no time on this sheet."

"That's strange, Detective. The receptionist has to put the time in and out. It's part of her job."

"What time does she come to work?"

"Seven o'clock on Sunday mornings."

"How did Ms. Ansalone get in earlier to feed her father an omelet?"

"Is that your idea of a joke, Detective?"

"No." Rooney read over his interview with Ansalone. It was clear that she said she fed Chicky his breakfast.

"Mr. Ansalone hasn't had whole food in four months. He's on a tube for feeding."

Chapter 66

"Dr. RED, DR. Red, to Waitsfield 3. Dr. Red, Dr. Red, to Waitsfield 3."
The voice boomed through the hospital's loudspeaker system, and all available restraint-trained personnel left their posts and headed to the locked psychiatric unit located on the third floor of Southwest Vermont Medical Center.

Libby Stark exited the elevator. She had been called at 5:00 AM. Her daughter Jennifer had been admitted to the unit through the emergency room. As she pushed the call button and observed the sign that designated this a Flight Risk Unit, she was almost bowled over by hospital employees rushing to answer the alarm.

She was carried along in the flow of traffic to where a small group of staff and bewildered patients stood outside an enclosed nurse's station.

"This will be like a three-hundred-pound baboon having a psychotic break. This is very cool." The speaker was about twenty-two years old and wore a nametag that identified her as a mental health aide.

Libby shrank back in fear as the object of the alarm screamed and kicked at the charge nurse who was waiting patiently for the restraint team to get in place. The nurse stood, legs apart, four feet from the patient, and talked softly but firmly. Her hands were by her sides, and her keys dangled from her belt. Other curious patients were walking away from the scene, ordered to their rooms. Libby thought she could make out Jennifer's hair as she turned a corner into a far room.

"My name is HAYSOOS, not Jesus." The man was huge. He was naked from the waist up with his stomach protruding over the waistline of gray pajama bottoms from which protruded an erect penis. His eyes darted back-and-forth, almost as if he could see the totality of his surroundings. Crudely drawn jailhouse tattoos on both forearms seemed to have a life of their own as the assault began. With a silent signal, the restraint team went to their assigned arms and legs, and in a second, the man went limp. They guided him, still screaming and resisting, to a small room with a wooden bed. Six people held him down, while the restraints were fastened to his arms and legs. Libby could just see a part of the room and noticed someone hand the charge nurse a syringe. The screaming dissipated behind the closed quiet-room door.

Libby sat, shaken by what she had witnessed. She looked around at the patients who were standing near their rooms. They hardly seemed ruffled. Most of them stared straight ahead. Dear God, how can my daughter be among these people? she thought.

"I'm sorry you had to witness that outbreak, Mrs. Stark. Can I get you something? Coffee or water?"

"No, no thanks, just let me get my breath."

"He doesn't belong in a unit like this, but we have to take him. He is severely psychotic and has almost no English. We don't really have a counselor who can translate and do effective clinical work, so he will leave here medicated and passive for a short time until he spends his money on tequila and pot. Then he will end up here again, if he's lucky."

The young psychiatrist began explaining the nature of Jennifer's illness to Libby. Although she had read and listened to explanations before, she heard, as if for the first time, "genetic, incurable, but it is treatable."

"Can she stay here awhile until she gets more stable?"

The doctor picked up the binder that contained admissions records and progress notes. She shook her head. "I can fight for three days maybe four, but that's it. I'll stabilize her on Depakote and try a new antidepressant, but that's about all your insurance company will allow. Your daughter has had multiple admissions over the last three years and now they direct us to stabilize and release. I'm, sorry, but that's the only thing we can do because the administration here can't provide the care without a payer. Has your daughter talked of suicide, Mrs. Stark?"

"Not really. Why?"

"Your husband's planned death bothers me. Patients with manic depressive illnesses are far more likely to commit suicide than individuals in other risk groups."

"How about sexually? Does she act out?"

The doctor leaned closer to Libby and waited while she said with resignation, "Doctor, when Jennifer's off her meds, she sleeps with anyone."

"Is she easily agitated?"

"She can go from sweet and clear, to out and out madness in a short period of time. I never know who's going to come down the stairs to breakfast in the morning."

"Are you getting help for yourself, Mrs. Stark?"

"I don't want help for myself. I want help for my Jenny." Libby sobbed and reached for a box of tissues the doctor offered.

"I'll hold her as long as I can, Mrs. Stark. Please get some help for yourself."

Chapter 67

October 1997
Washington, DC

THE BLACK LABRADOR retriever raced through the snow. Behind him stood the white painted brick Victorian house that was home to the vice president of the United States and his family.

"My parents have a summer house in Maine and I grew up with the Wyeths. This is beautiful, Mrs. Palmer." She stood, admiring the painting that adorned the foyer of the house that had been built for the superintendent of the Naval Observatory in 1893.

"Thank you, Barbara. Would you like coffee or tea?"

"Love some coffee. Thanks."

Barbara Potter had come to the vice president's home to meet and discuss strategy for the upcoming presidential primaries. She was a graduate of Boston University's College of Communication and over the years had developed an enviable reputation in Massachusetts's politics for picking winning issues for otherwise lackluster candidates. She had been recommended highly by the junior senator from Massachusetts as a person who could guide Marion Palmer through the primaries looming in New Hampshire and Iowa less than two years away.

"I have read your proposal and I like it very much. Obviously, as you state, it's time I carve out my positions. Tell me, what you think I should do with this Vermont trip?"

"Mrs. Palmer, this woman in Vermont has reached out to you for help with this issue. She is close to getting a bill passed that definitely is close to your heart, so nobody could accuse you of jumping on the bandwagon for publicity. Your leadership on mental health issues is unquestioned. Now it's time to go one step farther."

"What do you suggest?"

"I would release a statement to the national press that you're going to Vermont, not only to award Senator Stark an achievement award for her work on the parity bill, but also to embrace the victims as well."

"I don't follow you."

"Present the award to both the senator and the daughter. If the daughter is stable, she could be a poster child for this issue."

"What will I gain?"

"Name a woman whose contributions to society have been primarily through the platform of her husband's office."

Marion Palmer didn't hesitate for a second. "Betty Ford."

"You got it. She chose to speak on issues that up until then had been closeted. You have the opportunity to do the same and at the same time, cast a warmer light on your husband's candidacy."

"The Secret Service has some concerns about my safety on this trip."

"To Vermont? I have been skiing there for twenty years, I can't think of a safer place."

As they walked out of the home office, Marion Palmer told her secretary to find Libby Stark and tell her that she would be calling that afternoon.

Chapter 68

October 1997
Salem, Massachusetts

"*THERE BEING COMPLAINT this day made by Capt. Jonah Walcott and Nathaniel Ingersull, both of Salem Village. In Behalf of their Majesties for themselves, and also for several of their Neighbors against Sarah Cloyce, the wife of Peter Cloyce, of Salem Village, and Elizabeth Proctor, the wife of John Proctor, of Salem Farmes, for high suspicion of sundry acts of witchcraft.*"

Brian Rooney kept the three-hundred-year-old warrant on his desk in a clear plastic cover. He had read it hundreds of times in eighteen years. It was there to remind him that overwhelming evidence gained out of ignorance never served the purpose of justice.

The witness came to the Salem Police Department on his way home from work at Salem Hospital. He was tired and looked anxious, but a can of Coke and a few supportive words from Red Nolan soon had him ready to tell his story. "Just tell these officers what it was that you saw that morning, Mr. Rojas."

"I didn't see anybody kill anybody, but I saw the truck go like hell out of the parking lot. It almost hit me. I screamed at the driver, but they didn't stop."

"What kind of truck was it? Do you remember the color?" Assistant District Attorney Courtney Malone spoke carefully and directly to the hospital maintenance worker who responded with a description of one of Ellen Ansalone's vehicles.

"Green. Dark green, Ford or Dodge pickup, I think."

"You think it was green or you think it was a Ford or Dodge?"

"I think it was a Ford, but definitely green."

"What else? Did you get the plate number?"

"Not the number, but the first three letters of the plate were BKB, and the next thing was the number 3, I think."

"Massachusetts plates?"

"No, they were green and white, either Colorado or Vermont."

"How do you know the color of out-of-state plates, Mr. Rojas?" The female prosecutor looked skeptical.

"Kids, you don't travel with kids, lady, do you?"

"No, I don't have kids."

"We just came back from my sister's in New Jersey. My kids play a game where you get points for spotting license plates."

"Did you see the driver of the vehicle, Mr. Rojas?"

Brian Rooney held his breath for just a second as Rojas answered.

"A woman. Dark skin, long hair, but I couldn't tell you more than that 'cause she was flying out of there."

"When we asked you these questions in July, you didn't mention any of this. How come?"

Rojas looked at Red Nolan and hesitated. Rooney read through the incident report and reread the first interview with Rojas.

"What's going on, Mr. Rojas?"

Courtney Malone looked around the room, seeking answers from Nolan and Rooney. Both men shrugged as if to say, "We don't know."

"One more time, Mr. Rojas. How come you didn't come forth with this information until now?"

"My job. I didn't want to lose my job."

"Why would you lose your job?"

"I thought the cops would tell my supervisor that I was stoned. I can't afford to lose my job. I got three kids."

"You were stoned on what?" The ADA looked troubled as she asked the question.

"On weed, but I hadn't lit up until after the car almost hit me."

"Do you have a history of drug abuse, Mr. Rojas?"

"I've never been busted, if that's what you mean."

"Thank you, Mr. Rojas."

Rooney shut off the tape recorder as Nolan escorted the man out of the office.

"It's thin, Brian. What else have you got that goes to motive?"

"It turns out that the recording studio's profits had gone up during the last year. If McGowan and Ansalone could get Johnny to sell, they stood to make a lot of money."

"Why kill him then?"

"Absolute rage. I think Dwyer agreed to sell to McGowan, then for some reason changed his mind or the terms of the deal."

"Where's McGowan fit in all of this?"

"He's a patsy, I think. He just doesn't show me a killer mentality; he's too pretty, too correct, too bloody full of himself."

"This is getting personal for you, isn't it?"

"Not enough to try and railroad this woman," Rooney answered defensively.

"What about your buddy's theory that this woman was involved in a major crime in the sixties?" asked Marlow.

"Wilson's convinced that Ansalone was part of a group that robbed a bus carrying a lot of cash between banks in '63."

"Has he got anything solid?"

"She had means, and a short time after the robbery, she had access to a lot of cash."

"Is it true that her old man was mobbed up?"

"He was laying off bets to the guys from Winter Hill, but he was a small player as far as we can tell."

"Then how come somebody tried to kill him?"

"From what Nolan's buddy at Lynn PD says, it was a territorial dispute. There was a huge turf war going on between some people from Charlestown and the Somerville guys that Chicky was in bed with."

Rooney's phone buzzed. "Hold on a second, Courtney."

"Long time, Brian. Don't tell me you want to bust me for smoking dope in the seventies." The caller was Doug Lapham, a longtime favorite singer/songwriter on the happy-hour circuit in New England. Lapham, had once recorded an album at Frost. He and Rooney had met at a club in Gloucester where Rooney had moonlighted as bouncer his first three years on the Salem PD.

"Thanks for calling back, Doug. I need to pick your brain, or what's left of it after the seventies."

"Rooney opened his notebook. Tell me what can change the profit picture in a small recording studio like Frost up in Vermont."

"Lots of things can change the picture, but my guess is they're getting ready to sell their book."

"What kind of book?"

"It's the trade term for their publishing rights. What's different about Frost is that they're a publisher as well as a recording studio, and during the sixties and seventies they accumulated a lot of rights to people who are doing very well now."

"So they can just sell those to the highest bidder?"

"You bet. They will sell to some conglomerate that will repackage and rerelease. You know, like 'a hits of the seventies' album, the kind you see on TV late at night. What's this all about anyway, Brian?"

Rooney explained the situation, and Lapham seemed surprised.

"If they're doing this deal, Brian, they're keeping it low-key. Does Dwyer's family have any notice of an impending sale?"

"I don't know."

"Hey, Brian, I gotta run. I'm babysitting my grandkid this afternoon."

"Thanks, Doug. Can I call you again if I need more?"

"Anytime, pal. Good luck."

When Rooney hung up, Courtney Malone said, "Sounds like you got something."

"I think we got motive."

Chapter 69

October 1997
Boston, Massachusetts

"When is the last time you were in Boston, Wilson?" Brendan Leary sat directly beneath a portrait of the president of the United States. He tried to make small talk while Wilson and Rooney waited for Weldon to arrive at the Boston Secret Service headquarters.

Peter Wilson sensed that Leary was not much for small talk, or any other talk that didn't have to do with his job. Leary told Wilson and Rooney that the call from the vice president was firm. Mrs. Palmer and the secretary of commerce would definitely be making the trip to Vermont, then going on to New Hampshire and some early fund raising.

Leary spoke again before Wilson could answer. "I want everything you guys know about Senator Stark and this guy Carrier. I don't want to hear how safe the goddamn state of Vermont is. My ass is on the line, and there's a good chance this lady will be sitting in the White House at some point. What kind of shape is Carrier in Frank?"

They turned to Weldon who had come in last. He was drinking Starbucks coffee. "Much better than the initial report said. He's a tough bastard. It looks like he will be able to attend the award presentation in a wheelchair. We interviewed him for an hour the other night and all he wanted to talk about was the vice president's wife and the commerce secretary coming to Snow Mountain. He's an arrogant prick. If you listen to him, the whole state would have been collecting welfare if he hadn't come along."

"He's probably right. What has the sheriff's department come up with?" questioned Wilson.

"Eight expended shells. Twenty-two long rifle. No prints on the casings, and no footprints to speak of. The shooter could have walked away to one of the condos, or driven out the back way to Route 100," Weldon explained.

"Any chance it was random, Frank? You know, kids firing at a target?" Rooney leaned forward and yawned as he spoke.

"I doubt it; there would have been some evidence of a target."

"You think this is tied to a business deal, Brian?"

"I think Ansalone was trying to control a buyout of Dwyer's stock. My guess is that she's in hock to somebody. Maybe some friends of her old man's. I think she's desperate enough to try anything at this point."

"Where do you stand with the investigation, Brian?"

"We are close to arresting her for murder one."

"You think McGowan was involved too?"

"McGowan probably is involved from the standpoint of trying to fraudulently buy out the stock. I don't see him as a shooter, but we have to look at him as being complicit."

Brendan Leary took notes while they talked. He finished and said to Weldon, "What about the '63 robbery. Where are you guys with tying this woman to that?"

"Ask Pete. He's done all the scut work so far."

"Right now, we've got a lot of circumstantial stuff that ties her to the Green MT Trust robbery. The problem is that we can't directly tie her to the camp the day it went down. We also don't connect her to the Latimer kid, except for the initialed ring. The fact that she had access to keys and the possible ability to launder that much money, leads me to believe that she and someone else could have planned this thing. My guess is that Johnny Dwyer or the Indian Birdsong were involved, but they're both conveniently dead."

"How is Carrier involved in all of this? Any clues, Pete?" Leary further probed Wilson.

"It looks like that arrogant streak of his translated to not wanting any part of Ansalone involved in Frost records."

"That makes sense, Pete."

Rooney looked at his notes and said, "The day I interviewed Carrier, he made no bones about calling her everything but a whore, and I'm sure if I let him go on, he would have done that too."

"You think she did the hit on Carrier?" Leary sat back and played with his reading glasses as he spoke.

"Either she did it, or she had someone do it. I'm sure that she will have an alibi for the time he was shot," Rooney speculated. "So we try to remove her from the picture by focusing on Dwyer's murder and then try to squeeze McGowan for the rest." Rooney looked around at the assembled lawmen as if looking for consensus.

Leary said, "Look, Brian, I don't care how you do it, but I would feel a hell of a lot better if this woman was off the streets while Mrs. Palmer was visiting Vermont."

Chapter 70

October 1997
Warren Mills, Vermont

THE UNMARKED FORD Victoria exited Interstate 95 at Brattleboro, Vermont and drove along the commercialized area of Route 9, until it reached Vermont State Police Troop D Headquarters. Rooney waited in the parking lot as a Massachusetts blue and gray state police cruiser pulled alongside his vehicle and parked. Jim Roche of the Massachusetts State Police, as well as Frank Weldon of the Vermont State Police, would accompany Rooney when he served the arrest warrant on Ellen Ansalone.

"Porky says she's on the property," Weldon said as he gave a thumbs-up and entered his marked cruiser. The caravan pulled on to Route 9 and began the windy, mountainous twenty miles to Warrens Mills. Rooney thought about how many times he had traveled this road in a short few months. As they approached Marlboro, he looked at the road leading to the Boy Scout camp and thought about

Billy Latimer. He felt somehow connected to the old crime, maybe because of his newfound friendship with Ben Latimer and Peter Wilson. He tried to imagine the snowy day so many years ago when Billy pulled off the road and into a death trap. As they crossed over the mountain, he tried to figure why the Hogback Ski Area had been closed down. Its rusted old lifts stood like silent sentinels along the roadside. They passed the restaurant with the incredible views where he and Meggy had shared wonderful sausage and pancakes. He thought about Meggy and how she would feel about the arrest of Ansalone for Johnny's murder. The trees were past peak now and the fall was beginning to give way to early winter and graying skies. "Entering Warrens Mills"—the sign seemed like an old friend. They stopped near the municipal building long enough for Porky Atkins and Deputy Henderson to fall into the procession, then drove the two miles of newly paved roads that entered High Mowing and the office of Chicky Ansalone's daughter.

"How many roads in and out, Chief?"

"Unless she can fly, she'll have to come by here if she tries to run."

Atkins and Henderson stationed themselves at the entrance to the development. Weldon's cruiser led the way as they drove up the winding hill to the office. Ellen's truck was parked in front. The green and white license plate read BKB 342. Next to it was an older Toyota Corolla. Rooney took the safety off the chief's special and shifted it to where he could draw quickly if needed.

"Good morning. Can I help you?"

The receptionist recognized him. "Oh, it's you, Detective. Ellen's not here. Was she expecting you?"

"No. Do you know where she went?"

"She's on the property with the wood's boss, Flip Morton. He was all bent out of shape about something and she went for one of her rides with him. Maybe she's up at the clubhouse. Shall I page her?"

"No, in fact I want you to go outside and sit in your car for a while."

"I can't. There's no one else here to answer the phones."

Weldon produced his badge. She picked up her purse and cigarettes and walked out to the Corolla.

"Roche, why don't you stay with our friend here and make sure that Ansalone doesn't slip by us? She is on the pager with a walking gorilla named Morton."

The Massachusetts trooper produced a 9 mm, chambered a round, and laughed.

"Is this guy bigger than your buddy the Whale, Brian?"

"Shit, Jimmy, nobody's bigger than the Whale."

Rooney and Weldon drove up the narrowing road that dead-ended into the High Mowing clubhouse and pool. Ansalone's Porsche was parked in front.

"Go ahead in the front. It's your collar. I'll watch the back, in case she runs." Weldon drew his weapon as he walked around the car and headed for the back of the clubhouse.

The entranceway opened into a large red cedar room with a view that opened up for hundreds of miles.

Rooney didn't hear or see anything. If they were here, they may be up to something sexual. He chuckled at the thought of catching Ansalone and Flip Morton in the buff. The gurgling of a hot tub made him pause. The sound came from an elevated area about fifteen feet away. He could see Weldon through the glass slider, weapon in hand. He walked quietly up the three stairs that led to the hot tub and found himself staring at a very dead and bloated Ellen Ansalone. She was propped up, face bloodied, hands tied behind her; she was sitting in a whirlpool of blood and chlorinated water that bubbled and steamed like a geyser. Rooney's stomach turned, and he could feel the nausea sweep over him. Ellen Ansalone's corpse seemed to stare right through him as he vomited into the hot tub. He thought he could hear her voice screaming, "You asshole, Rooney."

Weldon came up the stairs, weapon in hand and stopped. "What the fuck happened to her?"

"Somebody beat us to it, Frank."

CHAPTER 71

STUPID RETARD. STUPID retard. Stupid retard. Fat pig. Fat pig. Fat pig. The voices wouldn't stop running through his head as he pulled into the abandoned monastery that had been his home for the past two years. Charles "Flip" Morton wiped Ellen Ansalone's blood from his steering wheel while listening to the screams and taunts of eight-year-old Porky Atkins. It seemed like every day when the short yellow bus would come to take him to Bennington and his special school, Porky would wait and taunt him. He had done nothing to Porky, but every day the taunts came. He unlocked the door to the former chapel and dining room the monks abandoned thirty years before. The back wall had a black crucifix mark where the former altar had been. Surrounding the crucifix were his pictures of Ellen taken secretly and not so secretly over twenty-five years. His pants were stained with blood, as was his shirt.

He drank from the half-full bottle of Chartreuse that he had taken from the clubhouse bar when he ran out. The liquor calmed the voices of confusion. His hands were slippery with blood, and he almost dropped the bottle. He gripped it harder, drank more, then sat on the wooden bench.

They would come for him. He took the lever-action deer rifle from the wall rack and emptied a box of .30-caliber shells into the pocket of his shirt. She lied to him. She always lied to him. *You stupid shit, keep your hands off me. Stupid shit. Stupid shit.* Her voice kept screaming in his head. *Don't touch me, you fuckin' dummy.* He just wanted to touch her as he had done so many nights in his monk's cell, touch her the way he had seen Brad McGowan touch her in the hot tub, touch her breasts the way the dirty little lawyer Romano touched them in her office.

She laughed at him when he told her about the pictures. *Just keep jerking off all you want to your pictures, but keep your hands off me.*

The shotgun was in his truck. He walked out and opened the toolbox that held the extra deer slugs and a box of pellets; then closing the truck, he walked back into the monastery chapel that had once been filled with Latin chants and prayers of supplication.

Her head had smashed against the tile that surrounded the Jacuzzi. Her face opened up after he continued to hit her. She kept screaming at him, but he knew that no one could hear anything. She was his now. Not Romano's. Not McGowan's. He tied her hands behind her back. She stopped yelling and begged him to stop. He took her blouse off and touched her breasts the way McGowan did. Her blood ran on his hands from her nose. He couldn't stop her from bleeding. He touched her breasts with his penis the way Romano did. She cried and begged him to stop. He hit her again and again, and she stopped crying and slumped into the whirlpool of bubbling, bloody water that was now up to her chin.

They would come for him soon.

Chapter 72

"It's a deserted monastery, abandoned by the monks of Charte who now live up on Mt. Equinox in Manchester. Some developers tried to make a go of it in the seventies, but its gone to shit now. We served him warrants twice before in there and I'll guarantee that's where he'll hold up."

Porky Atkins was nervous as he tried to take charge of the men who assembled to go after Morton. He wanted to wait for more backup, but the others were charged up and ready to begin the pursuit of the man who was last seen with Ellen Ansalone.

Atkins and Deputy Henderson had seen Morton as he left the development and watched as the town bully drove toward Warrens Mills. They stood like a vigilant posse preparing weapons and checking ammunition in the front of the Deerfield Valley Health Center. The last vehicle to pull in was the black jeep belonging to Peter Wilson. Weldon had called him to provide more firepower if they needed it.

Three members of the Deerfield Valley Rescue squad were assembled near an ambulance. They would follow at a safe distance to provide medical backup if needed. Massachusetts State Police from the Greenfield Barracks would act as backup and close Route 112 if Morton tried to run toward the state border. Passing through the village of Jacksonville, they picked up town Constable, Bucky Showalter, then proceeded the six miles to the overgrown entrance of the former monastery where the roads were ill kept and partially closed. They put on Kevlar vests and walked toward the small pond area and the old cells that once held two monks each and for years heard nothing but prayer. There were ten small buildings surrounding a cross-shaped building that served as a chapel and dining room. The woods had grown unchecked and all but hid the tiny wooden buildings that were remnants of the community of contemplation.

The pickup was visible as they split up in twos and surrounded the chapel area.

Porky Atkins bellowed into the bullhorn. "Come on out a there Flip, before somebody gets hurt."

Atkins ducked behind a tree after he spoke. The others had come within shooting range on all sides of the building. There was silence. No one moved. Rooney thought he was going to throw up again.

"Come on out, Flipper, and we can talk."

Silence hung in the fall air.

"We're coming in, Flip."

Porky's vest rode up on his massive belly as he stepped out from behind the tree. Peter Wilson tried to shove him back to safety at the last second as what was left of the stained-glass window shattered, and the barrel of Morton's .30-caliber erupted in the quiet of the Vermont day.

"You fat pig. I'm no retard, you fat pig."

The bullet entered just below Porky's waist. He went down and was dragged to safety by Wilson, who strained as he dragged the obese bleeding form into the tree line. A second bullet hit the ground next to Wilson. The others near Wilson returned fire into the building. Though it seemed an eternity, the firefight lasted no more than thirty or so seconds, and then, as if on prearranged signal, the firing stopped, quiet returned, and they knew they had killed him.

The deer rifle that had been to camp with Flip Morton for so many Novembers had fallen in front of the chapel. Rooney and Trooper Jim Roche smashed through the front door of the chapel and stopped. Morton lay on the floor in front of the crucifix and the wall of Ellen photos, bleeding from the head and face or what was left of it.

Outside, they could hear the sound of the paramedics working over the Warrens Mills' chief. Porky's bull elephant bellowing made Rooney laugh. He would live to eat another day.

Peter Wilson stood by himself and realized he wasn't hit. He felt himself all over and knew he was safe. The adrenaline was starting to leave. He sat on the rear of the pickup and felt his breathing return to normal.

"Who got Morton, can you tell, Brian?"

"Probably the shotgun. He took a lot of rounds to the face."

"Do you think he wanted to kill you that night at the fair?"

The question made Rooney think before he answered. Rooney walked inside the chapel and waved at Wilson to follow him. They stood before the wall and looked at the fifty or so pictures that were displayed next to the cross.

"He wanted to kill somebody. I think I was just the handy substitute for McGowan or Romano."

"What do we do about McGowan?"

Wilson picked a picture from the wall as he spoke. It was a shot of McGowan and Ellen Ansalone naked in the hot tub.

"Let the state's attorney deal with him."

"Looks like Meggy and Carrier will be running the record business."

"You know something, Pete? I think Meggy could keep that arrogant bastard in his place."

Chapter 73

November 1997
Warren Mills, Vermont

THE CARAVAN OF black Chevrolet Suburbans entered the valley and turned north on Route 100. Curious townspeople and a few tourists watched as the wife of the vice president of the United States, accompanied by the secretary of commerce of the United States, were driven the few miles to the Cold Brook Road. From there, they would drive to West Dover on Handle Road to pick up the day's guest of honor and her daughter. Six hundred guests were beginning to assemble at the new hotel that sat on the sight of a former farmhouse atop Snow Mountain. The guests were a curious mixture of professional mental health workers and small farmers and food producers. Politics took a backseat today as the bluegrass band began to tune in anticipation of the afternoon's events. The past weeks had seen rumors and newspaper stories abound. The Boston and Albany press corps jumped all over the tales of the Massachusetts transplant who had been murdered brutally before she could be arrested for the slaying of local songwriter and folksinger Johnny Dwyer.

Janet Palmer looked at the approaching house and knew she had made the right decision. "This has been a long time coming. I feel as though I've known you two forever." Janet Palmer hugged Libby and Jennifer Stark, standing on the porch overlooking the woods and meadows that made up the Stark property. Secret Service agents spread out around the house. "It reminds me of our farm in Virginia," she paused and feeling awkward said, "Jennifer, how are you feeling?"

Jennifer Stark looked like a model for wholesomeness. Her hair was combed long and tied with a bow. She wore a long skirt and a plain blouse beneath a beautiful knit sweater. She beamed when she spoke, "Like I've been lifted from a nightmare. I haven't felt this good in a long time."

Libby Stark hugged her daughter as she spoke. Janet Palmer could sense the pride that the woman felt.

"I am so glad we have this day to celebrate what I know will be a victory for you this year."

The three women got into the Suburban and chatted like old friends as they made their way to southern Vermont's largest and newest hotel—and their day of recognition.

Chapter 74

BRIAN ROONEY AND Megan Dwyer sat with Peter Wilson and watched as the long lines of guests were unceremoniously shuffled through metal detectors before they entered the master ballroom. The aftermath of the Ansalone murder and its repercussions had left both men feeling empty and unfulfilled. Rooney had wanted the satisfaction of putting Ansalone behind bars, for Megan's sake. Wilson felt that he had been close to solving the mystery of the Green Mountain Trust Robbery. Now the final pieces of the puzzle lay in the basement of a Lynn, Massachusetts, funeral home, awaiting final disposition. Brad McGowan and Frost Studios were being carefully scrutinized by the Attorney General's Office for possibly defrauding stockholders. Both Lyman Carrier and Megan Dwyer were cooperating with the investigation.

Wilson was struggling with a phone call he had received just that morning as he was returning from his run. The phone call was from the widow of Harlan Messicks, MD.

Messicks had been one of two doctors who had practiced in Warrens Mills. His death from cancer had left a large hole in the fabric of the town. He was the original country doctor. He had no normal hours and no set fees. He made house calls and delivered half the kids in the town. Many a night, Pete would have to drag him out of bed to minister to highway accident victims or an occasional overdose. He had been with Pete the day they had to cut down Earl Stark's body from the gondola. He had also escorted the young trooper to tell Libby that her Earl was dead.

Now Messick's widow wanted to make something right, and Pete was curious about her contrition for her late husband's sins. "Peter, I'm bothered by the report in the *Valley* paper that says the Ansalone woman was behind the bus being led to the old scout camp. You know, I never could stand her, but I have to tell you that there was no way she could have been in Marlboro that morning."

Wilson listened and sat up in his chair.

"Ansalone was in our office. She was with us for two hours, and then we rushed over to the Cottage Hospital. She was bleeding real bad. We were afraid as hell. Pete, my husband was a good man, but he had a soft heart for kids like her. He never should have done what he did, but that's water over the dam. She could have made trouble for us in those days because abortion was still illegal, but she never said a word to anybody. You know the only thing she said that day was that she hated Johnny Dwyer for knocking her up and not showing up to be with her."

Rooney said, "that's incredible, Pete. But it makes sense to me now why this woman hated Dwyer so much."

Megan had left them alone at the table. Wilson told Rooney the story to try and get his take on it.

"I'll tell you an even stranger story that's been bugging me." Rooney drank from a bottle of Bass Ale then looked at his friend. "This bother you?" he pointed to the bottle.

"No. Tell me what's been bugging you."

"Do you remember the day we interviewed your friend, the senator, and she confessed to sleeping with Dwyer?"

"Of course, she was all bent out of shape that we even asked her."

"It never happened. It turns out that Dwyer hadn't been with a woman in years."

"Hold on, Brian, why would anybody want to say they were sleeping with somebody that they weren't, especially after what happened to him? You must have your facts screwed up somehow."

"I pulled his medical records after an offhand remark that Karen Nelson made a while back. The last three times he was in Oak Hill, he was clear about being unable to sustain an erection. According to Wellman at Oak Hill, it is fairly common among longtime alcohol abusers." Wilson good-naturedly gave Rooney the finger.

"I suppose there's no hope I'll ever get it up again."

"None."

Megan Dwyer sat down at the table and the conversation shifted to the arrival of Lyman Carrier. He was wheeling himself into the room to a standing ovation from the assembled crowd. His beard had been shaved and he had lost a little weight. His face now clearly showed a childhood birthmark just below his eye.

"Did they match the gun that shot Carrier to anything they found at Morton's?" Rooney stood up while he spoke and put on a small gold pin with the letter *E* in the middle of a round circle. Wilson also put the same style pin on the collar of his shirt. The pins had been issued by Secret Service Brendan Leary to law enforcement personnel on site in order separate the good guys from the bad guys.

"No, not so far, but I guarantee they will."

The room buzzed again as Porky Atkins was wheeled in. He was wearing a brand-new uniform and boots.

"Porky's last hurrah," said Wilson.

Rooney laughed.

"You saved his ass but good, Peter. He's lucky you were there when he took the bullet."

"He's definitely what you would call deadwood, that's for damn sure."

The room was filled to capacity. Outside, a light dusting of snow was falling. From the large-glassed area at the rear of the room, a person could look up and see the top of Snow Mountain wearing its white winter mantle.

The five-piece bluegrass group broke into a rendition of "Columbia, Gem of the Ocean" as the wife of the vice president and the Starks entered the room. Applause broke out as they walked up to the head table and stood, basking in the warmth of the Vermont welcome. Waiters scurried about the room, filling water glasses and laying out monkey dishes filled with Cabot Creamery butter. Formal menus were passed, souvenirs of the day, bearing the gold vice presidential seal and highlighting the fact that each course served today was produced in Vermont.

Lyman Carrier smiled and spoke quietly to Libby Stark. This was their day and they both glowed with the satisfaction of having done a service to their home state. His wheelchair was placed to the right of a beaming Janet Palmer and her public relations specialist, Barbara Potter. The waiters were mostly new recruits brought in for the event. They ranged from college students on break to retirees looking for something to do with their days. They had been hastily trained and, for the most part, were able to handle the various courses and limited wine service that was offered. A local Episcopal priest said benediction.

The first speaker was Secretary of Commerce Ralph Michael, who had a long career at U.S. Steel and, in many cases, was responsible for the rebirth in the use of American steel. He lauded Carrier's work and gave a prepared history of the marketplace growth of Vermont products. He gave Carrier the award and had all the members of VisionVermont who were present stand and receive accolades for their efforts. It was obvious Carrier was still in some pain as he accepted the award for the members of his group. His comments were short and centered on the potential of Vermont farmers and food producers. During the speech, Libby and Jennifer Stark were visibly sharing the warmth of the event. Bluegrass music floated from the right of the stage as Carrier finished speaking and wheeled himself back to his center stage position. Janet Palmer, looking heavier than in her pictures, was cheerleading the musicians as they ran through a piece called "Foggy Mountain Breakdown." Ben Latimer stole the show as he picked out the banjo solo and drove the song. He smiled at the now-animated vice president's wife as she clearly let the down-home music of her childhood take over.

She led the audience in handclapping, smiling for the assembled press at the first three tables. Her fears of campaigning for her husband were fading as she felt the crowd sharing her enthusiasm. As Ben wound down, and the clapping slowed, Janet Palmer enthusiastically grabbed the microphone from the dais and led the audience in a round of applause for the musicians. The waiters were clearing the tables and bringing coffee and desert.

The break for dessert and coffee led Rooney and Wilson to the long line at the men's room.

"How's Meggy with all of this, Brian?"

"She's been real quiet."

"I don't think her brother was involved."

"What changed your mind?"

Rooney leaned against the wall outside the men's room as he spoke, "Ansalone and Morton. The pictures; the sexual fantasy; but more than anything, the way Birdsong was killed. I think that Ansalone was screwing Dwyer, and at the same time was setting up Billy Latimer for a fall. I think that Birdsong went along for a piece of the action, and Morton went nuts when they went to bury the bags."

"Who hit the power?"

"Birdsong. Then he went to meet Morton at the Fougere house to bury the money. Morton has the shotgun, and when Birdsong bends to stash the bags, he wastes him."

"What about Billy's watch and belt?"

"I think Morton dumped them. I think he found the ring and freaked out that Ansalone was screwing the Latimer kid."

"We're never going to know, are we, pal?" Rooney asked.

"No, but for Meggy's sake I think that's what we say. At least that's how it ends for me and that's what I'm going to report to Weldon."

"Thanks, Pete. For what it's worth, thanks. I think she doesn't need any more grief."

Chapter 75

"**T**HE MAN HAS birthmark bad, Sumner." Benjamin Wernickie pointed to guest of honor Lyman Carrier. Sumner Warren had brought his friend Wernickie to see the vice president's wife and to get out of the house that still haunted him.

"Had that as long as I can remember, used to take a ribbing at school. Guess that's why he wears the beard."

"You knew him when he was a boy?"

"Shit yes. His old man owned the property your house is on."

Peter Wilson listened to the two old men. He thought that someday that would be he. He hoped he would have a friend to talk to when he was that age. He sipped his third cup of coffee and thought about what he had just heard the old farmer say. "You getting old, Sumner."

The farmer turned and shook hands with Wilson. He introduced him to his Polish friend. "How do you figure I'm getting old, Pete?"

"The property where they found the body, that house belonged to the priest down at the Catholic church.

"Before him it was Ethan Carrier's property. He lost it in bankruptcy to cover his equipment when he lost the Snow Mountain work."

"Are you sure?"

"Shit yes. That property abuts my high pasture."

The sound of the microphone being tested grabbed their attention. Janet Palmer was introduced by the Democratic state chairman and received a standing ovation.

"Ladies and Gentlemen of the Green Mountain State, let me say to you what a proud day this is for me. I came here today to present the National Mental Health Service Medal to a remarkable lady. Most of you know Libby Stark as a senator, friend, and neighbor. The work she has done to promote mental health parity will reach much farther than Vermont."

Applause filled the room.

"Her work will enable those who need services the most to access care without the fear they currently face from their mental health gatekeepers. Before coming here today, my husband pledged to me that if he is elected, he will make mental health parity a large part of his agenda."

The audience cheered and stood in agreement. When they began to quiet, she spoke again, "I have never been one to step away from the limelight."

The audience laughed in agreement.

"Today, however, I am giving up this platform to a young lady of great courage."

The audience looked at Jennifer Stark, and she began to come to the microphone.

"Today, Jennifer Stark is going to tell you, in her words, what it means to live with mental illness and try to stay well in a system that is designed to fail all but the wealthiest of clients."

A waiter with long hair pulled back in a ponytail emerged from the kitchen and brought two large bouquets of flowers forward. He first went to Libby and then to Jennifer, who took the flowers and placed them in front of her at the speaker's podium. She read from the card attached "Best of luck to two of Vermont's finest ladies." The signature was that of the president of the United States. The audience stood and applauded.

As she waited for the audience to settle, she took a black notebook from her LL Bean canvas bag and placed it next to the bouquet.

As quiet settled over the audience of well-wishers, she began to read from the notebook. "On December 27, 1963, I took the life of a young man named Billy Latimer."

"What did she say?" exclaimed Barbara Potter.

The room settled and Jennifer repeated, "On December 27, 1963, I took the life of a young man named Billy Latimer."

Ben Latimer strained through the crowd to get nearer to the podium, only to be pushed back by a Secret Service agent.

"That's Johnny's notebook," Meggy gasped.

"If you are reading this, I am probably dead. I have stopped running from the past horrors and now know no matter what happens to me, it will be better than what the past twenty-five years of my life have been. When you read this, please try to find some way to forgive me. If Meggy and Ben discover this book, I can only say that I am sorry for what I have done to you. I know that nothing can bring Billy back."

"Get her off the stage. She's crazy." As Barbara Potter tried to move Jennifer from the podium, Libby Stark looked at Janet Palmer and said, "Let her speak."

Pete Wilson walked toward the head table and stood next to Ben Latimer. The agent in charge of the section looked at the *E* on Wilson's lapel and backed off his hold on Ben.

Brendan Leary nodded to the agent and then moved Barbara Potter back to her seat.

Newspaper photographers, realizing they had hit the jackpot, were busy snapping frame after frame.

Vermont ETV cameras were glued to the speaker as she again began to read from the notebook:

> He said all we had to do that day was to figure a way to move Peter Wilson out of Marlboro. He knew that E was seeing Latimer, and that the bus had been stopping at the camp on a regular basis where the two met. He had been following the bus and told E that if she didn't go along, there would be harm done to Latimer. We planned to just scare him, but it got out of hand. He said the money would stay in Vermont. For the most part, it has never left for any great period of time.
>
> My part was to create the diversion that would cause Pete to leave Marlboro. I had seen the master shut off on the pole for years and was surprised to see how low it was to the ground. The snow that fell that morning made my part easier. I drank a half bottle of rum to stop the shakes, and went to the pole and waited until 11:00. As the traffic lightened to almost nothing, I smashed the box.

The nearest repair crew would have to come from Searsburg, and I knew there wasn't much chance of getting them on short notice. Night after night, I had drunk with Bob Martin, the lineman from GMP. I knew they wouldn't come out and climb in bad weather unless there was a serious emergency.

"I can't believe what she is saying," a shaking Ben Latimer said as he was steadied by Wilson.

Meggy said nothing, tears rolling down her face as she listened to her brother's message from the grave:

Believe me, if you can, I never meant to harm anyone. I wasn't there when the bus pulled into Marlboro. I just know that Billy went to meet E at the camp and she believed nothing would happen to him. That all changed when the Indian got involved. I'm sure he's dead, too, but I don't know. E later told me that Billy came to meet her with a diamond ring in his hand. Oh God Ben, I hope you won't ever read this while I'm alive. Meggy, if you ever read this, I'm sorry. I have lived my life in fear that the madman would kill you. He held us both hostage for all these years.

I'm going to sing in Massachusetts in July. Then, if it's possible, I will make my peace with someone I let down on that horrible day in 1963.

I'm drunk now as I write. I promised myself, for the millionth time, I would face this sober, but now the whisky tastes good. I know now that the day I face him, I will be sober. I owe that to Ben and Meggy and especially to Billy Latimer.

Jennifer Stark was agitated and close to tears as she continued to read. "At one that afternoon, the madman told us that it was over and we could never speak of it again. He showed me pictures of Meggy and threatened to kill her if I didn't go along with his plan. For twenty-five years he has threatened E and me, over and over again, that our *families would die if we ever spoke a word.*

Jennifer Stark put the book down and began to speak. There was dead silence in the room as the bizarre events played out in people's minds. Through the large glass windows to her back, the snow fell harder now, swirling and blocking the view of the mountain.

"Today, the nightmare of my life is over," Jennifer Stark stated angrily. "It began to unravel when I broke into Johnny Dwyer's house and found this book."

Pete Wilson looked at the head table and saw, for the first time, the love of his and Billy Latimer's life. Elizabeth Allen—*EA, EA, EA.* The initials hit him in the gut and he felt sick. Jonathan had mentioned only briefly that he had a part-time secretary in the office. But Pete Wilson could only see Ellen Ansalone, and now it was too late to make it better. Elizabeth Allen Stark watched her daughter, tears streaming down her face, unable to speak or move as the reality of her daughter's speech paralyzed her.

Jennifer Stark was agitated as she spoke, "I wanted to blame Johnny Dwyer for all my problems. I went to his house to confront him for causing problems for my mother. My whole life has been spent listening to my mother sneaking around, whispering in fear. Now, I can only thank Dwyer for what he's done. I have told this story time after time to doctors and therapists to no avail. Now I know you can believe me. I'm sorry, Mother. It has to end this way." She reached into the bouquet and turned toward the wife of the vice president with a small .25-caliber handgun in her hand. The pony-tailed waiter who had once shared the stage with Johnny Dwyer had placed it there.

Without hesitation, Secret Service agent Brendan Leary moved to place his body in front of the future first lady and drew his weapon just as Jennifer Stark fired directly into the face of an unbelieving Lyman Carrier. The bullets entered his face just below his birthmark. The madman was dead.

Chapter 76

THE SOUND OF the bagpipe was the only sound that permeated the cold snow-filled cemetery overlooking the Deerfield Valley. The few mourners, gathered to place Johnny Dwyer's ashes to rest, were standing next to the stark snow-covered maple that would give comfort, as best it could, to the remains of the tortured man whose manuscripts had answered some of the mysteries of this small Vermont village. The sound of the backhoe, and its foul diesel smell, startled Megan Dwyer from her thoughts. Brian Rooney held the small black box that was to be interred. Newly appointed Police Chief Peter Wilson stood to his right.

"For Christ's sake, Porky, get that hole dug, we're freezing."

"Takes time to warm the machine and get the oil moving," Porky mumbled back.

Three weeks had passed since the revenge-filled slaying of Lyman Carrier. The revelations of the guilt surrounding Senator Elizabeth Stark and her role in the Green MT Trust robbery were spelled out in detail by the local and national media. The tabloid press was hovering around Megan Dwyer with offers to buy her story and her brother's journals for outlandish sums of money. The Vermont state attorney was still sorting out Lyman Carrier's computer records.

The cemetery had once again claimed the life of one of its young. Fresh flowers were placed, as if growing through the snow, on the recently closed grave of Jennifer Stark who fell in a hail of Secret Service 9-mm fire. The subsequent investigation of her activities and the confession of Mandolin player Jackie Burns to the break-ins and initial shooting attempt on Lyman Carrier had cleared Ellen Ansalone of all wrongdoings except trying to manipulate the stock price of Frost Records. Elizabeth Allen Stark was under house arrest pending a decision on her culpability in the Green MT Trust robbery. She had been allowed out under escort to bury her daughter next to her husband. In Lynn, Massachusetts, Ellen Ansalone was laid to rest with very little fanfare. Her father, Chicky, was brought to the graveside of his wife to offer a painful good-bye to the only other woman he had ever loved.

Epilogue

November 1997
Mount Equinox
Manchester, Vermont

"**WE HAVE DECIDED** to break with tradition, Brother William. We have prayed and asked for guidance on this issue, and we have agreed that you must be given the right to do as you will after reading the newspaper accounts that involve you and your brother. We knew this day would come, and as pained as we would be to lose you, we realize that any further danger to you is passed."

The speaker handed the *Brattleboro Reformer* and the *Bennington Banner* to the middle-aged robed man. The two had lived together in community for many years, and it was evident from the pain on the older monk's face that he saw the younger man as more than just another member of the Order of Charte; he saw him as a son or younger brother. The older man sat quietly and reflected as he watched Brother William read the paper.

He remembered vividly the snowstorm on that day in 1963 and the cries from the bushes where the man had been left to die. He had made a choice that day and had spent many hours in prayer and sometime fitful worry. He and other brothers had taken the beaten young man back to their sanctuary and nurtured him back to health.

It was months before the young man was able to tell the tale of that day. He told them how he had gone to propose to a wonderful young widow and had been viciously attacked and dumped by two men in masks and left to die in the old cemetery near the Auger Hole Road in Marlboro. It was there that the monks had been walking and praying while awaiting their regular visit with a dentist whose home office was just a mile from the old cemetery. Now the story unfolded in the newspapers and television, and their faith in the young man's story was finally vindicated. "William, go to the garden and ask God to give you the answers that you seek."

The young monk rolled up the papers and tucked them into his robe. He walked toward the door of the chapel where they had been talking, and he watched and listened as the few remaining Brothers of Charte began to chant quietly.

Outside he looked and, as if for the first time, saw the beauty of the surrounding mountains. He looked down to the valley that had been created by the merging of the Taconic and Green Mountains, and he wondered whether he could ever return to the world he had left so long ago. He wept.

Quiet enveloped him as he once again thought of Ben. He knew that if he left, it would give him great joy to see Ben and comfort him. They would be the Brothers Latimer again. He thought of the lake where they had been so happy as kids. He thought of his parents, and he knew they were at peace. He also knew that Ben had found a life of his own. He sat in the garden that he maintained for the good of the community, and he felt a kind of peace that he had not felt before. He began to prepare a letter in his head. He would write it later and he would tell Ben everything. But then a deeper peace settled in, and he knew it might never be mailed.

Brother William began to tend his garden as the sun turned warm against his face.

The End